A wonderfully clever mystery with gre[illegible] *style.* **The Wrong Guy** *is definitely on the money!*

~ Jen Wylie, best-selling author of *Sweet Light*

It's always a risk when a writer delves into reality to develop fiction, but Claudia Whitsitt pulled it off wonderfully. **The Wrong Guy** *is a solid mystery and won't disappoint readers. Well done!*

~ Book Suite Reviews

Claudia Whitsitt creates levels of tension and layers the suspense in this fast-moving and compelling novel set against the tainted campus atmosphere of Eastern Michigan University just after the arrest of real-life serial killer, John Norman Collins.

~ Gregory Fournier, author of *Zug Island: A Detroit Riot Novel* and coming soon, *The Rainy Day Murders*, the true crime story of the Washtenaw County Coed Murders.

Books by Claudia Whitsitt:
The Samantha Series ~
Identity Issues (Book 1)
Intimacy Issues (Book 2)
Internal Issues (Book 3)

Visit Claudia at:
www.claudiawhitsitt.com
Facebook:
Claudia Whitsitt, Author

Cover Design for The Wrong Guy by Littera Designs
www.litteradesigns.com

The Wrong Guy

For Denise,
I'm so glad we met!

Claudia Whitsitt

Claudia Whitsitt

Published in the United States by Twisted Vines Press

ISBN-10: 0991643003
Print ISBN: 9780991643004
ebook ISBN: 987-0-9916430-1-1

DEDICATION

This book is dedicated to Ann McCracken, my college roommate and lifelong friend. You have taught me the power of enduring friendship.

ACKNOWLEDGEMENTS

There are an abundance of people to thank. First and foremost, my husband, Don, who has an unfaltering faith in my ability to pen a story. For his endless reads, support and encouragement, I thank him. My children, Melissa Woodson, Noah Woodson, and Jenna Whitsitt also deserve my undying appreciation. To my writers group—Patty Hoffman, Barb Stark-Nemon and Kathy York—thank you for your tireless edits and suggestions. To my writing coach, Michael Thompkins, you know what you did. I am also indebted to the Southern California Writers Conference and its staff, especially Jennifer Redmond. This book, like the raising of a child, took a village. My heartfelt thanks to you all!

AUTHOR'S NOTE

The Wrong Guy is based on life at Eastern Michigan University after the real-life slayings (1967-1969) of seven young women, some who attended either EMU or the University of Michigan. The girls were brutally attacked, and their lives cut short too soon. Serial killer John Norman Collins was arrested for the last killing in July of 1969, and ultimately convicted of only that murder.

At the time, one of the murders didn't match the rest. Gary Leiterman, a retired nurse, was convicted of that crime in 2005, thirty-six years after the homicide was committed.

For the families of the girls whose murders went unresolved, they are left in limbo, even though all evidence points to Collins as the killer. Collins, was, in fact, linked to seven murders and countless other heinous crimes.

It goes without saying that this was a difficult book to write. The thought of dredging up painful memories for the families of the victims was never my intent, but my hope is that the knowledge of the true nature of this story reminds women of all ages to exercise caution at all times. Keep watch, remain alert, and don't take chances when it comes to safety.

To learn more about the true nature of the crimes, please visit my fellow author and friend, Gregory Fournier at www.fornology.blogspot.com. Greg is currently writing a true crime novel, *The Rainy Day Murders,* an extensive study of the Washtenaw County Coed Murders.

Chapter 1

LEAVING HOME

August 1969

Loading the '66 Chevy Caprice wagon with Katie's belongings would not have been a problem but for the human cargo. The car resembled a telephone booth stuffed with an entire basketball team, first string and the bench: Mom, Dad, and Katie in the front seat, the back of the car chock-full of brothers—Pete, Jeff, John, Jack, Dan, Ron, and Tom. The forty-five minute drive to Ypsilanti felt like an endless crossing of the Sahara, sans water. Bony knees and elbows, along with the sweltering eighty-five degree heat and ninety percent humidity put everyone on edge. Even with all the windows rolled down, the smell of overripe boys knocked Katie flat. Typical of her brothers, they high-fived and barked like circus seals when Dad finally pulled the wagon into the overly-crowded lot at the edge of the dormitory.

Once the tailgate opened, male appendages tumbled out like pick-up sticks dumped from their can, haphazardly toppling over each other amidst laughter and taunts. Wrestling broke out on patches of dry grass.

Katie's mother hollered from behind her Foster Grants, "Everyone grab an armload."

"Mom, wait," Katie commanded, unable to control the flush rising up her neck. "They can help once I've gone upstairs *alone* and introduced myself. If the boys tromp in there, they'll scare the poor girl away. Give me thirty minutes. Please."

The boys scrambled on to a new game, tossing an imaginary football and ignoring their mother. Years of practice. Katie would not miss, for one single moment, being embarrassed by her brothers or her mother. She eased her most precious cargo, the box loaded with her Nancy Drew books, to the back of the rear compartment. She would carry them up later, by herself. The last thing she needed was her brothers banging up her treasured hardbacks.

Katie craned her neck and gulped as she gazed at the bleak building. A huge rectangular box of brick and glass, it reminded her of a hospital, or worse, a prison—sterile, stony, and although bars didn't block the windows, she felt caged, even from the outside. One room appeared no different from another. Apart from the few maple trees lining the narrow patch of grass, she spotted no signs of comfort or warmth.

Her mom sputtered and choked. "You know how I feel about this. I need to come with you...get your room organized. I need to feel like I'm leaving you...safe... and sound."

Safe and sound. Right.

"We can hop right back in the car," Mom continued. "Stay home for a year. EMU isn't safe."

"Mom," Katie argued, "it's 1969. The world is a dangerous place. And besides, they caught the guy."

Mom started again, "But…"

"I know, I know. What if they arrested the wrong guy?" Katie couldn't help it. She rolled her eyes.

"You don't know what you're doing to me. How I'll worry. Every day, there's something in the paper."

"I'm staying. Now, could you please knock it off with the tears? Let me at least meet my roommate. I'll be back in a few minutes." Checking the dial on her Timex, she added, "I should have been here an hour ago."

Mom dabbed her red-rimmed eyes with a tissue.

Katie figured out early on her mom wasn't like other moms. Her barbs pierced deep, like hooks in a slaughterhouse. Wriggling out of them, wrangling free from Mom's constant need to be best friends, and to free herself from the role of "mother's little helper" felt like a full-time job. When her younger brothers had called her mom before she turned nine years old and the neighbor ladies tittered "how cute," she knew for sure something wasn't right. There must be a reason Mom put Katie in this role, something to blame. Mom seemed preoccupied…or overwhelmed…or too invested in her desire to look like a movie star and sing like some popular celebrity to focus on raising her family. Could it be a deep-seated psychological disorder? The thought of sorting it out exhausted Katie.

Right now, she didn't have time for it. She harbored her own worries. Between Eastern Michigan University and the U of M, seven young coeds had been brutally raped and murdered over the past two years—the last, only a month ago. No worries, she reminded herself. As long as she followed the recommended safety precautions, she'd be fine.

"If not for this, you'd find something else," she told her mom.

Tears flooded her mother's lids. "You're being obstinate."

Katie knew better.

Katie's dad wrapped his arm around his wife's shoulder. "We'll take the boys on a campus tour. They'll want to see the place."

She flashed Dad a look of eternal gratitude. He always came through for her.

Her parents reminded her of the Scale of Justice on the front lawn of the courthouse. Mom's side sunk deep into the soft earth—Dad's level head balanced the weight. Katie wished he didn't have to work three jobs to support them. In his absence she tried to keep the load from tipping, dipping, and spilling over. The few hours he spent at home allowed her to have a bit of her own life…having him here today meant she could get away.

While he rounded up his sons, Katie took a deep breath and hauled the two lightest containers out of the cargo hold of the wagon. She'd spent hours painting and decorating them over the summer. Only three weeks ago, on a blistery July afternoon, she'd set four sturdy beer cases on the newspaper-covered driveway apron. With her hair pulled back in a ponytail, she sprayed the high gloss black enamel in thin overlapping passes from the recommended twelve-inch distance. Three of her brothers, Pete, Jeffrey, and John, sat nearby squirting the water pistols she had filled earlier. The fine mist offered mild relief from the sweltering heat.

Katie fingered the pink construction paper daisies she had fashioned on the boxes as she inched toward the dorm entrance, glad she had used clear Contac paper to protect her work before consolidating her possessions inside. Her family didn't have a lot, but she and her brothers had everything they needed.

Her clothing, which included a brand new, prized pair of hip-hugger bell-bottoms, fit easily into the boxes, and she had tucked the most cherished volumes of her Nancy Drew collection in beside them.

Katie didn't care if anyone thought she was too old for Nancy Drew. Those mysteries saved her life. Nancy, her only sister in a fraternity of brothers, wasn't about to be left behind or tossed away. Besides, if people really understood Nancy's innate intelligence and courage, they wouldn't want to part with her stories either. Heck, once others learned the truth about Nancy, Katie might have to guard the books from thieves, or set up a personal library loan system.

All around her, college freshman lugged loads of clothing and bedding. Comet cleanser canisters peeked out of brown paper bags, toppling over other cleaning essentials. Laundry baskets overflowed with towels, Fritos snacks, and amid a sea of tattered dorm maps, the single escapee, an electric roller, speckled the landscape.

Feather dusters gathered stray dust bunnies as they brushed past. *How much housework got done at college?* Katie liked things tidy, but she didn't plan on spending her life cleaning.

Everyone seemed to have more than her. Funny, she thought, how my life fits simply and completely into four little boxes. *I have everything I need.* She nodded firmly in satisfaction. Life's finally taking me places, she thought. It's important to travel light.

She hoped she would fit in.

Katie studied the other girls, panic frozen onto their faces. She wasn't the only one fighting back tears and struggling to calm her quivering lip. Slipping past an old beater, its driver's door open in one of the metered spots, she cracked a grin as she listened to the blaring "Time of the Season." The Zombies music rocked the entire quadrant. A security guard asked a kid to turn it down.

Katie continued to nudge her way amid stalled groups with the appropriate "excuse-me"s and smiles. Mop handles and broomsticks tangled in the doorway and slowed her again.

"Here, come this way," a mother offered with a welcoming smile. She beamed with pride. "It's such a great day, isn't it? You girls moving in, about to be on your own."

Katie nodded and forced a smile as she edged by.

The woman faced her daughter. "Let me take a picture of you, Mary, so we can get the name of the hall in the background!"

Wow, Katie thought, so different from *my* mom! As she climbed the back steps to the third floor, she guessed

Room 313 would mark the halfway point down the long, narrow hall. Sweat dripped from her temple, and she hoped the single stream trickling down her back hadn't left a visible splotch on her shirt. She kicked the door a couple of times to signal her arrival. No answer. She smacked an imaginary hand on her forehead.

She should have stopped in the lobby at check-in to grab her keys. Too late now. Beneath her name, in bold print, she read: Jamie McCormick. Her stomach fluttered. She wanted to like this girl. She wanted this girl to like her. To hopes for a new best friend, she thought, then set the boxes at her feet and twisted the knob. The door fell open and she inched her way inside, kick-sliding the beer cases through the entryway. It seemed surprising keys were optional, especially considering the extensive letter she had received regarding safety precautions.

She scrutinized her new digs. The cinder block walls, painted banana-yellow, made the room feel frigid. Even on this, the most scorching of days, a chill passed through her. At the sliding glass window, she parted the heavy drapes. The EMU logo printed on them—a Huron Indian, in blue, white, yellow, and black—didn't even match the school colors.

In the courtyard, three lone maple saplings dotted the barren square. The previous April she picked this dorm for its newness, but now she questioned the wisdom of her decision. A brick and ivy dorm, one with character, would have been homier. Add the parched grass and dust-filled courtyard, and the place appeared deserted. Only the occasional fan in an open window provided evidence of human inhabitants. A flower arrangement, the one thing brightening her staid surroundings, sat oversized and out of place on the modular desk. It looked as if it belonged in a funeral home, not a college dorm room. All of a sudden its scent overwhelmed her and a sourness rose in her throat.

What am I doing here? Why did I think going away to college was such a good idea? To this college!

Sweet stale air filled her nostrils. She slid open the window and hoped the fresh air would calm her nerves, all the while reciting a simple prayer. "God, guide me through this day. Make the goodbye's quick, and help me not to cry." She crossed herself, and then added, "Oh, yeah, turn off the spigot in Mom's eyes, too, would you please?" She crossed herself again. *It's supposed to be about me, not her.*

Her heart bah-boomed like a bass drum and Katie swallowed hard. Stay busy, keep moving, she told herself. Unpack. Hopefully this Janie girl would make her appearance soon. If Katie didn't reach the parking lot exactly thirty minutes from now, her mom would allow her battalion of brothers to swarm the room.

She opened the top drawer of the dresser and found it stuffed with days-of-the-week panties, pair after pair, in pinks and pastel blues. Her eyes bulged. No one has this many sets of underwear, she thought. In the next drawer, sweaters galore spilled over—cable knit cardigans and pullovers of every possible hue. The drawer beneath held slacks and jeans. With each and every drawer stuffed full, not an inch of space remained for any of Katie's belongings.

Her muscles tensed. She twisted her neck to the left and then to the right. If only she had arrived earlier. Then, she could have staked her claim and felt situated, ready for all this. She placed her hands on her hips. The nerve, she thought, as she removed her roommate's clothing from one of the drawers. She stacked them in neat piles on one side of an imaginary dividing line on the desk, rearranged her own things in the top drawer, then closed it, and dusted off her hands.

From there, she headed purposefully for the adjoining bathroom. Delighted that no one had yet staked claim here, Katie arranged her toiletries on two shelves of the medicine cabinet. She placed her deodorant, toothpaste, and hair spray on the bottom shelf, and then organized her hairbrush, comb, toothbrush, and Heaven Scent cologne on the other. She set her electric rollers on the counter, and her bonnet hair dryer under the sink.

As she glanced in the mirror, her tie-dyed t-shirt and cut-off blue jeans looked suddenly out of place, and her long auburn hair too wavy and too plain. She wished she had ironed it straight. Even her deep-set eyes and slender frame were inadequate. *My eyes look flat today. Gray instead of blue.* She swiped the melting mascara smudges from beneath her eyes and inspected her legs. *I look like Olive Oyl, for Pete's sake.*

A sudden rap on the bathroom door startled her. She winced at her reflection. "Yes?"

"Hey, get out here! I want to meet you."

Katie smoothed her hair in a flash, strode into the room and froze, her mouth agape at this young version of Grace Kelly. Natural platinum-blonde curls framed Janie's round face—her blue eyes resembled reflecting pools of seawater. Dressed in madras shorts and a matching white poplin shirt, both crisply ironed, she could have stepped out of a fashion magazine like *Seventeen.* Red Dr. Scholl's sandals adorned her feet, and a gold locket hung from her delicate neck. Even from a distance, she smelled of Tabu, a far too expensive cologne. This day turned worse with each ticking second.

"Don't just stand there," Janie's voice rang out, loud and playful. "Tell me about yourself."

Flustered, Katie took a measured breath and began. "I come from a large family. From Detroit. What about you?"

"A Detroit girl?" She flashed a huge, perfectly-pearly and perfectly-straight smile. "I'm from Birmingham."

Well, la-di-da, Katie thought. She'd been to Birmingham once. Woman strutted through the streets, wearing high heels in the middle of the day. Used to Sears, JC Penney, and Woolworth's, Birmingham's stores sounded foreign: Gucci, Jacobson's, and Dittrich Furs. Underground parking kept the shoppers flawlessly coifed and dry—a scene from a Hollywood movie.

In spite of the fact that they came from different sides of the fence, Katie yearned for a connection. "Where did you go to high school?"

"Groves. The University forced me to attend some stupid summer school program before they'd accept me. Just what I felt like doing all vacation, staying up here and going to some shitty classes." She rolled her eyes as she unpacked a hatbox onto the desktop, then grinned.

"I barely got in. What about you? Where'd you go to school?"

Katie straightened, proud of her high school accomplishments. "I went to St. Mary's."

Janie's eyes widened as she gave her the once over. "Oh my God, you're Catholic? How the hell did I get a goddamn Goody-Two-Shoes as a roommate?"

"Don't worry. I'm normal. We'll get along just fine." Katie turned away and tipped her eyes heavenward. She lifted the second of her boxes and set it on the dresser with a thud. "I need room for my clothes."

Janie heaved a sigh and patted the folded stack of sweaters neatly piled on the desk. "I see you've made yourself at home," she teased. "I'll store a few things in the closet so you have some room."

"Thanks. I'll head down to check-in, then get the rest of my stuff."

Janie replied with a flip of her head. "Okey dokey."

Katie slipped down the three flights of steps, her eyes straight ahead. She needed time to think. How on earth would she live with this girl? By the time she arrived at the registration area, the line with her section of the alphabet moved quickly and she collected her cafeteria pass, room, and mailbox keys.

"I need to speak to someone about getting my room switched," she pleaded with the volunteer manning the desk.

"Sorry," the woman answered, "we're directed to take care of the most urgent concerns first. If you still feel determined to switch in a couple of weeks, talk to your housemother. Give yourself time to adjust." She glanced at the roster and raised her eyebrows. "But I must warn you, Kathleen, if you can't make do, word will get around. If you don't learn to live with this roommate, *you* may not work out, period."

"I don't think you understand," she rattled. "This girl is not normal."

"No one is, sweetheart."

From behind her, an experienced coed tapped Katie's shoulder. "It'll work out. I can't tell you how much I loathed my roomie first semester. Come semester break, I met a girl down the hall more my type and we swapped. This year, it's a breeze. Don't worry. You'll see."

Katie returned the girl's reassuring grin, hiding her doubt, and blew out a big puff of air. At home, at dinner, they ate all the food on their plates—a requirement—all the kids in her family maintained a permanent membership in the "Clean Plate Club." Her disgusting canned peas became tolerable when she mixed them with her mashed potatoes. She would find a way to blend this imposing girl into her life—stomach her. Who knows? She liked peas now. Maybe she'd like Janie after a while. *There is a reason for everything.* She stuffed the keys into the pocket of her cut-offs and pushed through the crowd to find her family.

Outside, Dad handed each brother a single item—a dust broom, a dustpan, a brown lunch bag of family photos, and a box of sanitary napkins. *How embarrassing.* She decided to collect the Nancy Drew's later, by herself. Mom sat sideways on the passenger seat…the door open, her head in her hands.

Why? Why can't I have a regular mom? I'll pretend everything is all right. Maybe that will work.

"Hi, guys," she said. "I met my new roommate. She's great! C'mon up, I'll introduce you."

Katie focused on getting settled and keeping the goodbye's simple. As the seven of them—from the tow-headed baby John, to the teenaged, freckled-faced, green-eyed Tom—lined up behind her with their hands full, she worried about them making do without her. "Mom," she said for the gazillionth time, "you have to keep an eye on John around the toilet. He loves giving his cars a wash in there."

"It's all right," her mother answered. "He'll be fine."

Katie knew better and blinked back tears. She'd been raising her brothers for so many years, she could barely imagine another kind of life. Only *she* noticed when one of them was sick, or sad, or lonely. Only *she* knew when Tom snuck in late at night and was too hung over to go to school.

I have to get out.

Since the ten of them wouldn't fit in the elevator, she guided them toward the staircase. They shoved through the steel fire door and tromped up the flight of industrial stairs—gunmetal cement with the requisite iron-gray railing. The boys howled like a pack of wolves all the way upstairs, just to listen to their voices echo.

She led the procession to her room. The door lay wide open and she stepped in first, the boys trailing behind.

Janie's rich laugh filled the room. "What are these, your footmen?"

Katie bit her lip as she pointed them out one by one. "These are my brothers: John, Jeffery, Pete, Jack, Danny, Ron, and Tom."

Janie shook her head and laughed at Katie's mom. "Whoa, you really are Catholic! The good old rhythm method. Not very effective, huh, Mom?"

"We believe in the sanctity of life, young lady," Katie's mom retorted.

Janie made a face behind Mom's back, waving her hands beside her ears and sticking out her tongue.

Katie tried to lighten the mood. "Let's get my things put away."

Her mom searched for linens and shooed the boys off the beds. She fired a fierce frown in Janie's direction and flagged open the sheet. "Which bed shall I make up for you, Kathleen?"

Katie, used to doing all things in a fair and equitable manner, looked at Janie expectantly. "Shall we draw for it?"

Janie smacked her pillow on the bare upper mattress. "I've already got dibs on the top bunk. I got here first."

Katie snatched a notepad and pen out of her bag. "Let's make it fair. I'll put an 'X" on one sheet of paper for you, and an "O" on another for me. Tom can draw it out of…" she tapped her lips and looked from brother to brother. "Ron's baseball cap."

Ron offered Tom his hat and Janie his sympathy. "She makes us do this at home, too."

Janie arched her brows and took stock of the boys, graduated in size like kitchen canisters. "Well, aren't you the little mother?" She chose a slip of paper from the hat and snorted. "It's an 'X.' You can make up the bottom bunk for your little darling, Mom."

Mom glared and balled up the sheet against her chest.

Katie reached into her pocket, hid her rosary in her palm, and snuck it inside her pillow as she pretended to smooth the case. The thought of sleeping beneath the princess in the closed up space unsettled her, but she spoke up to smooth the tension. "Fair and square, you win. I still have a couple of boxes downstairs. I'll go and get them."

Janie bounded off Katie's bed. "Hey, roomie, I'll give you a hand."

The girls left the unruly troops behind and began their first official walk, as roommates, down the third floor hall.

"Your family is weird," Janie said.

"They're a bit overwhelming," Katie admitted. "Once you get to know them, though, you'll really like them." Speaking of family, she thought, where's yours?

"And your mom," Janie continued with her critique, "are you sure she can handle this?"

"She'll be all right." Katie hoped, eventually, her mom would come around. As she pushed open the doors, she smiled at Janie. I'll follow the upperclassman's advice, she thought. *No doubt this girl is rich, clueless, and rude. Somehow, I'll have to make do.*

"Here we are!" Katie hoisted the tailgate. The two prized beer cases sat like trophies. She smiled as she smoothed her hand over the lacquered box tops and handed one to Janie before collecting the other.

Janie admired her handiwork. "Cool cases. Did you decorate these yourself?"

"Yep."

For an instant, Katie felt content. Maybe things would work out. Janie possessed at least one nice, normal bone in her body.

"What's in here? This is heavy for such a small box."

She glanced at the box Janie carted across the parking lot. "Oh, that must be the one with my books."

"You brought books?"

"A couple of favorite mysteries."

Janie shrugged, shook her head, and glanced in the crowd's direction. "I can't believe these girls."

"What girls?"

"You know, the ones moving in, like us."

"What about them?"

"They look scared shitless. Babies, all babies."

"Where is your family, by the way?"

"Dad dropped me off early. He didn't stay."

Katie couldn't imagine. He dropped Janie off? No trace of him? And no mention of a mom, or sister, or brother?

The elevator doors opened and a group filed out. Katie and Janie joined a waiting crowd of girls, also laden with boxes. Janie, in her haste for a corner spot, rammed Katie's box into the door of the lift.

She giggled. "Oops, sorry."

Katie prayed for minor damage. "Don't worry about it."

The roommates passed Katie's brothers darting through the hall as they strolled to their room chatting about meal and orientation times. They crossed the threshold, and Katie's mom threw her hands over her face and yelped.

Katie no longer hid her irritation. "Now, what?"

"Look at your case, it's ruined."

Sure enough, the case Janie carried had a good-sized crumple in the top corner. Katie hid her frustration. "It's a thing, not a person. No big deal."

"Yeah, Mom," Janie piped up, "cool your jets! It's not a big deal."

Katie's mother clamped her mouth closed and regained her composure, then pointed to the desk. "Look at the flowers."

"I noticed them when I came in," Katie said. She took a second look and admitted, "They are beautiful."

"Look at the card."

"They're Janie's. Not my business."

"Look again," her mom said. "They're for you."

Katie set down her box and plucked the envelope from the arrangement. The card, addressed to her, made her feel a tug of guilt for being so harsh with her mother. Maybe Mom had sent the flowers. She pulled out the tiny message card.

Janie snatched the tag from her hand and read it aloud, her volume increasing with each recited word. "Can't wait to come and visit you at college." Then louder and with more bravado, she cocked her head and shouted, "Love, Mark." She paused, unexpectedly serious, and narrowed her eyes at Katie. "Who the hell is Mark?"

Katie yanked the card from Janie's hand and faced her mother. "Did you open this?"

"I simply admired the arrangement," her mother answered.

Katie stomped her foot. "You read the card!"

"You know how I feel about *that* boy!"

Janie leaned over Katie's shoulder. "Who's Mark?"

"My high school boyfriend. Ancient history," she said flatly, facing down her mother.

Janie rubbed her chin like a reporter who just discovered the day's headline. "Well, now."

Katie puffed out an angry sigh and stared at her mother. "We broke up!"

Janie cocked back on her heels, licked her left index finger, and began leafing through a Nancy Drew mystery. "Did you know there are pictures in here?"

"The books are mementos. Favorites. Childhood treasures." Reaching blindly behind her, Katie snatched the book from Janie's hand and tossed it on her bed. Her mom recovered the novel and clutched it to her buxom chest, smoothing the cover.

Janie pilfered another book from Katie's shiny case. Her eyes widened, she set her shoulders back and began reading aloud in a deep, mocking, announcer-like voice, "Nancy Drew, an attractive girl of eighteen, drove home along a country road in her new, dark-blue convertible."

Katie's mom grasped the volume from Janie's hands and interrupted her oration.

Katie, monkey in the middle, felt the color rising in her cheeks. Meanwhile, her brothers raced up and down the hall. Only Tom stayed behind to feast his eyes on Janie. Suddenly overcome by the pungent scent of the roses, Katie steadied herself against the desk chair. "You know, Mom, it'll be easier saying goodbye if we do it sooner, rather than later."

Janie interrupted. "You okay, roomie?"

Mom took Katie's hands in her own and locked eyes with her daughter. "I can't stand this," she cried. "How on earth will I be able to live in a house full of men?"

Katie couldn't squelch her sarcasm. "They aren't men, Mom, they're little boys."

"You know what I mean, Katie. You're my salvation. I'll be lost without you." Her mom wrapped her arms around her and held on with all her might.

"You're gonna be fine, Mom," Janie said with unabashed authority.

"Stop being rude, young lady," Katie's mom commanded.

Katie bristled, stepped back, and swallowed. Her mom sucked the life from her like a heavy-duty sponge. "I'll call, Mom, and write. I can come home on weekends." She lied with a surprising fierceness. "You wanted me to go to college, remember? To have the opportunity you never did. Try not to make this harder than it already is."

Katie's dad's appeared in the doorway.

"We're just saying goodbye, Dad. I can't handle a long, drawn out farewell, all right?"

Dad laid his hand on Mom's arm. "C'mon, honey, let's get the boys home." To Katie, he added, "Let's all go downstairs and you can kiss your brothers goodbye."

"Really?" Katie threw her head back in thanksgiving. "Perfect. Let's say goodbye."

Already off and running, her dad led the pack.

Her back stiffened as she followed her parents and the throng of boys through the hall, down the steps, and out to the car. Dad opened the doors to let the heat escape while the boys fought for a place in line in front of her.

Her throat filled with tears and her chest tightened. Five minutes from now, she thought, it'll be done.

"I expect to see each one of you alive and free of major injuries the next time I come home," Katie said.

"Yeah, sure, Sis."

John and Jeffrey began to cry, both in anticipation of Katie's departure and from exhaustion, now long past their naptime.

She soothed them, stroking their arms and caressing their cheeks. "It's all right. Big Sis will be home soon." She wished with all her heart she wasn't lying to them. It was time for her to have her own life, even if she wasn't sure how.

Dad bear-hugged Katie and said, "Go get 'em, girl. I love you. You're gonna be great."

She softened in his embrace. "Thanks, Dad."

Mom gripped Katie's forearm with vice-like strength.

Katie's chest constricted, overwhelmed at the thought of her brothers without her, alone with their real mother. She felt like a traitor. "You're going to be fine. You'll all be fine."

From behind her came a voice soon to be the most familiar one in her life.

"Yoo-hoo!" Janie, swinging a purse over her head like a lasso, caught up to them, and nudged between Katie and her mom, breaking the fierce hold.

Mom looked spent, worn out. "My purse."

Janie placed the purse over Mom's shoulder, smoothing the strap over her breast.

"Don't worry." Janie waved a furious goodbye and led Katie away. "I've got her now."

Chapter 2

WARNINGS

September 1969

Another oppressive evening, typical of late summer, and the humidity hung thick, suspended in the air like a blanket. Katie and Janie sat on a stiff orange vinyl cushion crowded by their dormmates. They spotted their suitemates, Gwen and Cynthia across the room, but knew better than to wave or call out to them. Gwen had said, "We're black. We can't afford to mix with you in public." *Whatever.* Packed into the stuffy main lounge like sausages, they all whispered of things they'd rather do. The girls hated these mandatory meetings, the third of them in just as many days.

Katie stared out the window at her still new surroundings. Just outside, she spotted a distant sliver of blue poking through the threatening skies. The maintenance man, in his red suspenders and Wrangler jeans, made a final pass on his tractor. The fresh cut grass smelled sweet—the calm before the storm.

Facing an hour of tedium, she wished she could be looking out at the campus water tower instead. She closed her eyes and pictured the lingering petunias overflowing at its base. The water tower stood on a slivered triangle of land at the entrance of the university. Official bane of the university's reputation, it resembled a colossal phallus. Legend said, if a virgin graduated from the university, the tower would crumble. Katie chuckled to herself. With her strict upbringing, she might be the cause of its demise.

Sue Hutchinson, the housemother with the too-tight perm, began the meeting. "Now girls, you all know John Norman Collins is behind bars. It's dreadful what he's done. Some of those girls, students here at Eastern and our neighbor, the U of M…their souls have passed to a better place." Sue perched her heavy frame precariously on a metal stool. "I'm not telling you anything you don't already know. The Campus Police are running extra patrols, but some of you are still going out alone after dark. It's not a time to act foolish."

Behind her a girl whispered, "He strangled the one at the cemetery, shot her, and then slit her throat. Can you imagine?"

A voice answered, "And he left a copy of *Catch-22* next to her, along with her shoes. He positioned them side by side—staging them like some sick Hollywood horror scene."

"I think *I'm* gonna be sick," the friend said.

Katie's stomach took a dive.

Janie jabbed her in the side with a sharp elbow. "Will you be able to sleep tonight?"

Janie liked to make a joke out of everything, absolutely everything, but Katie's stomach knotted nonetheless.

They'd been roommates for a week and a half and she ought to feel some small tinge of loyalty to her by now, but at times like this, she wished Janie would just shut up.

"It makes me sad to think any girl on this campus would put herself at risk," Sue continued. "Please demonstrate common sense, and don't take chances. Stay inside after dark."

Katie wondered how the upperclassmen could have lived with this fear for the past two years.

"If you do have to go out," Sue said, "be sure you have a buddy, preferably a male you know and trust."

Don't go to the bathroom alone—always travel in pairs. Katie shivered as she remembered field trip warnings from her elementary days.

"There's an excuse to shack up with somebody if I ever heard one," Janie whispered as she grabbed Katie's wrist and made her jump. The girls behind them heard and giggled.

Shocked, Katie shook her head at all of them.

"Leave your handbags at home," Sue advised. "If you don't have a whistle, mace, or pepper spray, there are small canisters for sale at the Union which attach to a key ring. Keep your keys in your hands at all times when you're out, day or night. Lace them between your fingers, like sharp knuckles. Don't go asking for trouble. Remember, you're my girls. I want my girls to be safe. Don't be scared, be careful."

On cue, thunder boomed outside and a bolt of lightning lit up the lounge. The lights flickered. Sheets of rain blew in through the windows, and while Sue rushed to close them, the girls sat, either too dumbstruck or too bored to move. Katie, suddenly freezing, longed to gather her loose change, run to the pay phone, and call her dad.

"Come and get me," she'd plead. *"There's been some mistake. You've dropped me off at the wrong place. Young women have been murdered here."*

Even though Katie grew up in Detroit, a major metropolis, she spent most of her life within the secular boundaries of her Catholic parish, her school, and her friends' and relatives' homes. She attended college less than fifty miles away, still, she felt far removed from her safety net. The talk of the killings, the uncertainty of her new surroundings, it all left her feeling panicked and alone. The only one to steer her—Janie—seemed an ill-fitting guide.

Sue opened the meeting to questions and the room quieted.

Katie raised her hand and Sue pointed in her direction. "If John Norman Collins committed all of the crimes, why do we still have to be watchful...and afraid?"

Janie interrupted. "Oh, yeah!" She snickered in her sports announcer voice. "We got ourselves a real live Nancy Drew here. My roomie has the complete collection, and the deductive skills of a cat in a paper bag."

Girls joined in her laughter.

Sue glared at the crowd. "Questions are important. And yes, the authorities do believe this young man is responsible for all of the murders. Since he's behind bars, there have been no other..." She paused, carefully considered her words, then added, "incidents. However, the police want us to remain alert and exercise caution."

One of the upperclassman scoffed. "Who's kidding who?"

As the meeting broke up, girls helped each other off the floor. Katie twisted her arm through Janie's like a pretzel knot. "How did you stay here all summer? Weren't you terrified?"

"Trust me. I'm used to being alone. It's not such a big deal. Really. Don't get your panties in a bunch about these warnings. The university is making a fuss, even after they caught the guy. For God's sake, they need to give it up." Janie's huge blue eyes, white-blonde curls, and trim physique were at odds with her tough-guy personality.

She pulled Katie along. "C'mon, let's go upstairs."

The girls donned lightweight cotton baby-doll pajamas when they reached their room. Rather than clearing out the air and cooling it off, the storm left it thick, heavy, and hot. As Katie brushed her hair, she took in their space. Janie owned all of the forbidden appliances—a television, mini-fridge, and an iron. And she displayed them proudly.

"Aren't you worried about getting written up?"

Janie frowned from the bed and squinted at Katie like a horn grew from out of her head. "For what?"

"For having all this banned electrical equipment."

"You're kidding, right?"

"I'm a worrier. I can't help it. You and I, we're like yin and yang. I'm the voice of reason, and you...well, I'm not at all sure what you are."

Janie went uncharacteristically quiet.

A stuffed floppy-eared dog sat posed on Katie's pillow sham, along with her favorite doll, a baby in polka-dotted pajamas who talked when she pulled the string.

The posters plastered all over the wall above her side of the desk and next to her bed screamed personality. She had chosen them carefully—a picture of an old couple walking down a long winding road, holding hands. Another of a tow-headed toddler sniffing a daisy; it read *Take Time to Smell the Flowers.*

Katie had fastened a square of walnut-colored cork to the wall above the space between the two beds. Bubble letters fashioned out of gold-colored felt and thumbtacked to the board read "I GOT LOVE" after her favorite song. Next to it, a photo the RA had taken the first week depicted the roommates with their arms tossed around each other's shoulders, huge happy grins on their faces. Katie knew it was a long shot, but she hoped displaying the picture of the two of them, posed as real roommates, would mean something to Janie. Let her know she was trying.

She recalled drop-off day, and how as soon as her family left, Janie asked her to help take the bunks apart. It confused Katie. Janie had made a big deal about claiming the top bunk and then thirty minutes later, she wanted to take down the entire set. After Katie helped her lift the top bunk to the floor, Janie grabbed her hammer and started banging. Before long, she'd disassembled the bed, turned the frame upside down, and set the mattress four feet up in the air. It resembled a suspended bridge—to nowhere.

When Janie finished her reconstruction project, she added a simple flowered comforter, but nothing else. No evidence of Janie's star quality, just a flat worn-out pillow, tossed willy-nilly on the bed in a plain white case.

Katie couldn't push it from her mind. It seemed odd and a bit troublesome. Janie had stuffed the drawers and closet with loads of clothing, but the room said nothing about her.

Katie shrugged, afraid to broach the subject with Janie. Then, unable to turn off her optimistic nature asked, "Posters, how do you feel about posters?"

"Do whatever you want."

"I already did. But what about you? C'mon, don't you want to put up a poster that speaks Janie?"

Janie guffawed, arranging her hand behind her head and posing like a fashion model. "Speaks me?"

"Really, put up just one."

Janie placed her hands on her hips and pursed her lips. "You're not going to change me."

"What do you mean?" Katie teased. "I don't want to change you."

A recent family photo of a trip to Saginaw Bay with a wallet-sized studio pose of her grandmother tucked snugly into the bottom of its frame sat on Katie's desk. Her neatly stacked Nancy Drew volumes and textbooks lay on the shelf beside a carefully arranged cup with a highlighter, freshly sharpened pencils, and fountain pens with both blue and black ink. She selected a favorite mystery to lull her to sleep.

Janie crossed her arms. "What the hell? What's the deal with you and Nancy Drew?"

"They're treasures, sort of my security blanket. Think of it this way. Nancy got me through a lot of tough times. I'm holding onto her with both hands."

"Yeah, well if anyone needs something to hold on to, it's you."

"Meaning?"

"You're not twelve anymore!"

"Have you ever read her? Oh, I remember. You're not a reader." Katie's disdain hung in the air like a dense fog.

"Nice!" Janie stuck out her tongue.

"She's a great character," Katie defended.

"Well, fuck, so am I!"

Katie turned away and rolled her eyes. *Talk about characters.* "You know, you could say 'fudge' instead of using the 'f' word."

Janie laughed so hard, she held her stomach. "Yeah, and you could say 'booger' instead of 'drainage.'"

Janie turned the pages of a textbook.

"Would you like some help studying? I took a class on study skills. I'm happy to share what I learned."

Janie hooted, slapped her knee, rummaged under her bed, and retrieved a bottle of Mad Dog 20/20. She tossed back her head and belted down a slug.

Katie hated drinking. "Must you?"

"Just because your folks baptized you as an infant," Janie said, "made you a Catholic, you've swallowed this religion garbage, hook, line, and sinker. Don't you want to think for yourself? Face it, you've been brainwashed! You do the right thing all the time. You're motivated by guilt." Janie downed another gulp and then offered Katie the bottle.

Katie shook her head and turned away.

She had to admit it, Janie hit a nerve. Katie had spent her entire life caught up in doing all the right things, helping care for her brothers, getting good grades. When she strayed in the slightest, even in her thoughts, excruciating guilt tortured her long into the night. Janie's manner mostly put her off, but she found her irresistible at times, and the temptations, somewhat inviting. Not the drinking, but the attitude.

Katie took a deep breath and wished she could relax. Like Janie did.

Then again, as hard as Janie tried to hide her true self, Katie glimpsed the real Janie on move-in day. When Katie went to wash her hands before dinner on the very first night, Janie followed.

"Oh, no, don't tell me you wash your hands before meals," Janie had teased.

Katie stood stymied until Janie said, "Shove over." She nudged Katie with an elbow, grabbed the soap from her hands and washed up. "Just wait till you see the rainbow-colored ham, you won't worry about washing your hands anymore." Then she looped her arm through Katie's and skipped down the hall.

Katie liked that Janie was spontaneously affectionate and fun.

As she thought about her roommate, she glimpsed a lone photograph hidden behind the books on Janie's side of the dresser. Odd. Katie positioned herself so she could examine it without drawing attention. The woman in the photograph looked just like Janie. It had to be Janie's mom.

She pulled down her covers—the snapshot made her think of her own mother. Maybe having too many kids had done her in. Or maybe the cuckoo clock had hit her on the head once or twice. What about Janie's mom? Was she different?

Two minutes later Janie turned out the lights and Katie whispered, "Hey, Janie."

"Now what?"

Katie paused for a moment, then dove right in. "Your mom's picture. I saw it on the dresser. She's so pretty. Tell me about her."

Janie answered with her typical matter-of-fact brusqueness. "She's dead."

Katie murmured gently, "But there must be more to it."

"Not much. What else is there to say? I hardly remember her. She died before I turned five. TB."

"Did she ever live at home with you? Or did she stay in a sanatorium?"

"You're so stupid. Really, Katie. Panties. Bunch. Don't worry."

"Do you remember her living at home?"

"I remember once," Janie's voice softened, "when I was really little, she held my hands and danced with me in the kitchen. She wore a flowered blue apron, tied around her waist, and it fanned out when she spun around. She was so pretty, especially when she smiled."

"You must miss her a lot."

Katie turned on the night light, slid out of her bed, and over onto Janie's. She curled in next to her and smelled her roommate's perfume. Janie stared at the ceiling with her arms folded like a bow behind her head, and Katie waited. In the pale glow of the nightlight, in spite of her full-time attitude, Janie looked small and pure, like one of the cherubic angels painted on the ceiling at church.

"What else do you remember about her?"

Janie shrugged. "I don't know."

"C'mon. I want to know about her."

"I'll have to think."

Katie gave her a grin and a shove. "Uh-oh. Tall order."

She smiled back and slugged Katie in the arm. "Smart ass."

"Come on, tell me about her."

"She sang to me at night when she tucked me in," Janie recalled. "Moon River. With the prettiest, sweetest voice." A snuffle escaped her, and Katie held her sadness safe in the darkness.

Taking her hand and holding it, Katie gently stroked the top of it with her index finger. Janie didn't pull away.

"When we went to the sanatorium, they wouldn't let me near her. I couldn't be in the same room with her…I wasn't allowed to touch her. Momma sat in a wheelchair on one side of a window and Dad and I sat on the other. She would spread her hand out on the glass and I would put mine on top of hers, like a mirror." Janie closed her eyes. "The last day she put her whole face on the glass and kissed me. I kissed her back."

Katie blinked back tears and squeezed Janie's arm.

"At the funeral home," Janie tapped her fingers on her lips and continued, "my grandma stuck me in a dress. I'm a goddamned tomboy, for Christ's sake, I don't wear dresses. So there I am, flitting around, watching my skirt twirl, acting all normal. I ran up to the casket; I kept telling mom to watch me. 'See, Momma,' I said, 'I can make my skirt fly.' My grandma dragged me away and said I couldn't bother her now."

Katie shook her head. "You weren't bothering your mother."

"Shit, I guess not. Hard to bother a dead person."

"It wasn't fair. She shouldn't have pulled you away."

"I tried to crawl in the casket with her," Janie admitted quietly, "when my grandma wasn't looking."

"You did?" Katie pictured a young Janie sneakily hoisting a chubby four year old baby leg up on the side of the casket, securing a patent leather Mary Jane on the pall bearers rail, and climbing over the side, totally focused on the prize inside—finally getting to touch her mom, be skin to skin with her.

"Yep, and I almost made it. At the last minute, Dad snatched me by the scruff of my neck, and said something about 'come on, you little monkey,' like he was dragging me down from a jungle gym."

Katie's throat closed. "I'm sure he didn't know what else to do. I'm sure it hurt him, pulling you away. Maybe he tried making light of it in order to somehow keep you from hurting, too?"

"I didn't understand why everybody made such a big deal—they kept paying attention to me. Nobody ever paid attention to me. It confused me, you know? I just wanted my mom to play with me. I've thought about it. Finally, I had her from behind the glass, but she's lying dead in a coffin in front of me."

"You couldn't possibly understand. You were little."

"I always do the wrong thing. Even when I know better." A puff of air escaped Janie's lips.

"Did he try to explain it to you?"

"Who, stone face? No."

"Later? After you went home? Or when you got older and could understand more?"

"He hasn't mentioned her since the funeral."

"Honestly?"

Janie's nod lay shadowed by the nightlight.

"Did he at least take care of you?"

"What do you mean? Did he feed me?" Janie rolled her eyes. "I don't know. I guess. He left money in the cookie jar. I'd get up in the morning and get ready for school, take a couple of dollars and stop at the diner for the breakfast special. I parked at the same spot at the soda counter, and they'd bring me my bacon and eggs. I was a regular."

"What, when you were five? Seems like too much for a little kid to handle."

Janie shrugged. "Whatever. I lived through it."

"Did he come home at night and make you dinner?"

"Sometimes," she admitted. "But you know the worst part? When he went out at night, I'd take a butcher knife to bed with me. I'd lay awake, scared to death. If the wind so much as blew, I thought somebody was breaking in."

Katie wondered at the contradiction. On the surface, Janie seemed carefree and happy-go-lucky. She reminded herself not to judge a book by its cover. Janie had secrets. Deep wounds. How did she get from lost little girl to rich young coed?

"You're lucky you didn't hurt yourself with the knife."

Janie shook her head as if to shake off the memories.

"You didn't deserve any of that, you know," Katie said. She tried to give Janie a hug.

Janie waved her off.

"I worry about you. Sometimes you scare me. Don't go out so late, all right? At least not by yourself. And stop doing stupid stuff. Lying on the runway and watching the planes come in is dangerous. You've really gotta knock off the risky behavior."

"Ok, roomie," Janie whispered. "Whatever you say." She rolled over, faced the wall, reached out to touch the cinder block bumps, and then cleared her throat. "You know what this means, don't you?"

"What?"

"Next time, I get to ask you about your mom."

Katie gave Janie's back a quick pat and padded quietly to her bed. She fingered her rosary beads as she lay awake listening to the whirring hum of Janie's window box fan. Long after Janie's breathing evened out in sleep, Katie wondered about mothers, hers and Janie's.

Chapter 3

DIRTY TRICKS

September 1969

Monday's first class, an eight o'clock, meant early rising, so Katie tiptoed around in the dark to get ready. She didn't want to wake Janie. Only after she rode the elevator downstairs did it register—the total darkness, the missing scent of burnt coffee from the cafeteria—only she was up and about. Loaded down with her five-pound government text and binder, she squinted at the wall clock above the front desk. It read 5:40 a.m. It should have read 7:40 a.m.

At first, she wondered if there was some mistake. Maybe the clock stopped. Had the electricity gone out during the night? But her alarm clock plugged into the wall, it wasn't a wind-up like Janie's, and it woke her at the regular time.

Okay, great. Janie, the practical joker, had messed with her alarm. Her blood simmered. How could she? After last night when they shared something so deep. *How could I have been so naive, to trust Janie, feel close to her?* She gave herself a swift mental kick.

Too mad to wait for the elevator, she pushed through the back door to the stairway, the one desecrated with the Nixon/Agnew bumper stickers. Protests against the Vietnam War, the government, anything bureaucratic, were plastered all over campus. In light of Janie's practical joke, Katie planned to wage her own demonstration. She stormed up three flights of stairs and tore into the room.

Her books thudded on the desk. "I can't believe you tricked me!"

Janie rubbed her eyes, then propped herself on her elbow and snickered. "Don't tell me you're mad!"

"How could you think I wouldn't be? Do you like waking up two hours early? It's bad enough it's my earliest class, but if you call yourself my roommate..." she screamed, shaking. "What the heck, are *you* twelve?"

Janie tossed her head back onto her pillow and laughed even harder. Katie grabbed her books and tucked them securely under her arm.

"Boy, you don't have a much of a sense of humor, do you?" Janie muttered.

Katie glared at Janie. "I do, too, when something is funny. So much for considering you a friend." She swung around to march out, and fired again, "By the way, if I used foul language, this would be the time." She couldn't spend one more minute in the same building as Janie. She flew down the steps and out of the dorm.

In the pitch black, with no students around, Katie swiped back her tears as she scaled the steep hill to the ivy-covered library.

Her dad always teased her, to toughen up her thin skin, he said. He and her brothers would sing their own special tune reserved just for her, 'she has freckles on her butt, she is pretty.' But the desired effect never hit home, it just humiliated her and made her cry. Too bad Katie hadn't developed a thicker skin, then she wouldn't feel so gullible and miserable, offering friendship to an undeserving brat like Janie.

Everything happens for a reason, challenges make you stronger—she reminded herself as she slowed on the library steps. *You will learn to love this girl. You will learn to love her.* Her thoughts chugged like the little engine in the storybooks. She settled inside the library and distracted herself.

The extra two hours spent studying pushed her way ahead. After classes, she avoided returning to her room. It felt like giving in. Where the heck else could she go? Dismayed, she owned up to the fact her roommate retained the upper hand.

Then again, maybe not.

She had a leg up on Janie in the academic department. And in the organization and neatness category. Janie made messes. Her top drawer looked a shambles, and she forgot important items like due dates for papers, and the closing time at the library. Even if Janie dressed with more flair, and was prettier, and funnier, at least Katie's priorities demonstrated true character. A college education, the most important endeavor of her life, would provide her ticket out, to somewhere new.

Katie faced her troubles head on. At home, she learned to count on herself to get things done, get herself through hard times. She could turn her attitude around if need be, and a simple adjustment could make life not just bearable, but better. She decided to take a stand.

When she entered her dorm room at 3 p.m., Janie sat on her bed watching *General Hospital* and crunching on Better Made potato chips. Lounging there, she appeared not the least bit worried. Katie sighed as she set her books on the desk.

"Hey," Janie said cheerfully. "Want some chips? There's Coke in the fridge, too, if you want."

First of all, Katie thought, how can she ignore my feelings like this, and second of all, it will be a cold day when I accept her food. She inhaled a deep breath and shook her head.

Janie tossed the bag of chips in Katie's direction. "You're not still mad, are you? Check it out. You have no sense of humor at all! Besides if you are so into Nancy Drew, shouldn't you have figured it out? Too bad you're such a moron. You fell for it."

Katie caught the bag of chips, held it up between her thumb and index finger, looked straight ahead, and glared.

"Fine, I won't do it again," Janie said.

Katie flung the chips back at her. Her heart raced and her hands trembled. "I'm not going to put up with your stupid tricks. Either we're roommates or we're not. Real roommates don't treat each other like this."

"Have a chip." Janie tossed the bag back to her and blew her off. "You'll feel better. Do you want a Coke?"

Katie caught the bag in mid-air, folded the top over, and pitched it onto Janie's desk. "I'm not hungry or thirsty."

"Well, there's Coke if you want one."

"Thanks, but no. I prefer Pepsi."

She'd skipped breakfast and been too mad and too upset to eat lunch, but she didn't want to spoil her dinner, just two hours away, or grant Janie the satisfaction of forgiveness.

Janie sipped her Coke, engrossed in her soap opera. "Really, have some chips. You'll like *General Hospital*."

"I'd rather read."

"It's really good today. Jessie found out Phil is fooling around again."

"No thanks." Katie kicked off her shoes, climbed onto her bed, sat Indian style, picked up her favorite Nancy Drew, *The Hidden Staircase*, from the bedside table and began to read what she could have recited by heart.

Blasted Janie.

Twenty minutes later, she finished her chapter. She scrambled out of bed, sure to make plenty of noise, emphasizing she hadn't yet absolved Janie of her insensitivity. Out of the corner of her eye, she tried to catch Janie's reaction. The girl lay sound asleep.

Katie waltzed over to the mini-fridge and chose an ice-cold Coke. On her desk, she placed a paper towel and pilfered a hefty handful of chips, then wrapped her snack like Little Red Riding Hood off to see Grandma. Chips in one hand, Coke in the other, she settled herself in bed, and, once situated, laid the chips across her chest and positioned her drink safely between the bedside rail and the wall.

In spite of her miserable day, this moment felt better, way better than being at home with Mom.

Chapter 4

NEW POSSIBILITIES

October 1969

Katie blushed. For six weeks now she'd been lusting after Bobby Kirsch—a twinkly-eyed, sparkly-smiled, steamy hunk of man. The sight of him triggered all the classic signs: her heart fluttered, her knees knocked, and her arms tingled. He stood at the podium, giving his "My Most Embarrassing Moment" speech. He seemed so confident. Katie laughed all the way through, maybe a tiny bit louder than necessary. Mesmerized by his clear blue eyes, she melted like marshmallow on hot chocolate.

Class ended, and Katie lingered a bit, holding her books.

Bobby paused as he passed by her desk. "Hi, Katie."

She acted nonchalant and poised. "Oh, hi."

"Where's your next class?"

"It's at Strong," she said.

He reached out to take her books. "I'm headed to Pierce. Walk with you?"

"Sure." She donned her cardigan and arranged a flowered scarf around her neck before she and Bobby, instantly the man of her dreams, climbed Eastern Michigan University's hill, the steep-sloped sidewalk outside the Library. The crisp October wind blew jewel-colored leaves across their path.

"How many hours are you talking this semester?"

She barely managed an answer. "Fifteen."

"Are you working, too?"

She glanced at him, forced a deep breath, and willed her pulse to slow. "I'm a cashier in the staff lunchroom at the Union. What about you?"

"Twelve hours this term, plus working for the Campus Police."

"Sounds heavy."

He tossed back his head and laughed, grinning at her with a sideways glance.

She felt, right to the tips of her toes, every movement he made.

He shook his head. "Not so. Mostly I file papers and answer the phone."

His elbow brushed her arm as they fought the wind. She battled her nerves and said, "Oh."

"What? You're disappointed my life isn't more exciting?"

Katie apologized. "No, no, I guess I just assumed working for the Campus Police would be like Dragnet or something."

Another hearty laugh and a drop dead smile. "It's a campus job."

"Do you like it?"

"Pretty much. I'm struggling with a bit of a tricky situation there lately. Just trying to sort it out."

"What's going on?"

"I was an M.P. in 'Nam. Now I work with a guy I served with." He noticed her raised brows. "I know," he added with a grin, "what are the chances? Anyway, I pulled the plug on him, turned him in on something over there. He still holds a grudge. At least I think he does. And now he's a detective and I'm his grunt." His lips tightened into a thin line. "Tables are turned, you know? It's dicey."

Katie stopped dead in her tracks. "You served in Vietnam?"

"Yes, ma'am." He talked like he would to a superior officer.

She laughed, then asked in a serious tone, "What's it like over there?"

"It's a mess."

She looked at him through clearer eyes and with growing respect. "Are you going into law enforcement?"

"That's the plan. I'd love to be a detective one day. What about you?"

"I'm majoring in psychology, with a minor in music." She rattled on as she relaxed. "Combining the two seems like a stretch, but I'm going to stick it out as long as I can. My advisor says the music minor will wind up pushing me over the edge, and at some point, it'll become too difficult for me to manage. But I'm committed to both, and I don't like anyone telling me I can't do something. Guess I'll have to wait and see how it goes. Your major intrigues me, though. I love mysteries."

"How come?"

"Just always been drawn to sorting out puzzles."

"I can relate. So, a music minor, huh? Do you play an instrument?"

"Sort of," she joked. "I sing. I play voice!"

"Are you from around here?"

"Detroit, what about you?'

"I'm from Saline, a little farm town off US-12. Country living, not like where you come from." He chuckled. "Pretty boring compared to the big city."

"Detroit isn't the same as it used to be," she admitted. "A couple of years ago, before the riots, my girlfriends and I used to ride our bikes everywhere for hours, and sometimes, on Saturdays, take the bus downtown to shop at J. L. Hudson's. Then, the looting and the fires started on my birthday in '67. I remember lying in bed at night, listening to the gunfire and army tanks rolling down the street, wondering if I'd wake up in the morning. It didn't feel safe after the riots." She shook her head. "So many people high-tailed it to the suburbs. It was a mass exodus. If my folks could afford to, I'm sure they'd be gone."

"And you ended up in Ypsilanti, home of the coed murders," he reflected. "Not likely to increase your safety quotient."

"I know. I'm trying not to freak out. My folks bought me a coach's whistle." Her shoulders sagged. "They want me to wear it around my neck for protection. It makes me feel like I'm wearing a necklace with 'freshman' plastered all over it. Plus, I'm such a klutz." She paused and laughed. "Chances are I'd get tangled up in it and choke myself to death before some demented maniac could do the job."

Bobby shook his head. "I hear you. It's scary. No one wants to live in constant fear, or be afraid to go outside... or silly because they're taking precautions. But seriously, you can't be too careful. This guy they have locked up, John Norman Collins, is a real pervert. Serial murders—seven of them. He actually raped and killed the girls in one place and then moved them to another. Only a depraved animal could do that."

Katie shivered and noticed Bobby's expression. He looked concerned, like he cared about her. She flushed and felt safe in his presence. "You know a lot."

"So do you. Psychology is important. In fact, maybe you can help me understand what makes this Collins guy tick."

"I don't know enough yet, but I sure would like to figure it out some day."

"Be careful on campus."

"I don't go out alone after dark," she reassured him. "I take stock, check my bearings when I'm out alone, even during the day, and walk down the middle of the sidewalk, away from dark doorways and shrubs. During the riots, I learned about hate, and fear, and safety. I don't want to be scared every minute though. Sometimes I throw caution to the wind, and leave my mace in my room."

"The cops think he did all of them, and I tend to agree, but nobody really knows for sure. Between you and me, one of the killings was different. My bet, they'll pin six of the seven on him. Be careful. I'm not trying to scare you but seven—seven girls. I'd hate it if anything happened to you."

"Thanks," she said, "it's sweet of you to be so concerned."

"It still bugs me. They put so much weight on the farmhouse."

"The farmhouse? What farmhouse?"

Bobby paused for a moment, as if considering whether or not to say more. "The task force figured he held the girls at this old farmhouse. The cops call it a body farm."

Katie trembled. "Is it close by?"

"It's off LeForge Road, about two miles from campus." He slowed in front of Strong Hall.

"Okay, now I am freaking out," she admitted.

He patted her on the back. "Just be careful."

Katie nodded. "Here's my stop."

"I've got to head to class, too," he said. "Hey, I apologize for the topic today. Next time, I promise to make it lighter."

"It's all anybody talks about."

"I know." He reached out, rested his palm on her forearm, looked smack dab into her eyes and said, "Would it be all right if I called you sometime? Maybe we could go out."

She squelched a gulp so she could recite her number. "I'd like that."

How she would focus on her music theory class for the next hour, she couldn't imagine.

Chapter 5

PILLOW TALK

October 1969

After class, Katie raced back to the dorm, her books jostling along with her major organs. She couldn't wait to tell someone about Bobby, even Janie. But Janie wasn't home, so Katie spent an eternity rifling through her roommate's snack stash, switching channels between the soaps and pacing. Three long hours later, Janie sauntered through the door.

She tossed her books on the desk. "What's happenin'?"

Katie planted her hands on her hips. "Do you know what time it is?"

"A little after seven?"

"It's pitch black. You shouldn't be out alone after dark."

Janie plopped down on her bed cross-legged. "It's not late. Cool your jets."

"Where have you been? Your last class ended hours ago."

Janie grinned.

"You were with Jim, weren't you?"

Janie's grin widened.

"Well?"

"He's heaven on a stick."

"Gross."

Janie twirled like a ballerina. "Let's go eat. I'm famished. Sex makes me hungry. If you want, I'll give you details."

Katie grabbed her room key. Her news could wait. First, she wanted to hear more about Janie and Jim. "You're on. I want details."

Katie liked Jim. She, Jim, and Janie sometimes hung out together in the lounge. As good looking as Bobby but with piercing green eyes, "bedroom eyes," Janie called them. Jim Phillips seemed like the right guy for Janie. Older, like Bobby, he was all man with his solid build. He wore a tight t-shirt regardless of the weather and drove a jet-black late model Pontiac Firebird Trans Am as shiny as his hair. Every girl found him irresistible. When he showed up in the lounge, the ladies hung around, whispering their fantasies, envious of Janie. A thick spattering of freckles, the only thing boyish about him, made him even sexier.

Janie had met him during summer school when a flat tire waylaid her in the parking lot. She waited patiently, maximizing her cuteness factor, posed as a damsel in distress. Jim showed up thirty minutes later and stuck around ever since.

Katie sized-up the two lovebirds, amateur shrink style, and decided they had a fair amount in common. Both hardened and sarcastic, they mouthed off constantly, grabbing a drink or a cigarette at the first twinge of tension. They spoke their minds, regardless of the circumstances. Feeding off each other's acerbic natures, they entertained like the George Burns and Gracie Allen comedy team.

Katie knew why. Janie lost her mom early. Jim lost his dad at age eight.

Like Bobby, he grew up on a farm. One night his dad didn't return from the fields by dinnertime. Jim went searching and found him dead under an overturned tractor. He sped home and broke the news to his mom. Jim instantly became the man of the house and helped his mom raise his two little sisters. Wise beyond his years, he grew up all at once. To Katie, it seemed natural the two of them wound up together.

Katie and Janie headed to the cafeteria and lazed their way through the line.

"I'll never get used to this food," Katie muttered. "Did you see the spaghetti?"

"Looks like red glue."

"Disgusting."

"Hey, I have a speech due next week," Janie said. "Want to write it for me? I'll give you a pack of cigarettes."

Katie raised her brows and flipped her hair off her shoulders. "Yeah, if I smoked." She told the plump, hair-netted cafeteria lady she'd take a burger and fries. Janie ordered the same and they squeezed between the cream-colored Formica tables and steel-legged chairs to search out a secluded table for two.

Janie placed a cigarette between her lips, just so, and struck a pose. "Maybe you should start smoking. It's sexy, you know. You might want to start working on sexy. You could be if you tried, little Miss Prim and Proper."

"Yes, Miss Sex Pot, now tell me about your afternoon. What happened?" She removed the plates from their trays and arranged them like fine china to add hominess to the meal.

"He let me drive his car." Janie shimmied her shoulders. "And he never let's anyone drive the Trans Am. Ever."

"For real?"

Janie revved a pretend engine with fisted hands. "It's got some serious vroom, vroom, vroom."

"Did you speed?"

"I did some serious bookin' for a while, but mostly I tried not to get my twat stuck on the gear shift when we parked."

"Seriously?"

Janie looked at Katie like the stupid stick had hit her. "You really did grow up in a cave, didn't you?"

Katie leaned forward. "Tell me."

"Whenever he sees me he gets excited." Janie raised her eyebrows. "Comprende? He gets hard. Not surprising is it?" She danced a French fry seductively in a mound of ketchup.

Katie squelched a smile. "You're filthy."

"If you want, I'll tell you all about it."

She rested her chin in her cupped hands, listening intently. "I'm ready."

"Nah, I'm gonna let you guess. More fun."

In frustration, Katie threw up her hands. "Shoot!"

Janie tossed back her head and laughed. Teasing Katie seemed like her second favorite pastime.

"Did you do it in the car? Really?"

"Is the sky blue? Is the grass green?"

Katie shrugged and shook her head. "Just wondering. It can't be comfortable."

"It's not, but it's still fun."

"Are you sore?"

She cocked her head, suddenly serious. "I'm surprised you haven't asked about it before."

"I feel funny asking you about it. It's personal."

"I'll tell you whatever you want to know," Janie offered.

Katie rimmed her plate with fries, creating the perfect halo, and wished she could be less uptight. While desperate for information, she just couldn't say some words out loud. "In the middle of the day, you did it in the car?"

"We love doing it in different places. Once, at Jim's apartment complex, we stopped the elevator between floors, did it right there on the indoor/outdoor carpet, then started her up again and stepped off all nonchalant like. What a blast!" Janie hooted.

Katie winced. "Ouch. I see rug burns. I'd be mortified someone would see…or even suspect."

"You're so lame," Janie said.

"It must be possible to make love with someone special in less than broad daylight, and feel happy then, too."

Janie arched her brows.

"You do this on purpose, don't you? Just to get a rise out of me."

Janie just laughed.

Katie shook her head, flooded with feelings she couldn't even name. "I'm waiting for the right guy. Jim might be the right guy for you. But all of this sex in college, in the car, during the day...I want to wait."

"You're just a scaredy-cat. Sex is natural. What do you think Carole King meant when she wrote that song?"

"What song?"

"Katie." Janie shook her head. "For a smart cookie, you are dumber than dog doo-doo." She began to sing, "You make me feel like a natural woman. That song. Sex is part of being a woman."

"Oh my gosh, I can't imagine. I think about it all the time. How will I know I'm ready? How will I ever wait until I'm married? I'm embarrassed for someone to see me naked..." her voice trailed off.

"You're so, so stupid," Janie said.

Katie turned and studied her. "Did you really ever decide to have sex, or did you just do it on a whim?"

"Not all of us are as thoughtful about our decisions as Miss Catholic Goody-Two-Shoes. Sometimes you just have to go for it. Trust me. It takes about five seconds to get from a guy feeling you up to a guy sticking it in you."

Katie shook her head in horror. "Sick."

"Fine. I like Jim. He's my special guy. There's gonna be a special guy for you, too."

"You're right. I'm scared."

"Of course you are," she teased. "But aren't you curious?"

"Well, sure."

"What are you scared of?"

"Does it hurt?"

"Good question. It might. Not bad though, not enough to kill you. But I'll tell you right now, the first time? It may not hurt, but there probably won't be any bells going off either. You just have to get used to it."

"You don't like it?"

"I'm just saying there's a curve, you know? A learning curve. For a guy, they get off pretty quick. It takes us a while longer. We have to figure out what works for us. Then, it's fabulous!"

"I'm not sure I ever want to do it."

"You'll be fine. You just have to give it a chance."

Katie's head spun, one thought firing after another. "And I sure don't want to wind up pregnant and ruin everything."

"It's the guilt, isn't it? Shit girl, the church has fucked you up."

"I don't know," Katie paused. "I want it to be special. I've waited this long, it might as well be the right guy, you know? The guy I'm going to marry."

"Think about it this way. Suppose you hold out, wait for the 'one.'" Janie dramatically placed her hands over her heart. "Then you get married. Later, you see some foxy guy walking down the street. You wonder, what if I waited for someone like him? What if he has hidden talents my husband doesn't?"

"Must you always be so irreverent?"

"I'm serious. It's like checking the water ahead of time to be doubly sure you'll have a great swim...You know, the temperature is good, there aren't too many waves, the sun is shining and the bottom isn't too slimy. Or, you wait to get pushed in and find out the water is freezing cold, the waves toss you on your ass because a storm is winding up, and the sand is full of rocky pebbles and muck."

"Very poetic," Katie's voice dripped with sarcasm. "I see your point, but I'm not sure."

"Now or later. Trust me. You'll always wonder if you don't try it."

"How the heck do you know these things?"

"I raised Janie, remember. I figured it out for myself."

"Yeah, well. Doesn't mean you're right."

Chapter 6

IT'S A DATE

October 1969

Janie cleared the dishes from the table to the gray plastic tubs on the counters then skipped back to Katie and brushed her hands together. "We're all set. Let's go upstairs. There's Fig Newton's under my bed."

"You're gonna share?"

"Yes 'm."

They linked arms, skipping down the hall like schoolgirls. At the elevator door, they braked and waited. Once they landed at their floor, they continued dancing down the hall to their room—making far too much noise. Doors opened and those who spotted them nodded a "what else is new" and ducked back inside.

Katie unlocked the door and they shoved each other into the room, laughing as they began an imaginary boxing match. "I can't believe I forgot. Guess what?"

"I don't know, what? You said a bad word?"

Katie leaned forward. "No, not yet. Now shut up. I have something to tell you. This guy..."

"Ooo, Katie looked at a boy! Was he alive and breathing?"

"Stop it." Katie laughed. "Really!"

Janie's jaw dropped. "Who? The one who looks like Robert Redford?"

"The eyes are totally Redford. Seriously. He walked me to Strong today. And," she paused for effect, "he asked for my phone number!"

"Cool." Janie cocked her head in wonder.

"He's going into law enforcement. He served as an M.P. in Vietnam," Katie said proudly.

"So he's older." Janie bit her lip in deep contemplation. "And law enforcement. A perfect match for our own little Nancy Drew."

"Cut it out."

"How unlike you to go for it. An older man. He's gonna want sex, you know."

"Shut up...I think he likes me. I know I like him."

Janie hopped off her bed and rested her hands on Katie's shoulders as if breaking disappointing news to a child. "Now you have to hope he calls. Sometimes guys say they'll call and then they don't."

"I had a boyfriend. I'm not stupid." She brushed Janie's hands off her shoulders. "You have to stop thinking I'm a complete dipstick."

"Teasing, Katie. Panties. Bunch. Remember?" Janie rifled underneath her bed for the cookies. She skimmed off minuscule pinches with her front teeth. Then she spoke, completely focused on her eating project, "I'm just worried with all that religion, the nuns drove all the good stuff out of you along with the evil. Did they teach

Catechism classes on the devil? Or did they perform an exorcism on you before you graduated high school?"

Katie frowned and knitted her brow. "Very funny."

Janie tossed her a cookie.

She flipped it over in her hand as she thought. What if he didn't call? How would she go back to class? She'd feel foolish. If she pretended it didn't matter, like she had been so busy she hadn't noticed, maybe she would save herself some embarrassment.

"Some guys are real jerks," Janie advised. "They just want to see if you're attracted to them. It strokes their ego. They really have no intention of calling."

"I know. Can we talk about something else for a while? I don't want to think about him not calling. It's depressing."

"Okay," Janie tittered, "let's talk about your old lady."

"Pleasant detour," Katie said, snatching a second Fig Newton and shoving the entire thing in her mouth. "Do you have to start trouble all the time?"

"Hey, you asked me about mine." Janie gently peeled another cookie from the package and went about eating the crust from around the fruit.

"Fair enough," Katie admitted. "What do you want to know?"

"What's her deal?"

"I'm not exactly sure."

"C'mon, you must have a clue. You are the 'Nancy Drew' of the dorm."

"I've been trying to figure it out pretty much my whole life." Katie talked and chewed. "I always suspected something wasn't quite right, but I didn't know any different, you know? She's in way over her head with my brothers is all."

Janie's eyebrows lifted heavenward. "No, it's more than that. She's seriously messed up. I know I'm messed up because I didn't have a mom, but you're messed up, too. Your mom is weird."

"I know. All of us are messed up. Some of us a little more than others." She turned her eyes in Janie's direction.

Janie stuck out her chin. "What's your point?"

"No point." Katie giggled. "I need to get some reading done." She turned and reached for her Music Theory text. "I sure hope he calls."

"He'll call."

When the phone finally jingled a little after nine o'clock, Katie instantly became paralyzed.

"What if it's him?"

"You are so dumb. Answer it."

"I can't. I'm too nervous." Katie rushed over to the TV and turned down *The Newlywed Game.*

"Shit." Janie reached over her head and yanked the receiver off its hook. As she said hello, she hopped up, turned, and walked away, stretching the long spiral telephone cord around the corner and into the bathroom.

"Yes, she's here, but I'm not sure if she's available. Can I tell her who's calling?" Janie looked back at Katie and smirked. "Bobby?" She emphasized his name and winked. "Just a second, I'll check. She might be down the hall."

Katie wrestled to grab the receiver. "Give it to me," she hissed through an excited grin.

Janie slapped at Katie's hands.

"Hey, you're the fool who made me answer it."

"Yeah, well, I've come to my senses."

Janie placed her hand over the receiver and warned with a hoarse whisper, "Don't blow it, idiot. This is your big chance."

Katie's hands trembled. As she grabbed the phone, she cleared her throat. "Hello?"

"Hi, Katie. It's me, Bobby. From speech class."

The mere sound of his voice made her heart beat like a bass drum. "Hi."

"How ya' doin'?"

"I'm fine. Just catching up on some homework." She pulled a chair from the desk, sat down, and pushed her free forearm firmly against her knees to stop them from bouncing.

Janie stood in front of her bobbing up and down, making silly faces, sticking her tongue out and forming rings around her eyes with her thumbs and pinky fingers. She whispered, "Play hard to get."

Katie couldn't help laughing out loud.

"What's so funny?" Bobby asked.

"It's Janie, my roommate. She ate idiot stew for dinner. Now she's doing jumping jacks and making faces."

"She sounds like a lot of fun."

"I'm afraid so." Katie made a mental note not to introduce the two of them. "What are you up to?"

"Just finished up some homework and found myself thinking about you."

She felt like a star-struck kid. "You did?"

"I wondered if you'd like to go to a movie Friday night."

"Sounds great." *So much for playing hard to get.*

"What do you want to see?"

"I'm totally open." Katie flew out of her chair and jumped up and down. Janie hooted, way too loud. Katie mimed slicing Janie's throat with her finger, threatening to hurt her if she didn't shut up.

"Let's see *Butch Cassidy*. Can I pick you up at your place?"

"Sure! I'm in Putnam Hall. Just dial my room from the front desk. #313. I'll come right down."

"Perfect, I'll pick you up a little before seven."

She hung up the phone and turned to Janie. "I can hardly breathe."

"Let's go buy ice cream and celebrate!"

"No," Katie said. "I have to finish reading."

Janie moaned. "You're such a drag!"

"Am not."

Janie left and came back thirty minutes later with two huge bowls of chocolate ice cream drenched in syrup and sprinkles.

"Where did you get this?"

She chuckled, setting Katie's bowl in front of her. "I have my ways."

In their pjs, they climbed into their beds, sighing happy sounds as they savored their sundaes. Katie scooped Janie's bowl from her hands when she finished, carried both bowls to the bathroom sink and rinsed them out. "Thanks for the treat." She climbed in bed and cuddled under her blankets. "I love ice cream."

Janie drew the heavy curtains closed, turned off the lights, and climbed into bed. The room turned pitch black and went quiet as a forest.

"Janie?"

"What?"

"What if he wants to kiss me?"

"Kiss him back," she said with a groan. "I can't believe you're so stupid."

"So it's like riding a bike? I've never kissed a boy other than Mark," Katie whispered.

"The high school boy, right?" Janie turned on the light, leaned on her elbow, and locked eyes with Katie. "What's he like?"

Katie sat up in bed, flipped off the light, and continued. "All right, I guess."

"Doesn't sound all right." Janie turned on her back to listen.

"He was a little possessive is all, and angry most of the time. Almost paranoid, like the world was out to get him. I secretly started calling him 'Mad Mark.'" Katie gazed into the dark, turned her hand toward the wall, and fingered the cinder blocks.

"*Was* the world out to get him?"

"Didn't seem like it to me. I broke up with him."

"Sounds like a weirdo."

"I guess he's a little weird."

"What's his deal?"

"I'm not sure. When I dated him, I didn't notice so much. But after…"

"What?"

"I felt bad about breaking up with him."

"Guilt. That goddamn Catholic guilt is going to kill you." Janie shook her head. "How long did you date him?"

"A little over a year, I guess."

"What does he look like?"

Katie shot up in bed, suddenly animated. "Mark? He's big—not tall exactly, about five foot ten, but he's built like a truck. Wide body, great shoulders actually, and nice strong hands."

"So you still like him."

"No, not at all. Anyway," she added, "it's nerve-wracking to think about kissing someone else."

"Kissing a new guy should be fun."

"I think it's a little scary." Katie paused, not sure if she really wanted to ask the next question or not. "Janie?"

"*What?*"

Katie pulled up the covers. "Never mind."

"Do you want me to tell you exactly how it works?"

"Of course not. You and I, we're not the same. Sex is going to be special for me, not just some idle pleasure."

"Yeah, well if you change your mind, you know where to find me," Janie quipped.

Chapter 7

DATE NIGHT

October 1969

Two interminable days later, Friday arrived. Katie spent hours preparing for her date. She turned her head upside down in the sink and scrubbed her hair with emerald green shampoo until it squeaked clean, then carefully applied Dippity-Do gel on each precisely parted section and rolled her hair onto juice can sized curlers. After she donned the bonnet-style hairdryer her grandmother gave her as a going away gift, she laid down on her bed, quickly lulled to sleep by the soft hum of the motor and the steady stream of hot air.

An hour later, she woke from her nap and showered, lathering her legs with shaving cream and stroking the razor over them twice to be sure her legs were silky smooth. She felt like Cinderella dressing for the ball. Unfortunately, only Janie was available for the position of fairy godmother.

Janie evaluated Katie's style as she pulled a soft brown cable knit short-sleeved sweater over her head.

"You're looking sexy." Her plaid wool A-line skirt fit her to a "T" with hues of rust and gold. She smoothed her hands over the fabric, slipped her toes inside her brown pumps, then stood back and posed in front of Janie's full-length mirror, taking in her reflection. "So?"

"How do you feel about looking sexy? You're not thinking about putting out are you?"

"Of course not." Katie threw her hairbrush at Janie as she swung her head upside down, fluffed her hair with her fingers, and tossed it back. She checked her locks in the mirror, twirled a curl on one of her cheeks and spritzed it with Aqua Net. *Darn it!* Janie guessed right. Since Bobby's call last night, she'd been thinking about sex.

"You have no idea what you're getting yourself into."

"I do, too." Katie applied lipstick and blotted it with a tissue, then shot the wadded Kleenex at Janie, pursing her lips like a demure debutante as she glanced at the clock. Ten minutes to seven. Perfect.

Right on schedule, Bobby called. "You ready?"

She smiled to herself. "I'll be right down."

Janie pinched out a square foil-wrapped packet from a box in her desk drawer. "Here, you might need this." She tossed it in Katie's direction.

Katie snagged it, rolled her eyes, and pitched the condom back at Janie. "I don't think so," she said as the thought *maybe* crossed her mind. After one final glance in the mirror, she tucked her room key into her handbag. With a smile and a nod, she stood in front of Janie, waiting for her approval.

Janie grinned. "You look pretty. Have fun."

"Planning on it." She pulled the door closed and began to sashay down the hall. Cloud nine, she thought. I'm on cloud nine. Her hips swayed with a new rhythm, and as the elevator doors opened, she stood taller. On the ride downstairs, she thought about Bobby's warm lips meeting hers. A sigh escaped her lips as the elevator bumped to a grinding halt. She stepped off, trying to calm the rumba in her chest. As she rounded the corner to the front desk she spotted him, and lit up like the harvest moon.

His back turned toward her, he glanced over his shoulder and flashed one of the most incredible smiles in the entire world.

He walked up to her and took her hand. "Outstanding."

She blushed. "Thanks."

Before he opened the door, he paused to zip his suede jacket, placed his hand on the small of her back, and then guided her out the double doors leading to the metered parking.

Katie eased herself into the passenger seat of his '64 Chevy Bel Air and felt a surprising new confidence—poised and pretty. As she fantasized about snuggling a little closer to him on the bench seat, he eased the shift lever into reverse. "How 'ya doin'?"

"I cleared a mid-term off my plate today—I filled the entire blue book. I'm getting better at padding my answers." She giggled. "I met my roommate a month and a half ago and already she calls me the queen of BS. Enough about me though, tell me about you."

He cocked his head and smiled. "About me." He mulled it over, picking the highlights. "I worked in my dad's lumberyard for a year after high school, got drafted, and completed my basic training in Georgia. After basic, they sent me to MP school at Fort Gordon, and then I wound up in Saigon. I spent a year in-country, and made it home last March."

"The other day you mentioned 'Nam. It must have been horrible. Did it change you?"

Bobby laughed nervously. "I'm down to a nightmare every week or so. But it used to be every night. The jury's still out."

"What are the nightmares about?"

He turned his head, watching traffic.

Maybe he hadn't heard her.

"Aquarius" by the Fifth Dimension began playing on the radio. He turned up the volume and sang along. Katie joined in.

When the song finished he said, "You sound like Karen Carpenter."

She breathed in the compliment as if inhaling a fresh-baked chocolate chip cookie.

They held each other's gaze as the seven o'clock train stopped traffic. The train's whistle blew and a rush passed through her.

He parked in a tiny city lot around the corner from the theater, then came around the car and opened her door, offering his hand and helping her out. A streetlamp illuminated the cover of fallen leaves. She stepped onto the rain sodden sidewalk and held onto his arm as they walked to the box office.

Butch Cassidy and the Sundance Kid would begin playing at 7:30 p.m. They purchased a tub of freshly popped corn at the concession stand and found a middle aisle seat. Bobby laid his arm on the back of her chair, and she held the popcorn in her lap. He laughed when she looked dreamy during the romantic parts, and she laughed at the way he sat forward when the shooting started.

His cheek rested on the top of her head now and then, and she wished she could stop time and stay there with him, in the dark quiet of the theater, forever. But the two hours sped by, and she held his arm as they made their exit.

"How'd you like it?"

She giggled. "I loved it when Etta asked Butch if he knew what he was doing."

"Right before they got on the bike?"

She nodded. "And he says, 'theoretically.'"

They both laughed. His broad smile made his eyes sparkle as he held the door. She climbed into the passenger seat.

Bobby settled in behind the wheel.

Katie wondered if he, being into law enforcement, might have been put off by the duo's deeds. "Were you upset they were such bad guys?"

"They're outlaws, not bad guys."

"Just trying to be sensitive to the cop side of you."

Bobby rested his hand on her knee. "What do you feel like doing?"

Katie's heart arrested, and she inhaled for strength. "We could go back to the dorm and hang out in the lounge. It's uncomfortable though. The vinyl upholstery reminds me of a doctor's office, but it's somewhere to go."

Bobby shivered and leaned over to adjust the heat. "We could go to the little snack bar by your dorm and get something warm. There's a fireplace."

Katie grinned. "The Grill? Sounds perfect."

He shifted into drive, punched the eight-track, and headed back to the dorm. They parked and he brushed a quick peck on her cheek before he stepped out and came around to her door. He extended his hand and helped her onto the rain-slick walk. "Mademoiselle."

A royal blue awning sheltered the steps down to The Grill entrance, keeping them clear and dry. The smell of burgers and fries wafted through the door, overpowering the scent of falling rain.

Katie spotted room on the couch near the fireplace and she staked out a space while Bobby ordered two hot chocolates. She wound her legs beneath her and breathed in the earthy scent of the burning oak. His hand brushed hers as he handed her the drink.

"Summer changes to fall awfully darned quick, doesn't it?" He sipped his drink.

Katie nodded and her heart quickened as she looked into his eyes. "Michigan." He acted so self-assured. Katie surprised herself and blurted, "Tell me more about you. Do you like to read?"

"Can't say I'm much of a reader. What about you?"

Her eyes lit up. "I love to read."

"What do you like?"

"I started reading Nancy Drew right before I turned ten. I love mysteries, so it fascinates me you're into law enforcement."

"Nancy Drew, huh?" Bobby scratched his temple. "Can't say I've read any of those. But with your psychology major, it makes a lot of sense. The two are related."

Katie was glad he didn't tease her about Nancy Drew like Janie always did.

"Now, tell me something you hate."

"Rhubarb," she answered definitively.

Bobby chuckled. "Nobody likes rhubarb."

"What about you? What do you hate?"

He arched his brows. "Getting up at the crack of dawn." A sip of cocoa later, he fired the next question. "What do you want to do with your life?"

Marry you, Katie thought, but she didn't tell him that. "Eat plenty of spinach. I want to have muscles like Popeye. And you. Do you like green stuff?"

"Brussel sprouts." He paused slightly. "Do you like to dance?"

"I love to dance."

"You want to go sometime?"

Her stomach flipped. "Absolutely."

The lights flashed in The Grill signaling ten minutes until closing and Bobby said, "Should we head out?"

"We don't have much choice. I need to be in by curfew anyway."

They linked arms as they walked the short distance to the dorm. He held the door for her and she stopped in the vestibule and turned to face him. The reflection of the interior hall lights made his eyes twinkle, and she smiled. He took her face in his hands and kissed her.

His lips were tender and warm, and when she kissed him back, her passion surprised her.

A grin enveloped his face. "Goodnight. I had a great time."

"Me, too," she whispered. He squeezed her hand and she turned to walk toward the elevator as he headed out the main door. Unable to resist, she sneaked over to the glass doors and watched him stroll to his car. Already, she felt as if she'd known Bobby Kirsch forever. She loved his eyes, the blueness of them, and the way they saw inside her. An image of the water tower flashed before her and she chuckled. It wouldn't crumble because of her.

Chapter 8

SWEARING JAR

November 1969

No one ever said so, but everyone knew not to mix with the opposite race, even at this so-called bastion of open-mindedness, the university campus. A week after her date, Katie thought about it on the way back from the library. The whole thing was dumb and wished she could just say hi to Gwen and Cynthia. She felt weird breezing past them in the cafeteria, or passing them on campus without at least saying hello. Katie sighed. *They wouldn't acknowledge me anyway.*

Janie, on the other hand, messed with their two black suitemates all the time, anywhere and everywhere. They ignored her completely. Talking to a white girl might make them outcasts with the other blacks on campus. That they spoke to Katie and Janie at all was a miracle. At least they could visit each other's rooms regularly without anyone noticing.

Katie hitched her books up higher and smiled to herself. Even Janie stopped her gabbing when Gwen started talking about all the boys she dated. The girl even shared details about her orgasms. And Cynthia had "experience" with more than one boy, too.

Cynthia Jackson, thin as Twiggy, possessed fine, feminine features. Her eyes, big, bright, and brown, suited her sparkling personality. It took weeks to break the ice, but then Katie found out Cynthia majored in special education, and—in addition to being the oldest and only girl in her family, like Katie—she sang like a bird. Once she knew Cynthia better, she loved her. Cynthia was cheerful and fun-loving. Affectionate could have been her middle name, and Best-Friend-To-All the caption under her high school graduation photo. From Cynthia, soft-spoken and generous to a fault, Katie learned how to laugh at herself.

Katie's little brother, Jack, used the expression "full-size" in place of "grown-up," and it fit Gwen perfectly. With a woman's body Katie envied, curvy in all the right places, Gwen exuded sensuality—even when she wasn't trying to. She wore a turban-style scarf around her kinky hair and an old-fashioned housecoat like the one Katie's grandma wore. Gwen moved slowly no matter what she did, accentuating each movement with dramatic effect.

Janie and Katie cracked up and passed a knowing glance whenever they caught sight of her. Gwen, with her drop-dead figure, chose to cover it with an old-lady outfit she wore like a uniform. Katie couldn't for the life of her figure out why Gwen kept her killer body under wraps. If she had a body like Gwen's, and all that experience, she'd be inclined to flaunt it more. Well, maybe.

Gwen grunted whenever anyone approached her with a question. She saved words for special occasions.

Unlike Katie, she didn't feel pressured to be the person she thought everyone wanted her to be. Other than with Katie, Janie, and Cynthia, Gwen spent most of her time deep in thought. Occasionally Katie caught her smiling, but mostly, Gwen displayed the quiet confidence of experience. All the girls in the dorm scrambled for time in Gwen's presence, hoping for a tidbit of her seemingly secret life. Katie fancied herself as the one who would break Gwen's mysterious existence wide open one of these days.

Katie entered the room and was suspicious right off the bat. She couldn't put her finger on it—Gwen, Cynthia, and Janie sat on the side of Janie's bed, giggling and exchanging glances while they swung their dangling legs. As usual, Gwen wore her housecoat, and a hair pick stuck out from her Afro. Cynthia's tiny frame swam in a pair of flannel pjs. Janie, darling of the dorm, still wore a crisply ironed cotton button-down shirt and pressed Levi's, complete with creases. The three of them reminded Katie of the Three Stooges.

Katie narrowed her eyes as she set down her books. "What's going on? You look like you're scheming."

"It's like this," Janie started. "See this?" She held up a clear glass jar and waved her hand beneath it like one of the showcase models on *The Price is Right.*

The girls nodded in unison.

"This is Katie's Swearing Jar."

"What *are* you talking about?"

"When you swear…oh, sorry," Janie chided as she wagged a finger, "I mean say a bad word, each of us will chink a nickel into the jar."

Katie rolled her eyes. "Are you kidding me?"

"You can earn spending money by using 'bad' words. Think about it. Say forty bad words this week, you'll earn two dollars. At the end of the week, if you swear enough, we could order a pizza on Friday night. Comprende?"

Katie stifled a grin and huffed. "I understand, but I won't be paid to use vulgar language."

Cynthia nudged Katie with a bony elbow. "This is gonna be great."

Gwen rearranged the comb in her nappy hair. "We've taken bets on how long it'll take you to get in on the action. *All* the action."

Katie shook her head. "I'm serious. I do not swear. I never have and never will. It's unnecessary and makes you common. I don't feel the need to lower myself—to swear…or to have premarital sex."

Gwen dropped her normally stoic expression, fell back onto the bed, held her stomach, and kicked her legs in the air, laughing so hard the bed shook.

Katie couldn't help smiling, but she headed to the bathroom nonetheless. *Why can't I just let go and have fun?* Less than three minutes later, she trotted out of the bathroom and stubbed her toe on the lip marking the entrance. "Bummer."

"A nickel could have clinked in the jar," Janie scolded, touching the tip of her nose with her index finger. "Quit being such a prude."

"I am not a prude. Get over it. I don't use four letter words."

Janie snorted. "So, you're not hip."

"I don't think I'm unhip, or whatever you want to call it just because I don't swear. You guys overuse profanity. It's just plain raunchy."

Gwen slapped Katie on the back, then she clicked her tongue. "Too bad, so sad."

Cynthia, waxing sympathetic, wrapped a scrawny armful of excess flannel around Katie's shoulder. "Don't worry, hon, give it a little time. You'll come around." Her arms spread wide like a figure skater, she twirled four times on tiptoe, dropped a coin in the jar and pronounced, "Shhhhhhhhhhhiiiiittt," drawling the word out long and slow, like a song.

Gwen slid off the bed and bumped her curvy hips with Katie's, flipped a coin, scoring a direct hit into the jar, and said, "DddddaaaaaammmmmnnnnnN…" adding an extra kick of emphasis to the consonant at the end.

Janie shimmied and danced her way to the jar, dangling a coin above the opening. She cheered, "FUCK!"

Katie tried to stifle her laughter. She knew better than to turn this corner. Once she did, there'd be no turning back, like tumbling off a high dive board. She stomped her feet, pleading with the girls, "You guys, stop it. You're making this sooooo hard."

Janie clapped her hands in victory.

"It's time you joined the party, honey," Gwen sang.

Katie threw up her arms and moaned. *Believe me, I want to.*

Cynthia rubbed Katie's back and giggled.

"See, roomie," Janie hollered. "It's a fun way to earn money."

Katie fought the powerful urge to cross the naughty bridge. "I don't even know many swear words."

"We're happy to teach you," Gwen said.

"Think about it," Janie said. "You're going to be a psychologist. You can't be narrow in your thinking or experience. You need to be able to understand people. This is simple. Just try it. If it's not you, you don't have to keep doing it. C'mon. Just say 'shit.'"

What Janie said made sense. "I'll consider it."

Cynthia squinted at her. "Did you have fun with the new guy?"

"Incredible fun, but since when did we change the subject? Is this pick on Katie day? What does my date have to do with swearing?"

"Girl! Virginity, virginity. Someone afraid to swear must be too scared to do the nasty!" Cynthia paused for a minute, "Oooo, I wonder if he's a *good* dancer. You know what they say about *good* dancers."

"No, what?"

"It means he's good in bed," she replied. "Move into the sixties, girlfriend. Make love, not war."

Katie shook her head vehemently, paused, and reconsidered silently. "I'm not sleeping with him. You're taking this way too far."

Cynthia tipped back her head and hooted. "You think an older man is going to hold out for you? Damn. You're hot, but I'm not sure you're worth holding out for. C'mon, girl, didn't that high school boy want to have sex with you?"

"Of course he did, just look at me." Katie twirled and bowed before them. "But I wouldn't put out." She sputtered and laughed. "Mark used to say, 'I'm a man with needs.' I couldn't do more than make-out with him. He raised a hissy but I didn't feel *that* way about him. Plus I didn't want to compromise my beliefs. I'm not afraid." She tried to convince herself as much as her roommates. "I'll make love with the right guy!"

"Make love," Janie said. "Listen to her."

"We'll get you started soon, don't you worry," Gwen added.

Janie giggled. "This is going to be so much fun." She leaned over and whispered in Gwen's ear.

"What? What are you two up to?"

"We're drafting a manual, complete with drawings. *A Guide to the Male Anatomy.*"

Katie cried, "Stop!"

Then she pictured Bobby naked.

Chapter 9

LOVE IS IN THE AIR

March 1970

Katie peeled back the drapes to brilliant sunshine. Spring. Finally. Leaves burst open on the oaks and maples, and she smiled as she spotted sprouts of tulips and daffodils poking their way out of the solid ground. She opened the window a crack. Even the air smelled green. Everything came back to life. She stretched her arms high above her head and bathed in the sun's rays.

She'd hibernated all winter with her studies, and her efforts paid off. Although she often wore her four-point average like a badge of honor, it felt like small potatoes today. March 23, 1970. Hers and Bobby's six-month anniversary.

The phone jingled a little before noon. "Katie Hayes? There's a package at the desk for you."

It took her less than two minutes to pull on a pair of pants and t-shirt, run a quick brush through her hair, and slide into a pair of slippers. She raced downstairs. A sleek white box sat on the counter with her name printed neatly on the envelope. Bobby sent her six long-stemmed pink roses. And the card said:

I believe in the sun…even when it's not shining.
I believe in myself…even when I'm not sure.
I believe in love…even when I am alone.
I believe in you…even when you don't.
I believe in us…the hope and the promise.
To the most beautiful lady I have ever known.
Love, Bobby

Girls gathered round, hugged, and congratulated her. Katie felt like the belle of the ball. After murmuring her appreciation, she carried her flowers upstairs and arranged the fragrant budding roses into an old milk bottle. She stood back and admired them. With a perpetual grin, she began hours of primping.

It took forever, but she finally decided on the dress she wore for her senior homecoming dance, a pale dusty pink, made of a soft, sheer organza. Delicate pleats fell from the rounded neck all the way to the short-skirted hem. The sleeves flowed long and full. She slipped her toes into dyed-to-match pumps and added clip-on bows to finish.

Janie lent her a gold pendant with a tiny pearl accent. She fastened it around her neck and gently pushed faux pearl earrings into her newly pierced ears. When Katie sized up the finished product in the full-length mirror, she no longer felt like the silly schoolgirl who last wore this dress, she felt like a lady.

She peeked out the window and spotted Bobby, all decked out in his navy blue sports coat and tan dress slacks. Her heart skipped a beat; he looked so dashing. His thick blonde hair a little longer in back now, it brushed the back of his collar. As he walked confidently to the dorm entrance, Katie swelled with pride. Her man—so fine.

She grabbed her purse and keys and practically pranced down the stairs. By the time she arrived at the lounge, Bobby waited at the front desk. She threw her arms around him and kissed him full out.

Bobby took her hand and they strolled to the car. She scooted next to him on the bench seat and he put his arm on the seatback while he checked traffic, gently massaging her shoulder with his fingertips. The Carpenters song "We've Only Just Begun" played on the radio and they sang along—Katie loved their familiar routine—they drove around the back of campus and onto Huron Drive.

They arrived at the restaurant a few minutes early and Bobby suggested a drink at the bar. Katie climbed onto the barstool, arranging herself as she tried not to wrinkle her dress or slide off the slippery twirling seat. She wanted this night to be perfect.

When the bartender arrived, she smiled and said, "Just a Coke for me."

"I'll have *rum* in my Coke," Bobby said.

A minute later, their drinks appeared.

He smiled and clinked her glass. "To us. And to the best six months of my life." He took her hand is his, kissed it, and looked deeply into her eyes.

Tears welled in Katie's lids and she blinked them back.

He shook his head in wonder. "I never dreamed I'd meet anyone like you."

"I think you're the dog's bark, too." *Why did I say that?*

"Seriously, lady. You're the one."

The blood rushed up her neck and suffused her cheeks. "The one?"

He chuckled and hugged her close. "You're blushing."

She started sliding off the stool, caught the heel of her pump in the railing, and nearly landed on her ear. She laughed with embarrassment, spilling forward into his arms. "Sorry," she said, "I didn't mean to spoil the moment."

He easily lifted her at the waist and situated her back onto her seat.

She leaned over and kissed him on the cheek. "Go ahead. Tell me more."

"For a start, yours are the bluest eyes I've ever seen, and you smell so...clean."

"I do shower every day."

He flushed.

"Sorry I'm so nervous. I don't know why. The past six months have been the best of my life. Sometimes I feel like pinching myself. Other than you…I'm just not used to anyone being so nice to me. I never imagined. My whole life has been spent taking care of people: my parents, and my brothers. It's different with you. So magically, wonderfully different."

He rubbed the top of her hand with his finger. "I'm in love with you."

Her throat tightened and tears spilled over. "I'm so afraid I'll wake up one morning and discover it's all a dream."

He squeezed her shoulder and swiped a tear from her cheek. "It's real, lady. I love you. Now stop crying or you'll run your mascara."

Katie sniffed, smiled, looked at him, and said, "You just told me you loved me."

He smiled. "I did."

"And I started crying."

Bobby laughed.

"This is the best day of my life!"

"Mine, too."

"Janie would say it's impossible."

Bobby looked puzzled. "What's impossible?"

"You love me and I don't put out."

"Yeah, well I've been meaning to talk to you…" he said.

"Seriously?"

"No, of course not." He reached for her hand, studied it, and traced the outline of her fingers. "Do I want to make love to you?" He paused and smiled. "Absolutely. But I'll tell you something else. In 'Nam, I saw stuff. People doing unspeakable things. To put it simply, I'm a patient man." He locked eyes with her. "Hopefully, you won't make me wait forever. You deserve the best, and if you consider me worthy, I'm game whenever you are."

"You're going to make me cry again."

Throughout dinner, Katie couldn't take her eyes off of Bobby. He could be her husband, the father of her children, the one with whom she would spend the rest of her life.

After dinner, they decided they would each change into comfortable clothing so they could go for a walk.

Bobby pulled into his parents' driveway. He hated it, but since 'Nam he'd lived at his parents', and couldn't wait to afford his own place. Katie imagined the two of them alone, playing house. The day couldn't come soon enough.

"Wait right here," he said.

Katie squinted through the windshield. Bobby's parents, a typical Ozzie and Harriet, sat in the front room watching television and reading.

Bobby jumped back in the car five minutes later. "I'm back."

"You were quick."

"Motivated, lady. I'm motivated."

They raced back to the dorm. Bobby headed to the lounge to wait for Katie.

She double-timed the stairs and darted to her room. After she flung her dress on the bed, kicked her shoes willy-nilly on the floor, and left her hose in an accordion pile, she shoved herself into jeans and a heavy sweater, and raced down the steps.

Bobby retrieved a blanket from the back of his car and looped it over one arm. He held her hand as he led her down the hilly edge of campus, lush and shrouded by flowering dogwood trees. They strolled along the walk, hand in hand, and their arms swung in perfect sync as they wove their way amongst the trees. He spread the blanket under a slice of moonlight, sat down, and pulled her onto his lap.

What he said to her at dinner about her being special enough to wait for—it made her want him all the more. She inhaled his spicy sandalwood scent. Bobby ran his fingers up and down her arm and she took his face in her hands and planted her lips on his. His tongue greeted hers with a gentle longing. They settled back and wound themselves around each other, their mouths locked together in a mind-consuming kiss that pushed aside all meaning of time. Before long, frustrated moaning filled the air.

Suddenly afraid, mostly of herself, Katie backed away a fraction of an inch. "Whoa! This is getting way too serious."

"Still feeling like a good Catholic girl?" Bobby readjusted and pushed his hand through his hair. He lay on his side, propped up on his elbow, and gazed at her.

Katie lay on her back with her arms folded behind her head. She wondered aloud as she gazed at the stars. "I wish I could let go of my upbringing, but I might be sorry tomorrow. Besides, we have no protection, and I can't handle any more guilt or worry." She sighed as she sat up and pulled her sweater firmly down over her waist.

"But we do have protection. I'm a boy scout, remember?"

She winked at him. "Save it."

Bobby sat up and laughed as he patted her on the back. "You sure I can't change your mind?" Longing etched his tilted face.

Katie hated to disappoint him. "Bobby."

He chuckled. "Don't worry about me, I love cold showers. And who knows, maybe this will build my character."

Bobby continued to stroke her arm and Katie squelched the urge to tackle him right then and there.

Each and every time they were together, it became harder to push away her desire.

She groaned.

"Fine, we'll downshift." Under the starlit sky, he leaned toward her and placed a soft kiss on her lips.

She wished on the moon. "I don't want this night to end."

"I never want the nights to end when I'm with you."

Katie stroked his shoulder and laid her head on his chest. "You always know the right thing to say."

"I love you, Katie."

"I love you, too. Now take me home before I give in."

"I can't believe you won't let me."

Katie stood, brushed herself off, took his hand, and strode up the hill. "Me either."

Chapter 10

DEATH'S INTERRUPTION

March 1970

The next day, Katie arrived home from class a little after three o'clock. Still on cloud ninety-nine from her anniversary date with Bobby, her excitement bubbled over like fizz on champagne. She could hardly contain herself. Since he'd professed his love for her, she wanted to shout it from her third floor window. Instead, she propped her gold corduroy pillow on the bed, and tried to relax by turning on the soaps. But she couldn't sit still. She foraged under Janie's bed for snacks. The phone jingled mid-munchie-search and she grabbed it on the fly.

"Hello?"

"Katie, it's me."

"Hey, brother Tom. What's going on?"

"It's bad news. Mark Meyer's dad dropped dead this morning."

Katie clamped a hand over her mouth and started pacing in the eight-foot stretch allowed by the phone cord. "What? How? What happened? He's too young. It's impossible."

"The doc died at his office. Heart attack, they think," Tom continued. "Mrs. Meyers is his nurse, remember? She tried CPR, right there on the spot."

Tom reported the funeral arrangements to Katie, and she knew she'd better head home. As soon as she hung up the phone, she called Bobby and explained.

"I need to go home. I know Mark's family so well. I don't want to go, but I'm sure it's the right thing. It can't be more than a couple of days, what with the visitation and the funeral. To be honest, I'd rather stay here with you."

"Of course you should be there," Bobby said. "Don't worry about us. We're rock solid. I'll give you a lift."

"No, it's all right. Tom's picking me up."

"I'd feel better if I took you."

"Really, it's all taken care of," Katie said. She waited through an awkward silence.

"Let me do this. Let me take care of you."

"You're being silly."

"Am I?"

"A little. What are you nervous about? Do you think Mark's still hung up on me? I'm sure he's found some new girl at school by now."

"Don't count on it."

"Bobby."

A long silence followed.

"What?"

"I love you."

"You're right. I'm being stupid. Go, take care of things. Call me when you get back?"

"I'll call before then if I can, if mom's not bunched up about long distance."

"Gotcha. Hey, I love you."

Katie leaned over and inhaled the scent of her blossoming anniversary roses. "I love you, too. Thanks for understanding. You're great."

"Don't forget." He mustered a chuckle. "We were something last night, weren't we?"

Tom pulled the station wagon into the family driveway at exactly 6:00 p.m. "You ready for this?"

She gritted her teeth. She hadn't been home since Christmas. "Let's put it this way, I'm excited to see the boys."

Katie's three youngest brothers crawled over her shoulders and into her arms as she squatted down to greet them. They nearly knocked her over. She wrapped her arms around them, drew them close, and breathed the familiar whiff of brothers—sweat and cap-gun powder. "I've missed you guys!"

Mom wiped her hands on her apron as she hollered from the door, "Hurry in and wash your hands. Dinner's ready."

Dad met Katie with a bear hug. Seeing him felt better than she'd imagined.

"I've missed you, Dad."

He smiled and patted her on the back. "Not as much as I've missed you."

Katie exchanged a knowing glance with her father. "I'll help Mom."

He nodded.

With its wallpapered bold-flowered print, aging avocado-colored appliances, faded gold Formica counters, and cream-colored painted cabinets, the kitchen felt homey. Tonight it smelled of baked chicken and potatoes.

While Katie helped her mom fill the serving dishes, her brother Ron set the table for ten and they all crammed into their assigned seats. The meal began with a hushed prayer, then bowls clinked left to right.

Jeffrey whined as Tom pilfered a drumstick from the serving plate before it reached him. "I want one of those!"

Sitting around the oval table with nine mismatched chairs meant shoulder-to-shoulder seating. The highchair, tucked in next to Katie's spot, had been there her entire life. She cut John's food into teensy bites without blinking an eye.

Dad quizzed the elementary kids on their multiplication facts, and the older ones on church history. Twenty minutes later, the feeding frenzy complete, Katie shooed them out of the kitchen with a promise to clean the mess. They punched each other's arms and dashed to the living room floor for their nightly wrestling match with Dad.

Katie hoped for a moment to catch her breath.

Her mom stayed behind though, clearing the dishes. "I'm so glad you're home."

Katie frowned. "It's good to see you, too."

"I don't understand why you stay away."

"I'm not staying away. You know I have to study."

Mom poured herself a cup of coffee and sat down at the table while Katie rinsed the dishes and set them on the counter.

"You have no idea how difficult it is, being in the house without you."

Katie turned her back to her mom and sighed. *Here it comes.*

"My life is empty. All I do is cook, wash load after load of laundry, and clean the house. Even after all these months, it's not getting any easier."

"You need a hobby," Katie said. "You could take up knitting. You used to knit, didn't you?"

"Well, yes, years ago." Katie's mom looked into the bottom of her coffee cup, as if in search of answers. "I think maybe I'll go to college, like you."

She held her breath. *What the hell?*

"I'll bet, if I enroll for spring classes and get started right away, you and I could finish our bachelor's degrees at the same time."

"Great, Mom." *We could walk down the aisle together at graduation. Maybe you could even be my roommate next year.*

The next morning, Katie awakened to the sound of thumping. She rolled over, checked the time on the clock radio, and rubbed her eyes. Even at the crack of dawn, her brothers thundered through the house like cowboys chasing Indians. She suddenly hated being the only girl in the house and longed to return to Janie, Bobby, and her life at school.

As her seven younger brothers created havoc outside her bedroom door, Katie lay in bed. She spent her entire life being their second mother and never knew why. The seven of them kept her busy ever since she could remember. She fed them and changed their diapers—expertly wielding huge, sharp diaper pins by the age of five and snuggling them down for naps like her own personal baby dolls.

Once she turned ten, her mom decided she could handle the responsibility of babysitting for short periods. The dependable child, she did such a good job providing childcare her mom enrolled in secretarial courses, and two days a week for the four years she attended high school, Katie watched them after school and throughout the evening. She helped them with homework, as well as completing her own. Expected to maintain a four-point average and prepare the boys' dinner, give them their baths, and read bedtime stories, Katie became an expert organizer and negotiation specialist.

She rolled out of bed, yanked on her robe, and trod down to the kitchen to make bologna sandwiches and wrap them in waxed paper. As soon as Katie opened the fridge, Mom ran off to change John's diaper.

Being home is like jumping rope, thought Katie. *Once you learn to skip over the cord, you never forget.* She labeled brown paper lunch bags with a black marker, and filled each one with a sandwich, cookies, and a banana.

Five minutes later, the kitchen filled with grumpy boys—her own personal seven dwarves.

"I don't want mustard on my sandwich," Ron whined.

"It's ketchup," she said. "Relax. Eat your cereal. You're fifteen, right?"

Ron shot her a sheepish grin and slid his lanky body into a chair.

Ten minutes later, one by one, she handed out lunches to her school-age brothers as they raced out the door, late as usual.

"I'm coming to the visitation with you," Mom called from the bedroom.

Katie downed two aspirin and wished, like the genie on TV, she could cross her arms, and with one good nod, transport herself back to Ypsilanti. She heaved a deep sigh, wiped down the counters, and then ran the vacuum. Not only did she want to be back at school, she wanted it right this very minute. For good measure, in case God heard that, she dusted the first floor.

She put a few electric rollers in her hair and jumped in the shower. After towel drying, she pulled on a black A-line skirt and buttoned a ruffled maroon polyester blouse. Grandma Jo arrived to tend to the younger kids and Katie drove her mom the short route to the mortuary.

Katie hated funeral homes. Nobody liked them, she guessed, but they made her seriously queasy. She pulled open the entrance door and turned green. As soon as she walked inside, she checked for a place to stick her head between her knees without drawing attention.

"Quit being such a baby," her mom insisted. "Death's a natural part of life."

"Maybe for you."

Katie spotted Mark near the casket. Her mother grabbed her arm and reminded her, "I've never liked that boy. You're not getting back with him, are you? There's something odd about him. He's bad news."

"Let it go, Mom. His dad just died."

The first time she'd seen him in months, Mark looked drawn; he'd cut his once chin length hair short and trimmed his long sideburns. His face appeared thinner in spite of his powerful wrestler body. Mark saw her, waved, and smiled. Her stomach turned.

"Katie," he said. He hugged her, kissed her right on the lips, and held on tight.

She patted him on the back, squirmed out of his embrace, and swallowed breakfast for the second time that day. "I'm sorry about your dad. What happened?"

His eyes filled with a plea for comfort. "Heart attack."

She ignored the pleading gaze. "How's everyone doing?"

He wrapped an arm around her shoulder and caged her in with a firm grip. "In shock. It doesn't feel real. I thought Dad would live forever. Doctors aren't supposed to get sick, or die."

She twisted out of his hold and placed her hands on his shoulders to create more space between them. "Can I help with the kids?"

Mark nodded down the hallway. "They're all in the kitchen."

"I'll check on them. Don't you worry about a thing." She headed to the casket first, knelt down and folded her hands. With eyes squeezed shut, she paid her respects to Mark's dad, recited a quick Our Father, then kicked herself for being so nice to Mark. Bobby had guessed right. Mark still liked her. She never should have let him kiss her. Knowing Mark, he'd misconstrue it.

She crossed herself and opened her eyes, averting her gaze from the body, and stood. As she walked down the long hall to the kitchen, the untouched order of the place made her feel off kilter. Everything here stayed in its place—not only the dead.

Within minutes, Katie's mom marched into the kitchen. "I'm ready to go."

"I told Mark I'd take care of the kids," Katie said.

"You'll have to find a ride home then."

"Don't worry. Someone can drop me off."

Katie sighed in relief. Her mom's absence made her feel lighter, and Katie fed the younger kids and played rummy with them, glad she could be helpful but away from Mark.

Hours later, he arrived in the kitchen and folded into a chair. His sallow, gray complexion confirmed his suffering and exhaustion. Still, something odd stood between them, something weird.

Mark locked eyes with her. "I came to visit you at school, and I've written. Didn't you get my letters? And how about my last message? I left it on a *While You Were Out* note at the front desk."

"No, I didn't get it." *Had she received messages?*

Mark huffed, his eyes boring into her. "Doesn't seem possible."

Katie turned away and shook her head as she tried to figure him out. Growing up, his mother criticized his every move. Katie surmised that he had disappointed her by not having been blessed with his father's intelligence, charm, or good looks. When Mark couldn't please his mom, he vied for his dad's approval. No luck there either. Suddenly, Katie felt sorry for him.

She tried to distract him. "Would you like a bite to eat? There's leftover pizza. It's cold, but you like cold pizza, right?" Immediately, she kicked herself. *I can't let him think I'm interested in him.*

Mark grinned. "Thanks for remembering. I need you right now. You know me and love me."

She swallowed hard. She didn't love him. Not ever. She wanted to be with Bobby, not with him. *Get me out of here.*

"I'll fix you some food and grab you a soda." She ignored his advances and slapped two slices of cold pizza on a plate. Then, she handed the food and a cola to Mark.

"You look pretty. Older, like Farrah Fawcett."

He poked at her nerves, and she couldn't let it go, even if they were at his dad's wake. "Of course I look older. We haven't seen each other for a while."

Mark ate as he talked. "I still think of you as my girl."

Katie continued to wrestle with keeping down her breakfast. "Mark, it's over."

He folded in on himself. "I just want you to care about me."

She squared her shoulders. "I'm sorry. I care about you, but not in the way you'd like. I'm here as a friend. Only that."

"Sorry," Mark said. "I guess you're right. We're friends." He looked down at his lap and shook his head, almost repentant, then finished his last bite and looked up at her. "Thanks for staying. It means a lot. And again, sorry for assuming you were here as more than a friend. Wishful thinking on my part. Do you think you'll come back tomorrow?"

"I'm not sure."

Mark nodded. "I'm ready to take the kids home. I need to drop them off at the house first, but then I can drop you."

"I planned on walking."

"It's dark, Katie. Since the riots, it's not safe."

"I'll be fine."

"No, I insist."

"All right then, but I need to get straight home."

Katie cleared his paper plate and soda can from the coffee table. She rounded up the kids, put on their jackets, and shuffled them outside while Mark pulled up the car. "Let's go, guys."

After they dropped Mark's brothers and sisters at home, Katie sat as close to the passenger door as humanly possible, hoping the two-mile trip to her house would pass quickly. She relaxed when Mark turned onto her block, until he passed her house and drove around the corner—the corner where they used to park.

"I need to get home," she reminded him.

"I know I've kept you too long today, but I just wanted to talk to you for a minute. Like friends...like you said."

"It's over between us. Please, just take me home."

"I know it's over, but give me five minutes. My dad just died."

"I Want You Back" by the Jackson Five played on the radio. Could there be any worse timing? Mark's eyes filled with tears, he threw his arms around her, laid his head on her shoulder, and began to sob. His tears seemed genuine, still...She wanted to bolt, but instead, she patted him on the back, and told him it would be all right. He continued to cry, and she continued to console him.

An eternity passed before he calmed down. He gazed into her eyes and she detected the same wanting she had noticed earlier in the day. It made her uneasy. "It's late. I have to get home," she said.

He pulled her into him, and forcibly turned up her chin. "C'mon, just for old time's sake. Just one kiss. I promise. Just one."

"Knock it off, Mark. Take me home right this minute." Katie turned in the seat to unlock the car door. She'd walk home. *Damn it, Mark.*

He seized her arm and jerked her back.

"Stop it. Let me go. What's wrong with you?" Katie wriggled an elbow up against his chest for leverage and tried to peel his fingers from her arm with her other hand.

In a flash, he forced himself on top of her.

She pounded her fists into his chest. "Stop it."

"Come on, kiss me. One last time, baby." He pressed his mouth onto hers and bit her, grabbing her wrists and pinning them down on the seat. She squirmed with all her might, trying to free her legs from under his. His knee dug deep into her thigh, and she yelped in pain and horror.

She began to cry. "Stop it. Please. You're scaring me."

He clamped his hand over her mouth as he crushed himself against her. "Shut up!"

She reached for his hair, laced her fingers deep into his short, cropped curls, and yanked with all her might. He rose up and slapped her, his class ring smashing into her left temple. Then he took hold of her panties and ripped them down to her knees. She tried twisting out from under him, but she was no match for the State Wrestling Champion.

Her cheek stung as he slapped her again. He wedged her face between the back and the bottom of the seat with one powerful arm.

"I said shut up!" He moved above her, unzipping his pants. "You know you want to fuck me. Guess what? It's your lucky day." His voice sounded completely different, like a stranger.

She tried to talk, to reason with him, but the bench seat muffled her voice. Mark shoved his leg between hers. Pressed it into her. Hurt her. Too scared to do anything more, she cried. He plunged his hand between her legs, fumbled with her, and rammed his fingers inside her. He grabbed her thighs—forced his hardness against her. Her tears stung and her throat closed with fright. Mark moaned, lost in his madness, shoving to get inside her.

She took a measured breath and waited. As he reared back, she bent her knee and jabbed him hard.

He shrieked and crumpled on top of her. "Fuck!"

She rolled and twisted on the floor of the car, reaching for the exit. With a fumbled lift, the door handle gave way. She scrambled out, crawled onto the curb, and clambered to her feet.

Tears snaked down Katie's cheeks, the nakedness beneath her skirt reminding her she needed to hurry, to escape, to get away. She hopped on one foot and removed her remaining shoe. Then she gulped, choked back her tears, and ran—faster than ever.

Eight houses, seven, six...she counted backwards until she reached hers. She bolted through the side door and locked it. With a sudden jerk, she stopped and tried to calm herself. Noiseless in her bare feet, she entered the half bath just inside, closed the door and sat down on the toilet seat in the dark. Her skirt stuck to her stomach and she searched blindly for a hand towel, which she ran under water, all the while trying to quell the nausea that welled up from her stomach and into her throat. She fought for a measured breath and wiped herself, whispering, "make it stop" and then rearranged her clothing. Eyes squeezed shut, she splashed water on her face and listened for house sounds. The TV made a soft hum in the den. Trembling, and suddenly chilled, she wrapped her arms around herself and held on tight.

"Kate?" Mom called.

"I'm in the bathroom," Katie said, relieved to be hidden where she could fake it.

"Close up the house before you come upstairs. I'm going to bed."

"Sure, Mom."

Don't tell. Who would believe Mark tried to rape her on the night of his dad's wake? Who wouldn't feel sorry for him, out of his mind with grief? Her mom never liked him. Just this morning she'd called him "bad news." She'd blame Katie for accepting a ride.

She climbed upstairs in the dark, let herself into the bathroom, and turned on the shower. She stripped down, then stepped in. The warm water rushed over her and mixed with tears she could not control. She scrubbed her skin as she recited a mantra, "Get off of me. I want you off."

The soap stung as she washed her swollen, scraped, and aching body. Gulping air, she told herself to block it out. It didn't really happen. It was all a bad dream.

Katie fought waves of nausea. *So much for a reason for everything.* No way could she make sense of this. Ever.

She shut off the water, wrapped herself in a towel, gathered her clothing from the floor, and slunk to her bedroom. She wanted out. Out of town. Back to school. Home.

In a clean t-shirt and jeans, she grabbed the ripped and tainted clothes from the floor. Silently, she crept down the two flights of stairs to the basement and into the furnace room. Next to the old coal furnace, a gas incinerator sat, burning day and night. The suctioned door proved heavy, but she lifted it, and her clothes caught fire within moments. Through the small glass plate in the door, Katie watched them burn, holding herself and rocking, humming the song she sang to her baby brothers when they cried inconsolably.

"Hush a bye, don't you cry
Go to sleep my little baby.
When you wake you will find,
All the pretty little horses."

A light flickered in the back hall. Katie stopped and held her breath. Scared senseless, she edged around the basement stairs and whispered, "Who's there?"

"It's me."

"Tom, you scared me half to death."

"What the hell is wrong with you? Are you burning something? And what's up with the shiner?"

Katie lifted her hand to her face. Her eye felt swollen and sore to the touch. "Could you mind your own business, just this once?"

"Cool it," he said. "No explanation needed."

"Fine."

"Shit," Tom said, "What are you so damned touchy about?"

"Don't swear in the house. Mom'll kill you."

"Hey, your eye's huge. C'mon, I'll get you some ice. Does Mom know?"

"No, and she won't. Keep your mouth shut. Don't tell anyone. Not a word. And please, stop asking questions. In fact, will you do me a favor? Drive me back to school right now and I'll give you my last paycheck."

"I can't. Mom will kill me."

"Like you care. It's not like you've never been caught before. Besides, she'll never know the difference."

"Where's Dad?"

"Asleep, I guess. His car is in the drive."

"I've had a few beers. I shouldn't be driving."

"I'll drive. You can sober up on the way. Grab a Coke or something."

Tom wavered. He shoved his hands into his pockets, thought for a moment, then gave in. "All right, what the fuck. Let's go."

She threw her arms around him.

"Now," he said, "before I change my mind."

Chapter 11

THE COVER UP

April 1970

Katie pulled into the dorm parking lot just before eleven, and Tom woke as she slipped the gearshift into park. He slid into the driver's seat and rolled down the window as she gathered her bag from the back seat.

"Mark, right?"

"Don't worry about it. Not a word to Mom either. I can handle her. Blame it all on me. She'll rant and rave, I know. Blow her off. And thanks. You saved my life. Honest."

Tom paused and shook his head. "Take care of yourself, Sis. You know I never liked him. He's such an asshole. You want me to take care of him?"

She kissed his cheek. "Stay out of it."

Tom shifted the car into gear. "Mark's bad news," he said as he pulled away.

A soft light illuminated the hall. Katie slipped into the stairwell, desperately hoping to remain invisible on the way to her room. She'd kept Mark from getting all the way inside her, but it didn't really matter. He'd had his way with her just the same. *He ruined me.*

Her footsteps echoed in the staircase and reminded her that blood still flowed in her veins. She moved in a fog—thick, murky, and deep—but forced her shoulders back and blinked to clear her vision. She pretended to be all right.

She hoped and prayed she could sneak into the room undetected. Her feeble prayers were answered when the lock tumbled and she opened the door to a dark, noiseless space. She didn't turn on the lights, but grabbed a nightgown from the back of the bathroom door, and gingerly put her head through the neck hole. In slow motion, she broke some ice from Janie's mini-fridge into a washcloth.

The ice cracked like thunder and Katie looked up. If she woke Janie, she wouldn't know what to say. Janie snorted at just that moment and rolled over. Katie held her breath. Then, Janie threw an arm over her head and snored again. Crisis averted.

Katie hoisted her aching body into bed, placing the cold cloth over her swollen eye. With her pillow drawn over her fitful sobs, she tried to sleep.

How could I let this happen? Did I lead him on, just by showing up? I never should have gone home. Enough. Stop thinking, damn it. Exhaustion claimed her battered body and she drifted into a sound sleep. No dreams, no nightmares. Just sleep.

Hours later, she woke to the sound of her own shrieking. Someone shook her. She sat up and opened her eyes.

"Wake up. You're having a nightmare. You're screaming. C'mon, sweetie, wake up." Janie wrapped her arms around her and held her.

Katie wept as she took in her surroundings. She was home, safe with Janie, in the dorm. A sliver of daylight peeked underneath the closed curtains. "What time is it?"

"It's two o'clock in the afternoon, you goofball." Janie placed her hand under Katie's chin and turned her face to get a better look at her eye. "You've been sleeping *all* day. I thought you weren't coming back until tomorrow. Jesus, what the hell did you walk into?"

Katie broke down again, sobbing.

"What is it? What's the matter?"

"Nothing. Just a nightmare." She coughed and reached for a tissue, blew her nose, and lied. "I walked into a door at the funeral home yesterday. Klutzy, huh?"

"Wait just a minute. You show up in our room without warning, you're a basket case, and you have a black eye. What, did the fucking bad dream give you a black eye? You walked into a door? Listen to yourself. I'm not buying it. What's really going on?"

"Nothing. I told you."

The phone rang and Janie picked it up before Katie could stop her.

"Hi, Mrs. Hayes," she said with syrupy sweetness.

Katie shook her head at Janie and waved her off.

"Sorry, no, she left for the library about thirty minutes ago. She has an exam on Monday. Abnormal Psych," Janie paused and winked at Katie. "Yep, you know Katie. Always wanting to do her best. Crazy girl, she'll probably be there all day today and most of tomorrow. Yes...

mm-hmm. I'll tell her you called. Yes...I'll have her call you." Janie nodded and rolled her eyes. "Goodbye."

"You're a good bullshitter," Katie said. "Thanks."

"As much as I get a kick out of it, your swearing won't distract me. Why don't you want to talk to your mom? And why aren't you at the funeral? Tell me," Janie insisted, her hand resting on Katie's arm.

"Being home drove me crazy," she began. "It put me in a bad mood, you know? It felt so weird being there. And the funeral? I hate funerals. After being at the wake all day yesterday, I couldn't take another minute." She cocked her head in anticipation of Janie's agreement.

"Sure, I understand." Janie rubbed her arm. "Does your eye hurt? It looks pretty bad. Can I get you anything? Aspirin?"

"No, thanks." Nauseous, Katie laid down, wincing when her temple touched the pillowcase.

Janie narrowed her eyes as she examined Katie's eye once more. "I'm getting you some Excedrin...and some ice."

"Okay." Katie turned over to her good side and fell asleep in an instant. Later, she awoke to Janie's hushed voice on the phone.

"I don't know, Bobby," she said. "She showed up some time during the night. She's got one hell of a shiner and she woke up this afternoon screaming like a banshee. Someone or something scared the living shit out of her. I went to get her some aspirin, and when I came back from the bathroom, I found her sound asleep."

She quieted for a few seconds and Katie continued to feign sleep. She couldn't face Janie or Bobby. Hearing Janie talk to him made her well up again.

How can I tell him? How could I have let this happen? I've ruined everything.

She overheard Janie say, "I'll meet you downstairs."

She hung up the phone and left the room a few minutes later, shutting the heavy entrance door without a sound. Like a robot, Katie slid out of bed and walked into the bathroom.

She stared into the mirror and winced. The right side of her face was distorted and ugly—swollen, red, black, and blue. Katie used her baby finger to delicately apply layer after layer of make-up. She recoiled from her reflection. In the end, the meticulous operation seemed ineffective. It looked worse than before she had started. She dressed and focused on a plan. If she made it to the lounge under the guise of searching out Janie and food, maybe she could head off any discussion between the two of them. She didn't want them figuring it out.

She cautioned herself to act normal, but worried Janie and Bobby would see right through her. After all, they knew her better than anyone.

Why didn't I fight harder?

Katie entered the lounge. As if on the outside looking in, she watched herself search for Janie and Bobby. She spotted the two of them on a yellow vinyl couch at the far end of the room and was relieved to see them sitting a few feet apart. It reassured her that she could have a normal possessive thought in the middle of this vicious nightmare.

Bobby smiled. “Hey there. What the heck did you walk into, lady?”

Even through the added makeup, her goose egg looked purple. She dipped her head. “A wall.”

Janie frowned.

Did I tell her I ran into a wall or a door? Shit.

Bobby narrowed his eyes. “Are you all right?”

“Of course,” she said, choking on the words as she mustered a smile. “I’m just hungry and tired. I hate funerals. I couldn’t wait to get back here.”

“I’m glad you’re back.”

“Me, too,” she murmured. She felt woozy and her body swayed.

“Here,” he said as he patted the seat next to him.

“Sorry, I’m not feeling too hot. Maybe I need to eat.” Bobby draped his arm around her and she leaned on his shoulder. Quickly though, she felt herself giving in to her emotions. She worried he would sense something, so she faced him, bending a knee up onto the couch and resting her head on her hand. She couldn’t give it away.

Janie offered to make a food run. “Want me to go to Jack in the Box for you?”

“Would you? A fried taco would really hit the spot.”

Maybe if I straighten my shoulders, I won’t fall apart. What if he can tell anyway?

Bobby attempted to lighten the mood. “Here’s a funny story. My brothers and I went canoeing down the Huron River yesterday. You would have loved it, but water and I don’t get along. I dumped the damned canoe only ten minutes into the ride and ended up chasing the stupid thing. My brothers loved it. Me, on the other hand? Completely humiliated."

She forced a grin.

"At least I'm cheering you up." He smiled and for the next twenty minutes, kept up a steady stream of chatter about the trip.

The smell of grease and the ruffling of wrappers interrupted his light banter. Janie littered the table with deep fried tacos and Cokes. Katie realized she was ravenous and ate. She wanted to hold onto Bobby and Janie and never leave them again.

Twenty minutes later, pretending took its toll and fatigue set in. If she couldn't be with Bobby or Janie, she wanted to be asleep. When she slept, she couldn't remember.

She excused herself and went back upstairs. After she changed into a nightshirt, she sat on the bed in the darkened room, and let the tears flow.

Cynthia returned from her visit home and peeked inside the room. She spotted Katie, stepped in front of her, and gazed down at her. "What's wrong, sweetie?"

"I don't know. I'm not myself today. I can't stop crying, and it's for no reason. Nothing is going right."

Cynthia sat down on the bed beside her and placed her scrawny arm around Katie's shoulder. "Hey, it could be something as simple as the pull of the moon."

Katie, anxious to address Cynthia's pointed frown at her shiner, simply said, "I know. Stupid. I walked into a wall."

"Is it Bobby?"

"I'm just not sure I'm ready for a relationship. I feel all mixed up, like I'm in a giant mixing bowl and the beaters are battering me—pulling me through, throwing me up against the sides of the bowl, and pulling me through again."

Cynthia nodded. "You need to find yourself."

Katie gave her a puzzled look.

"It's your freshman year. Things happen fast, and you're still adjusting to being without your family, to being with a bunch of crazy girls. It's hard to be with a guy, totally with him, until you know who you are. Once you figure *you* out, it'll be super right, and you'll know."

"I feel stupid." Katie thought not of what Cynthia said, but of how she let herself down by not fighting harder.

"You're not stupid. When I first came to school, I still dated William. High school sweethearts, remember?"

Katie nodded.

"After four months or so, I met this other guy, a basketball player—tall, muscular, a strapping hunk of man."

"Really?"

"Yep. I broke up with William for a while, to be sure I didn't want someone else."

"What did you find out?"

"I needed to be alone. Totally alone. I'd been defining myself by my boyfriend. I needed to get comfortable with me, settle into my own skin."

"How did you do that?"

"By pursuing what I wanted to do—my education. I didn't go home for a while either. I stayed up here with

Gwen and did my own thing. It might sound silly, but I grew up a lot."

"Were you happy?"

"What, being alone?"

Katie nodded.

"Sometimes, but lonely, too. It's not easy. And I'm not saying just because it worked for me, it'll work for you. But it did help. I feel better for having spent time alone." Cynthia sat with her thoughts for a moment. "Let's put it this way. In the long run I've been a lot happier, and a better person because of it."

"I'm not sure it's about being alone for me. Maybe it's more about whether I deserve…"

"Deserve what?"

"A life, happiness, all of it…" her voice broke and she began to cry.

"It's gonna be all right, hon."

Katie couldn't answer.

"Things will turn out. You'll see. They did for me."

Katie nodded. She wanted to believe Cynthia.

"Can I tell you a secret?"

"Sure." Katie leaned on her arm and listened.

"William and I went to my parents over the weekend for dinner. He asked my dad if he could talk to him. They went in my dad's office, and came out shaking hands, slapping each other on the back, and laughing."

Katie's eyes brightened a little. "Seriously?"

"Really," Cynthia answered with a wide smile.

"At dinner, Dad banged his fork on the side of his plate." She took Katie's hand and continued. "My family is a lot like yours, I imagine, my little brothers all talking at once at the table and Mom trying to teach them manners."

She nodded.

"So Dad says, 'Listen up gentlemen,' and they all turn to face him at the head of the table. 'How'd you like to have a new brother?' I looked at my mom, wide-eyed, shocked she'd be having another baby. I mean, I'm twenty-one years old. But I noticed my mom looked as surprised as I did. Then, it hit me. He was talking about William.

"Before I knew it, William knelt down beside me, taking my hand and making a long speech about how much he loved me. I'm going to tell you, but don't tell anyone else...I can't even remember what he said. I mean, I knew William and I would get married someday. I just didn't have a clue he'd propose then, and in front of my whole family."

Katie threw her arms around Cynthia. "Congratulations!" She glanced at her friend's left hand. "Did he give you a ring?"

"It's being sized. The jeweler didn't believe I wore a size three and a half. He claimed I'd have to be as skinny as a dandelion stem to have such a small ring size. William said he tried arguing with him, but you know William, he doesn't like to argue with anyone."

"He's the gentlest big guy I've ever met." Katie thought of both Bobby, her own tall gentle guy, and then of Mark and his vicious attack.

Cynthia beamed. "I planned to wait and tell you all when I got my ring back, but you needed some happy news."

"Thanks for cheering me up. I'm thrilled for you and William. I just hope someday it happens for me. Right now, it doesn't seem possible."

"Honey," Cynthia said, "sometimes life serves you a shit sandwich without the mayo. Weird detours come along. It's not always so straightforward and easy. But sooner or later, you'll figure out the reason for the heavy serving of manure. And you'll be a better person because of it."

"I hope you're right."

With one last hug, Cynthia pulled down the covers, prompting Katie to scoot off the bed. "Hop in." Cynthia tucked the flowered sheet up around Katie's shoulders, gave her a kiss on the forehead and said, "Whatever it is, it'll get better."

As Katie drifted off to sleep, she thought about Cynthia and worried. Could she have said "no" in front of her whole family? But Cynthia seemed ready. She loved William. *Could I say no? Could I say yes?*

When she woke the next morning, she felt groggy. She grabbed a Coke, then reached for the phone and called home.

Her mom answered, gave a quick report of the funeral and started in on Katie. "You didn't even say goodbye to anyone. I don't know what's gotten into you."

Katie inhaled a measured breath. She'd anticipated mom's lecture, but it took tons of effort to listen, and to be nice. "Mom, you know how I am in hospitals and funeral homes. They turn me into a jellyfish. I'm sure everyone will understand if you explain it to them. I have to go and study."

"Don't you get in a snit with me, Kathleen Marie Hayes. I hope you're planning to come home again soon. I could use some help around here. Spring cleaning is just around the corner. And once school is out, you'll be home for the entire summer."

Her mother's words prompted a new bout of nausea. "Mom, why can't the boys help?"

"You know they can't get a job done decently. You're the one I depend on."

Mom hung up the phone and Katie felt more alone than in her entire life.

Great. Mom counts on me. Who can I count on?

Chapter 12

HIDING

April 1970

Two weeks later, Katie gazed out at the dogwood blossoms. She had always coped with unpleasant feelings by keeping busy. Maybe that somehow explained why her mom depended on her so much. She recalled hours spent cleaning out drawers, helping her brothers pick up their toys, pushing over a step stool to take clothes off the line, and placing the same stool next to the sink to wash dishes. She'd spent so much of her childhood like this. She hated it when the boys ran outside to play baseball with Dad, or when she heard them laughing during snowball fights while she remained stuck inside with Mom doing "women's work."

"You tried to hide it when you got upset," Grandma once said. "Why, I remember one time, staying with you kids, the boys wouldn't let you play Joan of Arc." She patted Katie's knee and chuckled. "You huffed off to the basement and folded three loads of laundry. Goodness, you were only six."

Today it felt reassuring to fall back into old patterns. She organized her notes for studying, cleaned out file folders, created index cards so she could cram for exams, and swept and scrubbed the floors in between.

When keeping busy didn't work, she tried praying. She felt like a deer, shot during bow season, bleeding out. She'd been in overdrive since Mark's attack, afraid to stop for fear of falling apart. She offered Bobby and Janie tons of excuses: "I'm tired. I have to study. I'm not good company today." If they suspected anything or knew she lied, they kept it to themselves. *Thank you, Jesus.*

Katie used a highlighter to mark passages in her music theory book and targeted her focus on harmonic intervals. When the phone began ringing, she kicked the trashcan. She wanted nothing more than to be left alone, but she picked it up anyway. It might be Janie.

"Hello?"

It was Bobby. "I'm off work in an hour. Feel like a break?"

"I wish. But I have tons of studying left for this Music Theory final."

"What's up? All of a sudden, we're not clicking?"

Katie tried acting nonchalant. "What do you mean?"

"Something's wrong. When are you going to tell me?"

Bobby's question rattled her, and she caught her breath. She'd never forgive herself if she let Mark come between them. Seeing her might distract him. "A study break sounds great. Why not?"

"Meet you downstairs in forty minutes."

She pulled her hair back into a ponytail, threw on a light sweater and tennies and ran downstairs to meet him. A trickle of her old self seeped back in and her heart warmed as she caught sight of him.

He wrapped his arms around her in a bear hug. She inhaled and took in his sandalwood scent. Her entire body relaxed. *Mmm. Bobby.*

She surprised herself and clutched him tight. "It's so good to see you."

He smiled and took her hand. "Where've you been?"

Shit, she thought, he's not going to let this go.

"I'm here right now."

"I'm a cop, lady. I take inventory, size things up. Things haven't been right with you since you went home for the funeral."

"I'm fine," she lied.

They walked hand in hand to the south exit of the dorm and headed west to their special place. Fifteen minutes later, they meandered down the winding sidewalk path, swinging their arms like a pendulum in perfect balance. *Maybe I can still be with Bobby in spite of what's happened.* The sun warmed their backs and she felt comforted and safe for a moment.

She tipped her face to the sky. "The sunshine feels good."

"Um hmm."

She smiled.

When the reached the towering oak, Bobby asked, "Want to sit?"

Katie loved their favorite spot on the hill. It overlooked the rear of the campus, facing the railroad tracks and commuter parking lot. "Absolutely."

He ran his hand over the ground, making sure it was dry. She melted into his arms as he pulled her down onto his lap, wanting nothing more than to turn to him for comfort. He took her face in his hands and gently brushed his lips across hers. She stiffened.

She faltered, trying desperately to keep herself in the moment—to keep from disappearing. *Why would I freak out now, when I'm with Bobby?*

He sensed her hesitation and wrapped his arms around her. "What's the matter?"

"Don't worry," she said, but she couldn't control herself and backed away from his embrace. As hard as she fought, the tears streamed down her cheeks. Shuddering, she gave in and let Bobby hold her.

"Tell me."

Katie bit her lip. "Nothing. It's nothing."

Bobby gently stroked her back. "Something's wrong. I'm not stupid, and I'm not going to ignore the fact you came back from that funeral with a black eye. I know you, remember? You're not yourself." Frown lines wrinkled his brow and he waited for an answer.

"Trust me. I'm all right. Please, don't push me on this. I'll let you know if I need anything. It's just a bit of a rough patch. Going home made me realize how much I need to be away from my family."

Bobby shook his head in frustration. "I'm keeping my eye on you."

"Thanks." She dug deep for a grin, trying to reassure him, then hopped up, pulling him up with her. "C'mon. I'm starving."

A little after eight, she said goodnight to Bobby, rode the elevator upstairs, walked into the room, and found Janie sitting cross-legged on the bed. "Oh my gosh! You're studying."

Janie stuck out her tongue. "Shut up, stupid. Oh, yeah, by the way, Mark called."

Katie froze to the linoleum square.

"Who?"

"I said your ex-boyfriend called. He wants you to call him back." Janie caught Katie's shock and a look of puzzlement crossed her face. "Did something happen between the two of you?"

"Leave it alone!" Katie shouted, throwing her hands up in the air. "You and Bobby *both* need to let this go! Nothing happened. And I'm not calling him back."

Janie shrugged her shoulders. "Hey, no sweaty-dah on my part. I don't care what you do."

"Sorry." She relaxed and offered a cow-eyed request for forgiveness. "I'm in a bad mood. Maybe it's exams. I don't know."

"Yeah, well, you're stupid."

Katie smiled. As out of character as Janie's all-out studying appeared, she could count on her roommate's predictable responses; they were reassuring.

"Do you want to do something?"

"Can't. I need to study. I never planned on getting back this late."

"Fine. Suit yourself, Miss Goody-Goody. I'm going out. I've been at these books way too long."

"It's late. Please don't go out by yourself."

"I'll find somebody to go with me. I've gotta get some food. Want some tacos or burgers?"

"No, thanks. I ate with Bobby." Not quite true. She just pushed the food around in circles on her plate.

"Okay, dummy, I'll get you some tacos anyway."

"Be careful."

"Don't be such a worry wart."

"I can't help it," Katie said.

The phone rang as Janie headed out the door.

"It's probably Mark. Just get it the hell over with."

"I'm not talking to him. The phone will just have to ring."

"Why do you have to be so damned stubborn?"

"I am not being stubborn."

Janie opened the door to leave. "Yeah sure, Sherlock. Some psychologist you're going to be. Face it head on, would you? Nancy Drew wouldn't hide behind her roommate."

"Give it a rest, Janie."

"Can't take the heat, can you?"

Katie pointed at the door. "Weren't you on your way out?"

Janie smiled and took a giant step over the threshold. "See you later, weirdo."

The door closed and Katie exhaled a long, choppy breath. What if she had picked up the phone when he called? *Maybe God is watching out for me.* She pressed her hand to her chest and tried to calm her racing heart, willing a vacant mind. She stepped into the bathroom, washed her face without looking at it, and then returned to her desk and opened her music theory text to page one hundred eighty three, *Dynamic Contrast.*

After her music theory final, she walked back to the dorm on automatic pilot, picking up the mail on her way through the lobby and setting it on top of her books. When she walked in the room, she tossed the mail at Janie, and the corner of one of the letters caught her right between the eyes.

Katie snickered. "Oops, sorry. Didn't mean to hit you."

"Yeah, right, shithead." Janie chuckled and stooped to pick up the letter. She turned it over in her hands. "Hey, it's a letter from that idiot boyfriend of yours."

"Bobby?"

"No, not him," Janie said. "It's from Mark."

Nausea rose in Katie's throat. *Couldn't he just leave her alone?* "What an ass."

Janie bounced across the room and chinked a nickel into the jar. "What's up with you and Mark?"

"What's up is I'm not in the mood for any more of his crap. We broke up ions ago, for God's sake. Is he a moron?"

"Just because he sent you mail doesn't mean you have to open it. Throw the *garbage* in the garbage. C'mon, Nancy Drew. You know enough to pitch unnecessary information."

A wave of relief washed over Katie. "Good idea. Sometimes you're smarter than you look."

Janie wagged her head and stuck out her tongue.

Katie plucked the letter from Janie and ripped it in two. For extra measure, she tore it again, tossed it in the wastebasket and stomped it down with her foot.

Janie looked proud. "Feel better?"

"Much."

"Well?"

"Well what?"

Janie placed Katie's hand on her back. Katie patted her.

"You're welcome!"

Katie rode an eternal seesaw, up one minute, down the next. She had felt such a high destroying Mark's letter, yet five minutes later when she leaned over to pick up her brush, she caught the pieces of it staring back at her and wanted to throw up.

She didn't want to read a single word Mark wrote, but curiosity ate her alive. Latching the door so Janie couldn't walk in on her, she unfolded the scraps, then fit the pieces together like a puzzle and avoided reading the words.

Once she reassembled the letter, a single sheet of loose-leaf paper, she lined it up alongside a copy of the obituary Mark had sent. She tossed the death notice into the waste can and willed the bile rising in her throat to stay put in spite of Mark's Old Spice cologne wafting from the torn page. Katie forced herself to read the letter.

April 24, 1970

Dear Katie,

How are things going at school? We should get together and talk. I know you. You're probably making something out of nothing. What happened on the way back from the funeral home—it's no big deal, Katie. You just looked really hot. I'm coming up next weekend to see you. I've called a few times, but you've either quit answering the phone or your roommates haven't given you my messages.

See you soon, Sweetie.

Love,
Mark

Chapter 13

SANCTUARY

April 1970

Katie hated her life. On rare occasions, she relaxed enough to feel a bit more like her old self, but those brief snatches of tranquility became the exception rather than the rule. Since the arrival of Mark's letter three days ago, she was totally preoccupied and depressed. She fought to block out the flashbacks and the knowledge that summer break loomed right around the corner. She would have to go home, within arm's reach of him. Somehow, someway, she needed to find a distraction.

Janie sprang into the room and Katie shot her a grateful glance.

"Wanna go on a double date?"

"Please, God."

"God's busy, do *you* want to go?"

Katie grinned. "I'll call the guys. Where are we headed?"

Janie whooped. "Bimbo's! It's time to get your tight ass into a bar."

Katie headed for the phone. Once she reached Bobby and he agreed to call Jim, she raced Janie for the bathroom, showered, dried her hair, and held out hope. With luck, tonight would put her back on track. She dressed in her best Levi's and a striped top, then stood back and looked in the mirror. "I'm ready."

"You look hot."

"You, too," Katie said.

Janie always looked hot. Tonight she donned her spanking new striped bell-bottom jeans with a white knit shirt tucked into her tiny hips. Katie watched as she buckled a fashionable wide belt around them. Janie remained the poster girl of style. Her blonde curls framed pale blue eye shadow and powder-blushed pink cheeks. Her irises looked like Easter eggs dipped in the dye for hours—the end result a shade of cornflower blue. Katie clucked her approval then ran across the hall to the third floor lounge window and peered down on the parking lot.

She shouted to Janie through the open doorway. "They're here."

Janie slipped her cigarettes into her clutch and they dashed downstairs.

"Do you have your license?"

"Of course, idiot," Janie said.

"I hear they check at the door."

"I love being legal."

Katie asked, "Really? I didn't think you cared."

"It only matters because you'll come with me."

Katie and Janie chatted excitedly about Michigan's new drinking age—nineteen—as the two couples pulled into the lot behind Bimbo's. They joined the stream of college kids lined up around the block and waited to pay the dollar cover charge for admission to a night of dancing and draft beer. Fifteen minutes later, Katie stood inside gaping. She'd never been inside a real bar before. Below log-beamed ceilings sat long farmhouse tables and benches. Wooden floors lay strewn with peanut shells. The lights hung low, and the air swirled and smelled of stale cigarette smoke. She threw her shoulders back and laughed. This was fun!

After she checked out the digs, she studied the people and noticed Joe Smokovich, Bobby's friend from work, settled on a stool at the bar. A fellow cop, Paul Bunyan tall, with a head of close-cropped thick dark hair, wide-shoulders, and a scare you silly aura, he served as Bobby's higher-up at the Campus Police.

Katie whispered in Bobby's ear. "Do you think he's trying to catch underage kids? Maybe I shouldn't drink."

Bobby laughed. "He's a friend. Remember, he was in 'Nam with me. Don't worry. You're of age, babe. It's all cool."

"I thought there was a problem between you two."

"Relax."

Katie hesitated and asked Bobby to get her a Coke. At around age three, she remembered having drained the dregs of her dad's beer bottle. The first and last time she tried Stroh's, she remembered the flat, warm, and slimy taste to this very day. Its color reminded her of urine. She shivered, doubting she could ever develop a taste for the stuff.

Bobby, Janie, and Jim, The Three Musketeers, tromped up to the bar, laughing and scheming about how they would get Katie drunk. Mostly Janie's idea, the guys went along as if entranced by the Pied Piper. They returned with a pitcher and four frosty mugs. Katie didn't see the Coke she requested. She let her mug sit there, half-hoping someone would fill it and eliminate her having to traipse to the bar for a soft drink. She'd look like a fool drinking soda while everyone else drank beer.

Thankfully, Bobby filled her mug and she immediately became captivated by the foam forming a pillow top on the golden slush. The guys raised their mugs in a toast and the girls hoisted theirs, clinking them in team spirit. Katie watched Janie take a deep, satisfying guzzle. Next, Bobby took a wipe-your-chin-off chug, then Jim joined him.

"Enough, Miss-Goody-Two-Shoes," she mumbled under her breath. She sipped, and as cold bubbles tickled her throat, a tingle sparked in her gut, and she giggled. She was officially a member of the gang.

The jukebox blasted, and Katie craned her neck to get the lay of the land and inventory her college cohorts' behavior. She tried to pick up some quick tips so she didn't stick out like an Amish girl on her first trip to NYC. Thirty minutes later, she relaxed and felt like she belonged.

The Spangles, a local group, began strumming top forty hits. When they played "Mama Told Me Not to Come" by Three Dog Night, Janie pulled Katie onto the dance floor. Jim and Bobby trailed on their heels and they danced the set like they'd been partners their entire lives.

As soon as the song ended, the girls made a bathroom run.

Katie grabbed Janie's arm and shouted into her ear, "Oh my gosh, aren't you having a blast?"

Janie elbowed her. "You finally loosened up and drank some beer. This is a big night for you, isn't it?"

Katie giggled nervously. "Did you see me?"

"You're quite the party animal."

"I'm not having any more to drink though. I don't know how it will affect me, and I'm having a great time as it is." She looped her arm through Janie's as they headed back to the table.

Janie gave her a friendly shove on the back. "There is no possible way you grew up in Detroit."

"I know, I'm a dipstick."

Katie pushed her hair back from her eyes, cut a path to the table, and found Bobby. He refilled her glass. She loosened up for the first time in weeks. It felt as if she were floating.

Janie yelled over the music. "I'm so proud!"

"What?" Katie feigned surprise.

Janie wielded her arms like a victory banner waving in the wind. "You're doing it!"

Katie's eyes widened. She had heard of liquid courage, and after she guzzled her second and third beer, she felt the effect herself. She jumped up from the bench, grabbed some change from her purse, and marched toward the pay phone.

Janie shot a quizzical look in her direction. "Where the hell are you going?"

Katie tossed a hoity-toity glance in Janie's direction as she shouted back, "To call my mom and tell her I'm not coming home for the summer." She slid into phone booth, closed the bi-fold glass door and deposited a dime into the coin slot.

Janie ran after her and tried to push the door open, but Katie braced her foot against it. "Leave me alone."

"Shit, stupid. You're drunk. Let me in."

"No!" Katie hollered.

"Quit being a goddamned idiot. Who the hell are you dialing?"

"My mother. I told you."

Janie shook her head and rolled her eyes at Katie. "Not now. Tomorrow. You're drunk! You're gonna say something you'll regret."

"Give me some quarters. It's long dishtance." The words slurred and Katie giggled.

By now, Bobby and Jim had joined Janie. "Fine. Come out and we'll find you some quarters."

Katie stood, catching herself on the door handle. "Hand 'em over." She wedged herself in the phone booth doorway.

"Lady, you're intoxicated." Bobby laughed, unleashed her from the handle, and guided her back to her seat.

"Me? No way. Not poshible. Now c'mon, gimme some coin." She paused, looked deeply into Bobby's eyes and batted her own. "Pretty please?"

"Did you eat today?"

She smiled and her eyes glazed over. "I don't bemember."

Bobby placed his hand on her arm. "I'm going to grab you a cup of coffee. Stay right there." (Like she could have gotten anywhere in much of a hurry.)

"Hey," she called after him. "Quartersh."

Clueless, Jim handed over three coins.

"Yippee!" Katie shrieked.

"Damn it," Janie yelled. "What'd you have to go and do that for?"

Katie, already back in the booth, held shut the door with her angled foot. She slid the coins into the slot and dialed home. Her mom answered on the third ring.

"Katie? Is something wrong? It's awfully late."

"I have an announcement."

"When are exams over, young lady?"

"Not until Friday, Mom. I still have the music theory exam," she fibbed, slowing her speech and concentrating on forming the words just right.

Her mom sounded suspicious. "Really. What's all the racket?"

"The girls are playing music."

"Well, that's not the kind of environment I want for you. I thought you finished classes yesterday. I've tried calling but you never answer."

"I'm either at the library or taking a final, Mom. You want me to do well, don't you?"

"It goes without saying, Kathleen. Now when should I have Tom come and get you?"

"I'm not coming home. I'm going to take classes and work. My bosh needs me at the Union. It's done. I can't change it."

"Have you been drinking? Where's Janie? Did she serve you something? I knew she couldn't be trusted!"

"Yeah, she poured liquor down my throat." Katie's giggle was followed by a hiccup.

"I won't talk to you if you've been drinking. It's enough Tom's been caught drinking underage. Not you, too."

"I'm of age."

"Hardly."

"I'm hanging up now, Mom. Love you."

Katie replaced the receiver and looked up. Bobby, Jim, and Janie's noses pressed against the glass, huge gaping expressions on each of their faces. She laughed and moved her foot to the floor in front of her. As soon as she did, Bobby pushed open the door and rested his hand on her arm. "Are you okay?"

A grin enveloped her face. "Shimply wonderful."

Janie shook her head. "Oh, boy. Did you call your mom? What did you say?"

Katie laughed. "Nothing shpeshal..."

Janie crossed her arms. "Oh, no. What have you done?"

"I just shared some important news."

Janie kicked peanut shells with her toe. "Holy shit. You've really done it now. You've lost it." Janie looked at Bobby. "You're the cop. What should we do with her?"

"Coffee," he said with authority. He reached inside, helped Katie up, and led her back to their table.

Janie, right on his tail and chuckling, sat down next to Katie and slapped her leg. "This is the most fun I've had since the bread slicer was invented! I never thought I'd see the day when saintly Kathleen Marie Hayes would drink too much. Woo-hoo. You're smashed!"

"You're sush an ash," Katie retorted.

Janie smacked her on the back, and the two of them laughed uncontrollably. They spotted Bobby packing two cups of black coffee. Jim, his faithful sidekick, trailed behind carrying a cute little stainless steel pitcher of cream along with a matching sugar container. Katie thought they looked like medics headed off to some dire emergency.

"Jush one mo' beer fo' me. I don't need coffee."

Bobby chuckled. "No, not a good idea. On second thought, c'mon, we're outta here."

They packed themselves in the car and Bobby drove around the corner to a diner named Bomber's where he plied them with coffee, eggs, toast, and bacon. He and Jim delivered them back to the dorm at a little past two. They'd missed curfew by a mile so they tiptoed around to the courtyard and called up to the Gwen and Cynthia's third floor window. Gwen shushed them, "Be right down."

Despite full stomachs, Katie and Janie's giggly tipsiness persisted.

"Shhhh," Bobby warned, "let's get back to the door. We don't want to keep Gwen waiting."

Janie let out an, "Ooo."

"Cool it," Jim said as he tapped Janie's behind. "Stop the shenanigans."

"How's it going to look if I get caught sneaking you back after curfew?" Bobby tried to be serious, but even he laughed at them.

Gwen's shadow finally appeared and the door opened, slowly and noiselessly.

"Get in here, you two," she whispered. "And shut up. It's one thing if the two of you want a conduct ticket, but I sure as hell don't need the aggravation. I'm graduating, remember?"

They snuck upstairs, feebly attempting to follow Gwen's instructions. Every few steps, Janie snorted, trying to squelch her laughter. Katie wrapped her arm around Janie's shoulder and whispered, "You're noishy."

Janie laughed louder.

"Shut up," Gwen barked hoarsely. "I'm hanging you two out to dry if you get us in trouble."

"Yeah," Katie snarled, "close your big trap."

Janie poked Katie's ribs with her index fingers, firing from both hands as she made machine gun sounds.

"Stop it," Katie hissed as she crossed her legs.

Janie continued firing her fake guns. "What? You gotta pee?"

"Don't either of you girls know how to sneak around? This is not how it's done," Gwen warned. She placed her index finger on her lips, tiptoed down the hall, opened her door, and stared them down.

The two teetering roommates whispered their way through the adjoining bathroom and into their own room. They fumbled in the dark, their clothes dropping where they stood, then foraged for nightgowns and yanked them over their heads.

"Go to sleep, stupid," Janie demanded.

"No. You go to sleep."

"You're so strange."

"You know you love me."

"Yes, I do, but shut your trap and go to sleep. If we wake Cynthia, we're in deep dung."

"I thought she went home for the weekend."

"She did," Janie said.

Katie heard the revelation in her voice.

"I saw another body in their room. I know I did," Katie whispered.

"Shit, Gwen's probably doing the nasty with Marcus in there right now."

"Uh-oh."

"Shut up, dimwit, and listen. Maybe we can hear."

At precisely that moment, the bathroom door opened and Gwen's looming silhouette appeared.

"Would you two youngsters shut the fuck up? My man is here and you're keeping us awake."

"Sorry, Gwen," Katie said. "We're going right to sleep," and for further emphasis, she added, "Night, Janie."

"Night, Dummy."

The next morning, a herd of elephants stampeded through Katie's head. She rolled over, peeked through a slit in her left eye, and listened. "Janie?"

Janie moaned.

"I didn't call home from the bar last night, did I?"

"Oh, yeah," Janie grumbled. "I'm afraid so."

Katie groaned. "Shit. What am I gonna do?"

Without a word, Janie plunked a nickel in the swearing jar.

"Call your mom. Apologize. Better yet, blame it on me."

Katie blinked the memories back into focus and thought hard. *I did, didn't I? I called Mom and told her I wasn't coming home for the summer. She's going to kill me. I don't care. I have to stay away from Mark.*

Feigning cheeriness, she turned to Janie. "I remember now." She giggled. "She thought it was your fault."

"What? Great. Your drinking is my fault."

"Yeah," Katie said. "She thinks you tempt me. And I'm weak and impressionable."

"If that's her bag, thinking you're succumbing to peer pressure, let her blame me. I'm used to the heat."

"Guess what?"

"What, there's more?"

"Yep." Katie sat up straight and smiled broadly.

"Come on, spill."

"I'm not going home this summer. For real."

"You...are a hot tamale."

Chapter 14

BREAKING FRIENDSHIPS

May 1970

"Let's go," Janie yelled.

"I've got the Frisbee," Katie said.

Three days later, a beautiful May afternoon, Michigan's spring was in full bloom. Daffodils, crocus, and tulips poked their heads out of freshly cleaned beds, and the scent of lilacs traveled on the breeze. Katie positioned the Frisbee and whipped it with all her might. The disc flew past Janie's head and out of the yard.

"You're such a girl," Janie shouted.

Katie laughed. "Yeah, well, too bad."

As Janie ran off to retrieve the Frisbee, Bobby and Jim turned into the quad. Bobby grabbed the disc and tossed it to Janie. Jim darted in front of her and wound up wearing her on his back, wrestling for the disc. Caught up in hysterical laughter, Katie missed the Frisbee and it hit her upper lip. The strong whiff of vinyl tossed her back into Mark's car, her face pinned to the seat. She slapped her hand over her stinging mouth and struggled to blink back the overflow of tears. Turning away from her friends to regain her composure didn't help. Katie doubled over.

Bobby squinted across the quad. "You all right?"

"I'm sick," she called between gulping sobs, holding her stomach.

Bobby raced to her, laying his hand on her back.

"I better go upstairs and lie down."

Should I just tell Bobby about Mark, about the phone calls, and the letter? And then she looked up at him, so sweet and concerned, and knew she couldn't. She couldn't risk losing him.

"Do you want me to come with you?" Bobby asked.

Janie whispered to Bobby under her breath, "She's not sick."

"No, you guys stay here. You're having fun. I don't want to spoil it for you." Katie's throat filled as if taking on water in a murky lake. "I'll go lie down. I'll feel better soon."

"I'll come with you," Bobby offered.

"No, I want to be by myself."

Katie couldn't avoid the hurt in his eyes.

Bobby frowned and shoved his hands deep into his pockets. "Can I at least walk you to the door?"

"All right."

Bobby draped his arm around her and walked her to the dorm entrance. He squeezed her shoulder and kissed her on the cheek.

"I wish you'd tell me," he said.

"I don't feel well. Maybe it's something I ate." *If he knew, he'd never want to be with me again.*

Bobby scowled and shook his head. "Call me later if you feel up to it."

"Aren't you going to stay and hang out with Jim and Janie?"

He looked sad. "No, I'm gonna take off. See 'ya."

Katie watched him climb into his car, back out, and drive off. She wished she could fix this.

After she rode the elevator upstairs, she shuffled into the room and climbed on her bed, her face planted firmly on her pillow. They had left the radio playing and a Beatle's song began.

Why couldn't she keep it together? Something as simple as playing Frisbee and wham, out of the blue, she turned inside out. Other times, the sting of Mark's hand haunted her, or she felt his hands on her, his fingers forcing their way inside her. No matter what she tried, she couldn't make it go away. Make it stop, she prayed. She swallowed, squeezed her eyes shut, and willed the flashback away.

But turning away from those thoughts didn't help. It just led to other issues. Her mother. Though she only remembered snippets of their phone conversation, she knew she should call home and apologize. She had never been so rude to her and the guilt chewed at her gut. No, she told herself. Stop the guilt. Stop the shame.

It's not your fault Mark attacked you. Not totally. And it's not your fault you need to stay away from home.

Her mother would be angry and hurt, but one day, maybe she would forgive her. *Go ahead, Katie, fool yourself. Let yourself off the hook. No way would this be pretty.*

Her thoughts bounced around like a ball on the end of a rubber band, pinging and ponging all over the place. She could scarcely breathe.

Katie rolled onto her back and counted the ceiling tiles, across and then down, imagining the square footage of the room in some simplistic math problem. Count this way, then count the other way, multiply. How big is this room? A little bigger than a prison cell, she guessed. "Hey Jude," Paul McCartney sang, suggesting Jude take the bad and make it better. She slammed the "off" switch.

The door creaked open and Katie held her breath.

"Hi." Janie peered at her with round blue eyes. "How are you?"

"I'm okay," she pretended, rolling onto her stomach and turning her face to the wall.

"I don't think so." Janie sat down beside her and rubbed her shoulder. "Are you ever going to tell me what's going on, or are you going to keep this all to yourself?"

Katie shivered. She knew Janie had a clue something happened with Mark. Janie was smart. She could add two plus two. Yet Katie couldn't stop thinking—if she hadn't gone home for the funeral, none of this would have happened.

Janie would be pissed Katie didn't get away from Mark as soon as he pulled up to the curb. She would say Katie shouldn't have accepted a ride from him in the first place. *You could have walked home and avoided the whole mess.* Janie might feel obligated to get someone else involved.

Bobby.

Katie had bit his head off and sent him away. He'd left. Of course, he left. He respected her.

She acted like a total idiot lately, avoiding him and crying whenever she did see him, not the fun-loving girl he fell in love with. That girl had all but disappeared. Just a matter of time before he dropped her.

Janie waited and after a few minutes Katie rolled onto her back. "It's Bobby. We haven't been getting along lately. I thought he was the one, and now I don't think it's gonna work out." Tears ran, matted her hair to her temples, and then pooled in her ears.

She didn't have to fake the tears. Tears for the loss of Bobby. Tears for the parts of herself she couldn't revive and for the sadness and shame she felt. Filled with hopelessness, her nose ran, her eyes ached, and the phlegm in her throat made it feel raw.

Janie offered a sympathetic gaze, and as she used a tissue to dab Katie's tears, said, "You're lying. You and Bobby are like shoes and shoelaces."`

"I saw it in his eyes when he left today. He's given up on me," Katie said.

"Maybe he just doesn't understand what's going on with you. You've been acting strange. Sometimes you seem so different, so...far away. Plus, you're crabby...and you're not eating much."

"What the hell?" Katie choked with anger. Janie did whatever the hell she felt like doing. What right did she have to criticize her? "Are you keeping tabs on me? I haven't been hungry and it's not like you eat. Dammit, do you think you're my mother?"

"You're so full of shit," Janie sneered. "I can't make you tell me, but I'd bet a million dollars something happened when you were home, something went on between you and Mark. Contrary to popular belief, I'm not stupid."

Katie sat bolt upright and stiffened. "Since when do you know me inside and out? You think you've got me all figured out, don't you? *Katie, you're such a goody-goody. Katie, you're such a prude. Katie, you're such a Catholic.* It's all simple for you, isn't it? You know all and I know nothing. Well, not so this time, Janie. You don't know everything."

"Shit. Fine. Have it your way." Janie stomped toward the door. Then, suddenly, she stopped, turned, locked eyes with Katie and stared her down. "Kathleen Marie Hayes. Damn it. Tell me."

"Oh, and now you're going to pull that parental name calling bullshit on me? You make me sick."

What was wrong with her? Mark could have raped her, gone all the way. It could have been worse. Still, even though she'd been totally freaked out by what happened with Mark, she'd made it through finals, hadn't she? And even though Janie and Bobby thought she was acting strange, to her way of thinking, she could have been acting a lot stranger. The more she thought about it, the angrier she became. Neither one of them had been through what she had. How the hell could they understand? Besides, it had happened to her, not them.

Janie faced her. "Oh shit, he raped you, didn't he?"

"Leave me alone," Katie shrieked. "Get out. Just get out."

Chapter 15

WORRIED

May 1970

The next morning, Katie peered through the dark at the illuminated hands on the clock. 5:00 a.m. Hours before she needed to wake, she threw one arm over her head, and went back to sleep.

The second time around, at 9:00 a.m., a sliver of sun peeked in under the drapes. Gilbert O'Sullivan's "Alone Again, Naturally" played as the wake up song on CKLW, and she twirled the tuning knob on the peach-colored clock radio hoping for something less sappy. Reports of the Kent State massacre droned on every station. Katie had first heard the news three days ago and couldn't bear to hear another word.

It hurt too much to think about those poor kids. In a way, Nixon started the whole thing. When he announced the invasion of Cambodia, it set off a firestorm of protests. She couldn't imagine what it must have been like to be on either side. Some National Guardsman, a guy like Bobby, serving his country and doing his job, was ordered to fire on Americans as they exercised their constitutional rights. What it would be like to face a soldier while she was demonstrating? The world has gone mad, she thought.

Three years ago, on her sixteenth birthday, she lay in bed listening to gunshots. She watched the reports on television. People looted, breaking storefront windows and hauling out goods—refrigerators, stoves—not just an article of clothing, but big-ticket items, and they seemed to feel entitled. Then, 'Nam. Guys her age being sent off to fight in a war no one understood. And now, the National Guard shot and killed college kids for speaking up.

Bobby compared the Kent State shootings to some of the things he witnessed in 'Nam. The wrong troops called to handle a situation—untrained, inexperienced youngsters summoned to control their rowdy, rabble-rouser counterparts. He told her about the My Lai Massacre: rapes, beatings, and the mass murder of unarmed Vietnamese citizens, possible Vietcong sympathizers, which the military wanted to keep secret. On a smaller scale, she lived the same nightmare. Rapes, beatings, and killings in her own backyard.

Everywhere Katie turned, she faced ugliness. *I wish I knew how to help.*

As she slid out from under the covers, she replayed last night's drama. She winced and glanced at Janie's bed, anxious to apologize for her asinine behavior. But Janie's dismantled bunk hadn't been slept in. If anyone should have slept somewhere else last night, it should have been her, not Janie.

Katie straightened her bed and pondered Janie's whereabouts. She probably spent the night at Jim's, too pissed off and fed up to come back. On second thought, Janie had come close to guessing the truth, so she might have gone to Jim's to get his advice. Katie cringed. The thought of anyone knowing what happened between her and Mark made her feel ashamed. She wanted to hide, become invisible, escape. How had Janie gotten so close to the truth? Had she somehow given her secret away? *Shit.*

Katie plunked a nickel in the swearing jar.

She felt hopeless and defeated, but padded into the bathroom and turned on the shower. Steam quickly filled the room and her sinuses cleared out. Working up a sudsy lather, she washed up, rinsed off, and stepped out. Only two options existed. Either she came clean with Janie, or she continued the charade. She remembered her Nancy Drew mysteries—lies and deceit never paid off in any of those stories. It was time to let Janie in.

Everywhere she looked prompted thoughts of Janie: the worn bristles of Janie's pink toothbrush sitting alone in its holder, the electric rollers stacked on the bathroom counter, the blonde curly strands of hair on the ceramic floor. Katie dried off, combed out her hair, decided to let it air dry, and threw on her work uniform, a tan shirtwaist dress. She gazed at her sallow reflection and realized how much she needed Janie.

It was still too early to call Jim's, so she opted for breakfast in the cafeteria. Instead of eating, she pushed overcooked scrambled eggs around her plate, and when she returned to her room half an hour later and began unlocking the door, she heard the phone ring. *Janie.*

She grabbed the receiver. "Hi, Janie! I'm here!"

"Kathleen? This isn't Janie. It's your mother." Her mom began firing at her like a machine gun. "Why haven't I heard from you since Friday? You call home in the middle of the night, inebriated, and then we don't hear back from you? Haven't you put your family through enough this year? And this cockamamie idea to stay at school the entire summer? Janie's idea, correct?"

Katie answered after a measured breath, "No, of course not. I can think for myself. I have a job. I've enrolled for classes. I have to be at work in an hour. Can I call you later?"

"Now you listen to me, Kathleen. I don't know what's gotten into you, but I don't like the changes I'm seeing. You used to be such a sweet girl. And now, well, you're starting to remind me of one of those feminists who think they should burn their bra and sing hippy music."

"What, it's not all right for me to make a decision for myself?"

"This kind of behavior is outlandish. You're turning into a headstrong liberal!"

This must be what she thinks of a woman who asserts herself. Janie's right, thought Katie, my mom is crazy. And annoying.

"I'm sorry you don't understand," she said. "I just want to get through school as soon as possible. I can't wait to be a contributing member of society." She felt like donning boots after laying it on so thick.

Mom blew her nose. "You have no idea how lonely it is here without you. Do you know how long the summer will be if you don't come home?"

She met her mother's words with a long awkward silence. "Sure, Mom. I miss you, too." She rolled her eyes. "I'll try to get up to the cottage with Janie on the weekends. We can spend some time together then, all right?"

"I hope so. We're leaving June fourth. Right after school gets out. You'll miss our five weeks, our whole summer."

"Don't worry. We'll work something out. Listen, I've got to get to work. Love you." She hung up the phone. "Shit."

She flipped another nickel in the swearing jar. Why did *she* have to call? Wasn't it enough trying to deal with the Mark issue all by herself? And the worry about Bobby. Her mom pulling a royal guilt trip on her right now pushed her to the edge. And then there was Janie.

Janie. She's not back yet. *Shit.*

Katie grabbed a handful of change, threw it into the swearing jar, and brushed her hands together. Should cover a day of swearing. Next, she dialed Jim's number and waited for it to connect. The phone rang endlessly. What the hell?

Maybe Cynthia knew where Janie had gone. Katie darted into her room. No one there.

She draped a cardigan over her shoulders, snatched her room keys off the desk, and headed out the door, locking up behind her. Maybe Janie had forgotten her key. Maybe she went to class without stopping home first. Or maybe Katie slept through her knocking. She checked her watch. No time to search out Janie's keys now. Surely, Jim talked her into spending the night.

Katie strode out into the morning. Near sixty and sunny, the day promised to be perfect. The sunshine granted her clarity. Janie would promise not to tell Bobby, and Katie would tell her everything. Janie would help her figure things out.

She entered the Union cafeteria, marched into the office, found her nametag on the bulletin board, pinned it on her uniform, and wound between the tables and chairs in the main dining room to her place at the end of the line. Perched on her stool and punching the keys of the cash register as professors and teaching assistants pushed their trays down the line, Katie felt official, like an important cog in the wheel. She grinned at staff as they wandered through and told them to "have a nice day," grateful for their familiar faces. Her four-hour shift flew by.

On her way home from work, she reminded herself of her mission and quickened her steps. When Katie saw Janie, she would give her a big hug and apologize.

She reached the dorm, decided not to wait for the clunky old elevator and double-timed the steps. Her desire to see Janie overwhelmed her—she couldn't wait to stop the pretending. But when she turned the door knob, she stood dumbfounded. The knob didn't budge.

She frantically unlocked the door and called out, "Janie? You here?"

The room lay untouched. No sign of her.

She grabbed the phone and dialed Jim's.

He picked up on the first ring.

"Hi, Jim. It's me, Katie. Why didn't you answer the phone?"

"I did."

"No, earlier this morning. Never mind. Is Janie still there?"

"What do you mean still here?"

"Didn't she stay with you last night?"

"I wish. Trust me, I asked her. Lately, she tells me to dream on. Why?"

"I don't know where she is."

"What do you mean? I walked her to the door after we finished playing Frisbee. I thought she went up to your room."

Katie's voice trembled. "She did come up to the room."

"Is something wrong?"

Katie fought for composure as she told Jim about the argument. "There's no way of knowing anything is wrong," she said.

"I'll be right over," he said.

While she waited for Jim, Katie called Bobby. No answer at his parents' house. She called the Campus Police. Not there yet.

Ten minutes later Jim banged on the door.

"Now tell me again. What happened?"

Katie admitted she'd hurt Janie's feelings and she stormed off.

"Maybe she went to her cousin's."

Jim stood in front of her, hands jammed in his pockets. He looked a little frenzied in contrast to Katie's faked calm, and she doused herself in guilt.

"I feel like an ass. I made her mad. Maybe you're right. She's probably just cooling off somewhere."

He headed for the door. "Let's go look for her."

"Maybe she's down the hall. She could have spent the night in somebody's room. I'll check," Katie said.

"I'm coming with you."

They headed out. Jim started at one end of the hall and Katie at the other. The two of them hammered on doors. Spring semester meant fewer students, and when they checked with the girls still at school, no one reported seeing Janie. They met back in front of Katie's door.

She cringed at Jim's wrinkled brow. "Let's not panic."

"You're right. Maybe she drove home."

"I meant to check and see if her keys are here. I'll do it now." With Jim close on her heels, she walked back in the room and grabbed them from the hook on the shelf. "Here they are," she said as she cupped them in her hand. "Let's see if her car's in the lot."

They climbed into Jim's Trans Am and backed out of the dorm lot. He gunned it, squealed a sharp left, and sped to the lot at the far end of campus—the resident's lot. They circled, searching for Janie's fire engine red Pinto. Both of them rolled down their windows, as if somehow they would have a clearer view. No luck.

"Let's make one more pass."

Janie's car must be here. Had they missed a row? Katie's hands lay clutched in her lap. Jim swerved the car three hundred sixty degrees and they searched again.

Katie hiked up in the bucket seat and pointed as she sputtered with relief. "There it is. There's the Pinto."

At the far end of a row, tucked snugly between two oversized sedans, Janie's car sat pulled forward, hidden from view. Jim threw the Trans Am into park and rushed out. Katie followed. Hands cupped over their eyes, they peered in opposite windows. The candy apple red Pinto sat locked up tight, neat as a pin, shiny bright, as Janie always kept it. Not a strewn paper cup or receipt on the floor. Unlike her cluttered desk, her spotless baby sparkled. Katie unlocked the door and checked the glove compartment. Nothing amiss. She pushed the locking pin, held the door handle and closed the door.

"What now?" Jim asked.

"I guess we'd better call her dad and see if she went home." A nervous tear dampened her face. She brushed it away with the back of her hand. Four o'clock already. Janie had been gone twenty hours.

Jim sped back to the dorm. When they arrived back in the room, Katie rifled Janie's desk and located the list entitled "Important Phone Numbers." In Janie's bold left-handed backward-slanted handwriting she found Dad-home, Dad-work, Cousin-school, Roommate-home.

Katie dialed long distance on the black rotary. Mr. McCormick's secretary asked if she wanted to leave a message. Katie froze. What could she say? *Tell him his daughter's missing—in Ypsilanti, home of the coed killings.* Instead, she asked to have Mr. McCormick return her call at his earliest convenience.

Then she tried him at home. After ten rings, she looked at Jim and shook her head. No answer.

"C'mon," she said. "Let's talk to Sue Hutchinson. That has to be our next move."

They ran downstairs and banged on Sue's door. No answer.

Katie turned to Jim, whose eyes filled with fear. She felt responsible and clambered for an idea. "I'll call Campus Police. Just as a precaution." He followed her upstairs where she located the number affixed to the phone stand. When she got in touch with the police department, she asked for Bobby. Still not there. She reported Janie's absence to the responding officer. Goosebumps rose on her arms as she gave a brief description of Janie.

"Sorry, miss, we only take official reports from a family member. I'll put it on the spindle, but I can't file it yet. Have her parents come in and make the report."

Katie's legs went boneless. "I can't find her dad, and her mother is dead. You have to do something."

Jim fixed his eyes on the floor and paced as he turned a cigarette end to end with his thumb and index finger.

"Don't worry," the officer continued, "she's probably at a friend's. This kind of thing happens all the time."

Katie's voice rose. "You're the ones who told us to be careful. I don't think you understand. Janie isn't the type to spend the night away without calling. And where would she go?" She paused for a breath. "Her car keys are right here."

She couldn't calm her racing heart, stop her teeth from chattering, or still her rattling limbs.

"Have her father, someone from her immediate family, come down and file a report, miss. Follow procedure."

Katie fumed. If she had been this cop, if she had answered this call, she'd have shown some compassion, and been properly concerned. She hung up.

"Something bad's happened to her," Jim said.

Katie reminded herself to stay calm. "Nothing's happened. She's fine. Calm down."

"I'm trying, but it's not working."

"Not for me, either," Katie admitted. "Let's call Bobby." She picked up the receiver and redialed. "Bobby Kirsch, please," she said when the same officer answered the phone. She crossed her fingers. He had to be there by now.

"Bobby Kirsch."

Katie sighed in relief. "Hi, it's me. I have horrible news. Janie's gone and we need your help."

"What do you mean?"

"We argued last night. I lost my temper and told her to leave me alone. She left. I figured she'd come back after I went to sleep but she didn't." Words raced from her lips, not a breath in between. "I assumed she went to Jim's but she didn't go there either. I really messed up this time."

"Don't worry. We'll find her."

She told him what time Janie left, and how they found her keys and her car still in the lot. She told him how Jim came to help her search.

"Stay cool." He paused and cleared his throat. "You've done everything I would do."

Katie could almost see his cop mode turn on.

"Do me a favor," he added. "Write down everything you remember about what she was wearing, and find a recent picture of her. Keep trying to reach her dad. I'll be there as soon as I can."

Katie felt better as soon as Bobby assigned her a mission. She hung up the phone, snatched a pencil and paper, and wrote "Jane McCormick" at the top, then began to list Janie's attire:

- Levi jeans, size 3 (ironed with a sharp crease)
- White button down oxford shirt, (tucked in, also ironed) size "S"
- Brown belt (2" wide with silver buckle)
- Gray sweatshirt (EMU logo: dark green iron on letters-3" high) size "M"
- Keds shoes, (clean, stark white) size 8
- Gold heart locket (with picture of mom on one side, Janie on the other) 16" chain

Jim stared over her shoulder as she wrote.

"She's probably wearing her Saturday underwear, too," Katie joked, hoping to lighten the moment.

Didn't work.

While Jim watched, his eyes became emptier.

"Go outside and smoke a cigarette, then we'll figure out what to do next."

Looking as if all the blood had drained from his body, he turned and left the room without a sound.

Katie scanned back over her list and added: 5'4", 98 pounds, blonde hair, blue eyes. Then she stood and removed a picture from the corkboard. In the snapshot, Janie wore a blue wool jumper with a white blouse. Around her neck hung the locket she wore, day and night, with the picture of her mom tucked inside. Katie paper-clipped the photo to the description inventory.

Jim knocked on the door and she let him in. He dragged himself inside and sighed. "I need to do something. I can't just stand around waiting. I'm going to try Janie's dad again."

The click, click, click reverberated as Jim dialed the rotary phone. They held their breath. The sooner they reached Mr. McCormick, the sooner they would know more. If Janie wasn't home, an official report could be filed.

He tapped his foot and chewed on his fingernail while he waited for the call to connect. "Mr. McCormick, please. Yes, hello, sir. This is Jim Phillips, Janie's friend at school. I wondered if she came home last night." He paused and waited for an answer.

"No?" Jim's brow furrowed and he continued, "I'm sorry to tell you this, sir, but Janie's been missing since around eight o'clock last night. Her keys and car are here," his voice cracked. "I'm here at the dorm with her roommate, Katie."

He paused while Mr. McCormick spoke.

"Yes, sir. We've checked."

While Mr. McCormick spoke again, Jim drummed his fingers on the phone stand, and then answered. "The police insist you come to school and make an official report, sir. They'll only take a report from you." He rested his forehead on his hand. Katie couldn't see his face, but she could hear the concern in his voice.

"We'll wait right here." He said goodbye and hung up.

"What did he say?"

Jim shoved his hands in his pockets and frowned. "He's going to call the Campus Police, then head up here. He'll need the list you made. And he wants a picture."

"What, he doesn't have a picture of her?"

"Yeah, this is fucked up," Jim agreed. "I hope you know Janie well enough by now to realize she's a softy inside. She's not as tough as she comes off."

"I live with her, don't I?"

"I know, but that's why I'm worried. Maybe she was pissed, but think about it. She's been pissed at you before and she's still come home."

"It's more like I've been pissed at her. She's noisy when I'm trying to study. She's off the wall rude to my family. I can't say I've pissed her off so much."

Jim groaned. "Trust me, you've pissed her off."

"About what?" Katie knew better.

He shook his head. "Not now."

"I'm sure she'll show up any minute." She forced a weak grin. "You know Janie. She likes to do things her own way."

Ten minutes later Bobby knocked on the door and stepped inside. He hugged her and nodded approval at her list. Katie felt the forgiveness in his touch, and curled into his shielding embrace. She told him that she and Jim had scoured the floor and the parking lot.

"I got ahold of her dad and he's headed up here," Jim added.

"He's stopping to pick up the list I wrote. Then, he'll go to the Campus Police and file a report. We should make a point of checking everywhere on campus as soon as her dad leaves."

"Smart move, but we need to sweep the entire building before we do anything."

"Let's do it now. We can make it through the dorm before Janie's dad shows up. He's coming from

Birmingham, so it'll take him a while. Between the three of us, it won't take more than thirty minutes to scour the building. Worst scenario, one of us will have to come upstairs before we're finished and talk to Janie's dad."

"When we find her, I'm not letting her give you any more shit about Nancy Drew." Bobby smiled and patted her on the back.

Chapter 16

SEARCHING FOR JANIE

May 1970

The three of them met back in the room after combing the dorm. Close to five o'clock. Still no sign of Janie, and no sign of her dad.

His hands jammed deep in his Levis' pockets, Jim reported first. "Some chick on the second floor—I think her name is Marge—saw someone headed across the railroad tracks about nine last night."

"Marge Miller," Katie said. She looked at Jim. "Janie *must* have been headed over to your place." Katie noted the time and the name of the coed on a sheet of lined loose-leaf paper.

Jim raked his fingers through his hair. "Then where the hell is she?"

Katie touched his arm. "Don't worry. We'll find her."

Jim turned away, closed his eyes in frustration, and folded his arms over his chest.

They heard a sharp rap on the door. Bobby walked over and opened it, and Mr. McCormick's frame filled the doorway. He stood with his hands on his hips and in his booming voice demanded, "What happened?"

Katie gestured toward Janie's desk chair. "Mr. McCormick. Please, come in."

Mr. McCormick waved his refusal and remained planted in the doorway. Katie reported the short version of the story, shielding both herself and Janie. For some strange reason she felt protective of Janie, even with her dad.

"We had a stupid argument. I'm afraid I made her pretty mad." She rubbed her temple with the tips of her fingers, massaging in tiny circles. "If I hadn't been so stupid, she'd be home."

Mr. McCormick again waved his arm in a gesture of dismissal. "It makes no difference what you said, Kathleen. I've been through things like this with Jane before. She overreacts. I phoned the State Police," Mr. McCormick continued in his commanding voice, demonstrating his authority. "Their post is south of here on Michigan Ave. I'll place an official report there."

"Excuse me, sir," Bobby piped up. "The report actually has to be made with Campus Police. They conducted the initial investigations for the other missing girls. I don't mean there's anything to worry about, sir, but since Janie disappeared from campus, the campus cops will be the first to look for her. They'll alert the Ypsilanti Department and the State Police if it becomes necessary."

"I can handle this, young man," Janie's dad directed.

Bobby nodded without agreement. Katie watched his calm demeanor turn into a slow burn. "The Campus

Police Station is west off of Cross St. on Hewitt, on the right, inside the parking structure on the second floor."

Katie handed Janie's dad the list and picture. "Here's the description I compiled."

"Fine." He folded it methodically and slid it into his inside coat pocket.

She glanced at Bobby and arched her brows. "Would you like us to come with you, Mr. McCormick? We can show you the way."

"No. Wait here. If Jane calls, you'll be here to answer the phone. If you hear anything at all, call my home and leave a message. I'll check with her mother periodically."

She's not Janie's mom, Katie thought. "Mr. McCormick?"

"Yes?"

"She's going to be all right. We're going to find her."

"It's not like she hasn't pulled shenanigans like this before," he murmured. As he turned, he blew out a puff of air, shook his head, and left.

After Mr. McCormick shut the door, Bobby turned to Katie and Jim. "Interesting guy."

"It explains a lot." Jim looked sad.

"I guess." Katie's guilt resurfaced and she quickly changed focus. "What next?"

"We don't know anything's wrong," Bobby said. "Janie could be cooling off somewhere."

"No way," Jim interrupted. "I would have heard from her. She always calls me when she's pissed at Katie." He looked at Katie apologetically as he paced the floor.

"It's all right. I complain to Bobby about her, too." Katie climbed on the side of her bed and jotted down questions.

Jim continued to mark the floor. Suddenly his head fell to his chest. "I'm afraid she was taken. Like the others."

Bobby rested his hand on Jim's arm. "First of all, we have to keep our heads if we're going to help Janie. Remember, the guy behind bars is the guy who killed those girls. Janie wasn't snatched. She took off of her own accord. My bet is she went somewhere to blow off steam, drank too much, and is sleeping it off. This is different from the other girls' disappearances. Janie took off for a decent reason."

Jim stepped into the bathroom and shut the door.

Katie whispered to Bobby, "I get what you're saying, but just because she left for a reason doesn't mean she didn't get picked up and dragged off. I'm sure the other girls were where they were for reasons, too. You're not making sense. Think about it, maybe the cops have the wrong guy locked up."

"I know. Maybe they do. But maybe there's another guy," Bobby said.

Katie's stomach sank.

"As far as the cops are concerned, it's over. They're sticking with who they have, John Norman Collins. Hell, the task force isn't even together anymore, and I'm not sure one new missing person would provide reason enough for them come back together. The cops aren't going to know what to do with this, trust me. There hasn't been an incident in almost a year. If Janie's been snatched, and if she's going to stand a chance, we're the ones who need to get moving.

"We may not have a lot of time," Bobby continued as Jim returned. "So, let's keep a couple of things straight. I'm not trying to scare you guys, but when the girls disappeared, they were assaulted and killed soon after. Brutal attacks. All raped, some shot, some beaten and strangled, and some stabbed. If the real killer is still out there, or a copycat, we need to hurry. I have some idea where to look. Are you two in?"

"I can't sit here twiddling my thumbs. We need a plan. Right here. Right now. Let's get moving." Jim opened the door and gestured them into the hall.

Katie peered at Bobby. "What about the farmhouse? You told me about it when we first met. Girls were killed there, and then their bodies dumped somewhere else."

She knew he'd seen files related to the crimes. Bobby knew more than the average citizen.

He mulled it over. "Sealed as a crime scene last year."

"Still," Katie insisted, "we should check places we know were involved in the previous crimes just to be safe. If there's someone out there, especially a copycat, it's the most logical place to look."

"You guys need to quit jawing. We need to get out there and search." Jim impatiently rolled a cigarette between his thumb and middle finger. "We could look at the farmhouse, but let's circle the campus first. We'll take my car."

They raced down the back steps and loaded in the Trans Am. Katie sat crammed in the backseat, her knees practically spiking her chin.

Jim made a sharp right out of the lot onto Ann St., heading toward the heart of campus. He drove slowly and methodically. They focused on classroom buildings, the paths adjoining them, and the lush landscape along the shorter streets that wound through the main grounds. It was late afternoon, and the campus was quiet. Katie passed Jim the picture of Janie. He rolled down his window, and as he came upon passersby, asked if they had seen a girl matching Janie's description or photo. No luck.

They decided to head to the farmhouse next, trying not to let their worry creep too close. Bobby directed them out of the parking lot back to Ann Street and down toward Jim's apartment. Jim abruptly pulled over to the side of the road.

"Let's try here first. I think this is where Marge thought she might have seen her. Bobby, take the other side of the road with Katie. I'll get this side," Jim directed.

They scoured the edge of the road. Beer and pop cans, cigarette butts and fast-food wrappers littered the gravel shoulder. Beyond the shoulder lay a field of tall thick weeds. Cars whizzed by as they parted the weeds and examined the ground.

Jim shouted at them from across the road. "Look deeper into the field. If Janie walked here, she could have been hit by a car and knocked off the road."

They sliced through the weeds, checking a five-yard swath on either side of the road with care and caution, but found only trash—the normal curbside rubbish. No Janie.

Within twenty minutes, they were back in the car. They passed Jim's place, north of Huron River Dr. and Katie's gaze panned the landscape for Janie. Her sunny blonde hair would shine like a beacon on this cloudy late afternoon. But no luck. No Janie.

Just past Jim's apartment complex, about a mile and a half down the road, stood the dilapidated farmhouse. Even from a distance, Katie saw the home as merely a shell of its former self. It barely stood. The structure bowed, and the roof caved in like the Big Bad Wolf had blown on it one too many times.

Bobby supplied some details. "He kept the girls in the basement for a time, some in the barn."

When they pulled up along the fence at the edge of the property, Katie climbed out of the back seat. Her hesitant footsteps followed Jim and Bobby as they crept through the weeds toward the old house. Off in the distance, it stood hunched over like an old woman, the buildings surrounding it—the garage, the burned-out barn, and the tin-can water tower—looking like the life had passed out of them long ago.

She stared at the tattered leftover yellow crime scene tape struggling in the wind to free itself from the old metal posts, and her thoughts turned to the last years' events in the life of this farmhouse. The house, its comfort and history, had been destroyed along with the lives of those girls. As much as she hoped to see Janie's sunny blonde hair a few minutes ago when they passed Jim's apartment, it was the last thing she wished for now. The evening sky turned to dusk, and darkness settled as quickly as a shade drawn for the night. Katie shuddered.

She looked ahead for Bobby and noticed he carried a heavy-duty flashlight by his side. Big enough and heavy enough, she guessed it could double as a weapon if need be. Her footsteps slowed.

Bobby grasped her hand, and led her in silence as they angled through one of the larger holes in the fence at the back of the property. Katie's shirt ripped as it caught on a broken wire, and the sharp jagged cable scratched her upper arm. Tears spilled over, the stinging scrape striking her wounded heart more than her flesh. She paused for a moment, fighting the memories of Mark and the haunting feeling gripping every cell of her being. She squeezed back tears. *Mark's not here. You're safe.*

Violent shivering consumed her as she followed Bobby toward the house. He shined his flashlight on the scattered beer bottles, used Kotex pads, crushed cigarette boxes—more like a trash heap—a garbage dump—than a home. Smells of dead animals, rotten eggs, cat urine, and a wet, open food scrap barrel overcame her. Bile rose in her throat. She tore her hand away from Bobby's, covered her nose with her palm and held her breath. Without warning, she tripped. Her hands flew out in front of her and she screamed.

Jim looked puzzled and concerned, but silenced her just the same. "Shh."

Bobby sheltered her with a protective arm. "It's okay."

Jim assumed the lead as they inched toward the basement window. Katie wedged herself between them, weak and wobbly. She felt herself fade, become smaller and smaller, disappear. It demanded enormous effort to put one foot in front of the other and she struggled to keep up with Jim, and watched as he peered into the narrow basement window. The paint on the casement and jagged edges of the broken window had peeled away. She focused on the window's frame, concentrating on it to keep dizziness from overcoming her. Unable to even glance into the basement, she watched the back of his head until he turned around. He said something she couldn't decipher, and blinked to bring him into view, as if to listen better.

"No sign of life."

Tears rolled down her cheeks and a sob escaped her throat. Mark's violation shrouded her like a heavy leaden coat. The air felt thick and still.

"I'm just saying I don't see anything."

"I know," she whispered. She forced herself in front of Jim, squinted to adjust to the light, and studied the inside of the basement. The cinder block walls, the cobwebs, the concrete floor—all of it right out of an Alfred Hitchcock movie—paralyzed her. A lone wooden chair, as if somehow suspended, sat out of place in the room. The smell of musty moss filled her nostrils. She shuddered and turned away.

They skulked along the edge of the house, Bobby taking the lead now, Katie and Jim continuing in single-file behind him. At each window, they stopped. Bobby flashed the beam inside then turned back, shaking his head. Jim took the flashlight and double-checked his efforts.

After a widespread inspection of the house, they made their way over the rest of the property. Katie studied the barn. It leaned like a child's toppled tower of blocks and only charred slats of fallen wood remained. The spring night cooled to a chill.

"We might as well head back," Bobby said.

Katie slumped as they began the long difficult trek back to the car. "Where could she be? Can you imagine her staying away this long? It doesn't make sense. Something's happened."

Katie tipped her head to the moon and remembered Janie's last words each night—*goodnight mom.* She prayed to Janie's mom. *Help me find her. Let her be alive.*

The beam from the flashlight caught a glint of gold. Katie reached for a gold chain tangled in the weeds. Bobby's eyes followed hers and he stopped her. "Wait," he said.

"You're right, it might be evidence."

"It's hard to say. There's a lot of garbage out here. But..."

"We should take it, just in case." Katie inhaled a deep breath. Maybe some good would come out of their search after all.

"I have a plastic bag in the car. I'll get it. Wait here." Jim retrieved the bag, turned it inside out, grasped the chain and folded the bag over on top of it. Katie lifted the bag from his hand and held it up close. Bobby cast a shaft of light on it so she could get a better look.

"There's a locket on the chain, like Janie wears." She examined it more closely. Not the same. "Thank God, it's not hers. We need to take this to the police, don't we?" Katie's spirits lifted. This could be a clue.

Bobby nodded. "We should turn it over, just in case." He gave her hand a squeeze and turned to walk to Jim's car. "Let's head back to the dorm and see if there's been any word."

Katie stopped dead in her tracks. "What if she's here? What if we missed finding her?"

Jim placed a reassuring touch on her forearm. "We searched high and low. It's time to try something else."

They walked to his car, loaded up, and headed south.

Jim's car bumped over the railroad tracks, and two minutes later he pulled into the dorm lot. He slouched down in the driver's seat, and thumbed the steering wheel. They sat in silence.

"I'll check inside." Katie raced up the back stairs, down the hall and into the room, then retraced her steps back outside.

"She's not here. We have to keep looking."

"Try heading up towards Summit Street," Bobby said.

Jim backed the car out of the lot and headed around the eastern edge of campus, driving the perimeter of the grounds. He passed the university apartments, the Catholic chapel, and the theatre hall, then pulled onto Cross St. where blue lights flashed in the distance.

Katie's stomach fluttered. "Oh, no! Look!"

More sirens blared behind him, and Jim pulled right to let the fire trucks pass. Lights and sirens sped by. Fire trucks, police units, ambulances—too many to count—screamed past them and onto the triangle of land at the base of the water tower.

Bobby pulled out his auxiliary badge and jumped out of the car. Jim and Katie followed, forcing their way through the gathering mayhem. Bobby flashed his badge and passed through the circle of cops, firefighters, and ambulance personnel. The city cop mistook him for a university officer. Jim pushed forward too, only to be stopped by a state trooper.

He turned back to Katie, frustrated and panicked. "Damn it."

She wrapped her hands around his arm. "Stay here. We'll see what Bobby finds."

"It's *my* job to find her," he agonized.

The crowd of onlookers grew on the three-cornered patch of land at Cross Street, Forest, and Washtenaw Avenue. Emergency vehicles blocked their view of the action, cordoning off the area.

It didn't make sense, but Katie felt Janie's presence.

The heavy doors of an ambulance clanked shut, and Bobby's head rose out of the crowd. Katie waved her arms and shouted his name. He nodded in her direction and hurried toward them.

"Give me the keys," he commanded. "Get in."

They jumped in the car, slammed the doors shut, and sped off.

Jim turned in the passenger seat. "C'mon man, I can't breathe. What's the deal?"

"It's her," Bobby said. "It's Janie."

Katie began to shake uncontrollably. "Just tell me, is she okay?"

"They found her bound and gagged. She's alive. Out of it, but she's got a strong pulse."

Bobby raced to Beyer Hospital, pulled up to the curb, and waited while the EMT personnel hoisted Janie out of the ambulance. They watched as the gurney rolled her to the emergency room entrance. One of the EMT's guided the IV drip as they steered the stretcher through the automated double doors. Katie climbed out of the vehicle, murmured a prayer, and rushed to the stretcher.

Chapter 17

RESCUED

May 1970

Twelve hours later, the big hand on the wall clock clicked. The stark white lights illuminating the hallways and lounge like a constant spotlight weighed on Katie's nerves. She and Jim had spent the entire time at the hospital, vigilant, like sentry guards. If it weren't for the cops demanding an interview, Bobby would have stayed, too. Katie tried shaking off a headache—a dull sleep-starved pain—and ignored her growling stomach.

The morning paper arrived in the fifth-floor lounge and she read the headline of the *Detroit Free Press*:

THE WRONG GUY?
EMU Coed Kidnapped—Found at University Water Tower

Specific names weren't mentioned but the major city press reported Janie's disappearance and subsequent rescue. Like crows on road kill, they offered the little scraps of information they pilfered. She glanced at Jim, passed out on the couch, and wished she could sleep. Instead, Katie pushed her stiffened body up and dragged herself down the hall toward Janie's room.

The Wrong Guy. Bobby, her mother, the news. They all used the same words. What *if* the cops had arrested the wrong guy? She wrapped her arms around her chest, numb with disbelief. The scent of disinfectant and stale urine made her feel like climbing in the bed next to Janie's.

Katie passed an elderly patient in a wheelchair. The hollowed-out form, an attached IV pole seeming more alive than the old woman, put her over the brink. She concentrated on the checkerboard floor, stepping on the green squares, not the black, to distract herself from the grim surroundings. When she reached the doorway of Janie's room, she leaned against the jamb. She could hardly stand seeing her precious Janie's face, so pale and fragile. Her stomach turned over, and she twisted toward the hall. Out of the corner of her eye, she saw Bobby and Jim.

For a brief moment, Katie laid her head on Bobby's shoulder and smiled for the first time since Janie went missing. "I'm glad you're back."

They watched Janie breathe, and after a few minutes, Bobby broke the quiet. "I managed a couple of hours of sleep, took a shower and went over to the station. Pretty interesting."

Katie shushed him and pulled he and Jim back to the lounge and sat them down in a private, far-away corner. She didn't want to disturb Janie, or for her to overhear. "What happened?"

Bobby drummed his fingers on the table and shook his head, his lips forming a thin line. "Joe questioned me."

Katie's brow furrowed. This couldn't be good news. "Joe? Seems weird. I thought he was a friend."

"Not today. Today he was all business," Bobby said.

"You've worried about left over bad blood from 'Nam," Katie said.

"Yeah, well, at first he asked the usual, 'Where were you last night and what were you doing?' Then, 'What led you to the water tower? Were you bored…looking for trouble?'"

Jim tapped a smoke out of its pack, lit it, and inhaled a deep drag. He offered the pack to Bobby, a cigarette poised for the taking.

Bobby waved him off and continued, "I guess he forgot. Bored is something I embrace. I don't go looking for trouble. I saw enough trouble in 'Nam. Bigger guys than him, with far bigger messes."

Katie wondered if there could really be bigger messes than this. She shook her head and admitted an embarrassing truth—she really had grown up in a bubble.

"Then Joe fired more questions, 'Where were you after Jane McCormick went missing? Why did you go to the farmhouse location? What made you think you could enter a crime scene? Why didn't you sit tight and let my guys do their job?'"

"He thought he could rattle you," Jim muttered.

Bobby closed his eyes and leaned back in his chair. "I've done this questioning thing myself. Way before he ever did. It's what M.P.'s do."

Jim narrowed his eyes. "So why's he drilling you?"

"He's pissed we went to the farmhouse. I'm not sure why. The last murder took place ten months ago. It's not like *they* went there looking. No one's been there in ages." He sighed and rested his elbows on his knees. "Maybe he still considers it a crime scene."

"They should be looking at the necklace," Jim said. "That's what I'd focus on."

"In one of my books," Katie started, "Nancy finds a broken locket. In the end they find the other half. You know, it's a heart, and half of it is missing."

Jim looked at her as if she'd grown horns. "You've lost your mind."

Katie felt the blood rise up her neck. "What?"

"Nancy Drew? Now?"

"Hey, it's just a thought." The absurdity of her words registered. She started to giggle and couldn't stop. "Some hot shot investigator I'm going to turn out to be."

Jim rolled his eyes and slapped her shoulder. "You're on fire, Nancy! Catch those bad guys."

Katie finally pulled it together, and she asked Bobby, "Where did you wind up with Joe?"

Bobby leaned back, glued his eyes to the ceiling, and stretched his arms over his head. "He threatened me. Said insubordination could cost me my job."

"I would have given him an earful." Jim flicked his ashes in the tray as if flipping off the cops. "What the hell? Do they think it's cool they sat on their asses while Janic was missing? Hell, they wouldn't even take a report from us. Instead of going out and finding her, they're parked at the fucking donut shop."

"You can't lose it with them. It'll make things worse. When your turn comes, stay cool. The cops are bent outta shape," Bobby continued, "because reports are questioning both the arrest and their tactics. Did they get the right guy the first time around?"

"Your buddy Joe thinks he's a bad ass," Jim said. "What's more important? Bad press or doing their job?"

"Both." Bobby let out a deep breath. "Try being a cop."

"Janie could be dead," Jim said. "Is that what they want? To lose another girl."

"And we found the necklace," Katie interrupted.

Jim started to chuckle. "Nancy's back."

Katie grinned. "Shut up."

Bobby ignored their stupid jokes. "Joe didn't seem concerned about Janie. He had a bug up his butt. He kept saying, 'Do you realize you compromised the scene?' I looked him straight in the eye and said, 'I thought I might be bringing you possible evidence.' I just walked out."

Katie studied Jim. Overnight, he'd grown a full beard and he'd been chain smoking for hours. In front of him, the round metal ashtray overflowed with butts. She stood up and tossed the contents, then wiped out the bowl with a tissue.

Jim couldn't stop shaking his head. "I can't believe they want to stick it to you."

"Keep in mind the cops aren't just dealing with her disappearance," Bobby said. "The Kent State stuff has everyone fired up. The cops are under a lot of pressure. Be cool. I'll handle the department. These are my people."

"Whatever floats your boat."

"Hey. We're lucky. Hardly anybody ever walks the triangle."

"By the water tower?"

Bobby nodded.

Jim locked eyes with Bobby, and a full minute later, softened. "Who found her? I'd like to thank them, do something for them."

"The shop owner next to Ned's Bookstore said it was four kids. Two boys and two girls…about twelve years old. I guess they were bouncing a tennis ball on the double doors of the water tower. They spotted Janie's body in the weeds and ran to the store to report it. The guy said they were frantic."

"Those poor kids," Jim said. "They must have been scared out of their gourds."

"Can you imagine? Four little kids?" As an afterthought Katie asked, "Our going out to the farmhouse won't cause you a problem at work, will it?"

"Big deal. We went looking for Janie on our own, without Joe's permission." Bobby kissed the top of Katie's head and grabbed a cigarette from Jim's open pack. "Joe thinks it's fishy we wound up at the farmhouse, but hell, he would have done the same thing in our position. I think they're going nuts about the necklace. It makes them look bad."

"How is that possible? It's small, easy to overlook."

Bobby lit his cigarette and sat back. "They fire me and the press will climb all over their backs. No, I'm safe."

Katie worried nonetheless. The cost of her stupid fight with Janie was adding up.

Bobby asked, "What do the doctors say?"

"She's stable. They're keeping her sedated, pumping her with fluids, and they've been taking her vitals on and off all night." Katie shivered. "The nurse said they checked for signs of sexual assault, but I haven't heard any results."

Jim rested his elbows on his knees and shook his head. "If only I'd stayed longer the other night. Maybe if I'd come upstairs with her, the two of you wouldn't have fought."

"If it's anyone's fault, it's mine," Katie said. "I'm the one who should have handled things better."

"After my dad died...Just the smell of hay, or hearing the word 'tractor' threw me off. Now Janie's going to have to deal with the same damn nightmares. I hate that." Jim kicked the stack of newspapers at his feet, then stood, shuffled to the vending machine and stuck a quarter into the coin slot. It spit out a cardboard cup and filled it with muddied slop.

"Stop blaming yourself," Bobby said. "Only one person is responsible for this. We just haven't found him yet. Don't worry. We'll get him. You guys need breakfast. I'll go down and grab something. How about some real coffee?"

Katie nodded and Bobby strode off to the cafeteria. He was back in the lounge within minutes and spread out two individual serving boxes of Frosted Flakes, two containers of milk, plastic spoons, and fresh-brewed coffee. While they devoured their food, he suggested a plan. "You guys need to head down to the Campus Police. If you don't show up, they'll track you down and haul you in. It's better if you beat them to it."

"If Janie's dad would visit, we could do that," Katie said, "but I'm not leaving her here alone."

"I'll be here," Bobby said. "Don't worry."

Jim averted his eyes from the doorway, hunched his shoulders, and whispered, "Speak of the devil."

Mr. McCormick looked lost for a moment and then spotted them. "There you are."

Bobby spoke on their behalf. "Did you need something, sir?"

"Katie."

"I've got it," she murmured under her breath. She led Mr. McCormick to a couch in the corner.

He rubbed his shaky hands over his sallow face. New creases had appeared overnight. He had all but vanished from Janie's life, but now, he had no choice but to give his attention to her. Katie thought about it and figured he would have been about thirty when Janie's mom died. And Janie's mom had been sick for years before that. She felt a sudden pang of compassion for him and placed her hand on his forearm. "How can I help?"

He pulled away and jammed his hands in his pockets. "Janie needs someone to keep an eye on her. She's impulsive, and irresponsible."

"With all due respect, Mr. McCormick. This is not Janie's fault. I made her leave, I pushed her away."

"Promise me you'll keep a special eye on her. I'm entrusting her to you. She needs..." He paused, gazing out the window.

"A mother," the words flew out of Katie's mouth.

Startled, Mr. McCormick faced her and locked eyes.

Katie lowered her eyes and wrung her hands. "Sorry."

He stood, stared blankly ahead, and walked out of the lounge.

Bobby gazed at her. "What's his deal?"

"He's just worried."

Bobby nodded and put his hand on her shoulder. "You and Jim head over to the station. You'll be back before Janie comes to."

"We'll get back as soon as we can," Katie said.

They stood wordlessly and headed down the long antiseptic hall to look in on Janie. The three friends stared at each other, tied together by a series of events none of them could yet comprehend. The ties tightened, and in spite of their exhaustion, she imagined each of them secured to Bobby like the posts of a tent, held strong by his sturdy stakes and lines. His steady gaze assured them they would hold up—at least for today.

Chapter 18

QUESTIONED

May 1970

Ninety minutes later, showered and dressed in clean clothes, Katie and Jim walked into the Campus Police station hidden on the second floor of the parking structure. They announced themselves at the same marred Formica counter where Katie usually visited Bobby. Mike, the desk officer, asked them to wait, and pointed to a set of maple chairs. Katie was intrigued by the police end of all this. She could see herself working in this field someday, applying psychology to police work. Jim, on the other hand, appeared to be crawling out of his skin.

"You've got to relax," she whispered. "If you go in there all wound up, they're going to think something's fishy. Bobby said to tell them what we know. Let's tolerate these interviews, put them behind us, and focus on Janie."

Jim lit a Marlboro and inhaled deeply. "Yeah, right." He blew smoke rings over his head.

"Don't be so uptight."

Detective Joe Smokovich, with his close-cropped hair and linebacker shoulders, sported a shiny polyester suit, and called Jim first. Katie followed him to the counter.

Smokovich peered at Katie, his recognition of her clear. "No, miss, I need to speak to you one at a time."

Katie dipped her head. "Yes, sir." She patted Jim's forearm and walked back to her seat.

"We'll call you next," Joe said before he ushered Jim down the hall.

The wait felt endless. Jim finally returned, the deep circles under his eyes spelling exhaustion.

"Does he want me to come in next?"

Detective Smokovich appeared at the front counter and called Katie's name before Jim could answer. Seemed like he didn't want her and Jim to compare notes.

"Follow me, miss," Joe said. She glanced back at Jim, hoping for some gesture telling her what to expect, but his eyes were closed. She had not choice but to walk in blind.

She entered the stark interview room and assumed a seat in the cold metal folding chair, her hands clasped on the table, her back straight; she girded herself for questioning.

"Let's start with the night of your roommate's disappearance."

Katie tapped her lips and began. "Janic and I had a fight. She upset me. I'm afraid I lost my temper. I yelled at her." In spite of the fact that Katie fought for composure, tears filled her eyes. "She got mad…not mad exactly, but hurt. She left."

"What did you argue about?"

"Stupid girl stuff," Katie lied.

"Such as?"

"Janie wanted to know about a boy I dated in high school. I didn't feel like talking."

"Any special reason you didn't want to talk about him? Was there a problem?"

She shrugged. "No. I broke up with him a long time ago and didn't see the point of rehashing it."

"She didn't tell you where she was going?"

"No, sir." Heat rose up Katie's neck. "If Janie told me where she was going, I would have looked there."

"And you wound up at the farmhouse?"

She couldn't believe Joe treated her like a suspect, but she tempered her irritation. "Yes, sir."

"What did you hope to find there?"

"Janie, sir."

"You know you compromised a crime scene."

She narrowed her eyes, confused. "Pardon?"

His lips formed a thin line. "We have a suspect behind bars—the Coed Killer. Why did you think *you* should enter the farmhouse?"

Katie stiffened. "We didn't intend to cause a problem, sir. You have to understand. Janie's life might have been in jeopardy. I felt especially responsible. I would have done anything to find her."

"You stuck your nose in the wrong place. You could be charged with interfering in an ongoing investigation. Is that what you want?"

"Respectfully, sir, didn't we help? We found the necklace. It's a new lead, right?"

"I'll ask the questions, miss."

Katie tapped her foot, jiggled her knee, tried a deep breath, and attempted to slow her rising anger. "Yes, sir."

"Whose idea was it to go to the farmhouse?"

"I'm not sure."

"Try to remember."

I am trying, she thought. She took a minute, gazed at the ceiling, and tried to retrieve the scene. Once she did, she felt even more clueless. Bobby said tell the truth and be done with it, but if she did, she'd be admitting she knew about the farmhouse because of Bobby. And she didn't want Bobby in trouble.

"Searching your memory? You're a young woman. It shouldn't take so long."

"I don't want to get it wrong. Please understand, I was beside myself. We all tossed ideas around. I remembered reading about the farmhouse a while back. I'm not sure who of us decided to look there for Janie."

"Who made the final decision?"

"We all did." Katie's nerves got the better of her. "Jim stopped the car and we searched alongside the road—along Ann Street—we split up. We searched in the weeds on the other side of the shoulder, in case she'd been hit by a car."

Joe drummed his pencil on the tabletop and studied her. "All right."

Katie held his gaze.

"That'll be all for now. I'll be in touch."

She stood and shook his hand. "I'm sorry I wasn't more helpful."

Katie stepped into the waiting room, frantically searching for Jim. More rattled than she'd expected, she needed to see a familiar face. She peered out the window and spotted him on the sidewalk below, smoking like a fiend. She flew down the steps.

"That detective creeped me out."

Jim shook his head and inhaled a serious drag from his cigarette. "I know. 'When you say Janie, who are you referring to? Do you have a sexual relationship with Jane McCormick?' He's an asshole. He made a federal case out of everything, like *we* did something wrong."

"I don't get it," Katie said.

Jim assured her. "Bobby'll know what it all means."

Katie nodded. "You're right. Let's go find him."

Chapter 19

SAFE AND SOUND

May 1970

Jim and Katie reached the hospital fifteen minutes later. They entered the elevator and punched the button for Janie's floor. Katie wanted nothing more than to sit with Janie and hold her hand.

Jim agreed to search for Bobby and ask his opinion about the interview. He headed for the lounge and she wandered off to Janie's room. The possibility of sexual assault wouldn't leave her mind. Not that. Not Janie. She inhaled a deep breath and said a prayer, but was unable to keep her tears at bay.

Katie wiped her eyes as she entered Janie's room and quietly eased the visitor's chair closer to her bed. She watched her friend breathe—in and out, slowly and silently. If only Janie could feel as peaceful and serene as she looked.

Katie gently grasped Janie's fragile hand. She owed Janie so much. Janie had tried to help her, and she had pushed her away. None of this would have happened if she hadn't. It was her turn to help Janie now, to push aside her own shame and guilt.

A middle-aged woman with sympathetic eyes entered the room. She introduced herself as a social worker named Mrs. James and offered Katie a sympathetic gaze. "You look tired."

Katie waved her off. "No, I'm fine."

"Your friend has a long road ahead of her. Physically, she's fine, but it can take years to recover from the trauma of an attack like this."

Katie could only imagine. While Mark's attack had left her splintered, she guessed this trauma would be even worse for Janie. "Can you tell me anything?"

"What do you mean?"

"About what she's been through," Katie pleaded. "I'm her best friend. I have to help her."

"Well, the good news is there is no sign of sexual assault, and she can recover from the physical injuries. She's making good progress, and the doctors say they should be able to discharge her later today or early tomorrow. As far as the emotional toll, it depends on how much she remembers. From talking to her, she doesn't seem to have any idea what happened."

Katie heaved a sigh of relief. This was the best news she could have hoped for. "She's conscious? She woke up?"

"This morning, for a little while."

"I wish someone had let me know."

Mrs. James patted her hand. "She's getting all the care she needs."

"She can't remember anything?"

"Nothing," Mrs. James said.

"I'm not sure I understand."

"Later, she could have flashbacks."

Katie cringed. She knew all about flashbacks. "How can I help her?"

"She'll need to talk. Need reassurance that it's normal to have bits and pieces return to her memory."

"So, can I tell her what happened?"

"She doesn't want to know."

Katie nodded. "That's Janie. But I can tell her, right?"

"Let her decide when."

"And then she could remember more of what happened?"

"Yes."

"But it could frighten her again? Traumatize her all over again?"

"Yes, but more than that," Mrs. James said soothingly, "remembering will help her heal."

Remembering is healing? For her, she hadn't found that to be the case. But maybe it would help Janie. The possibility brought her hope. "Janie is the type of person who likes to put things behind her. She doesn't like to dwell on the past."

"We recommend follow-up counseling for her. I came by to drop off my card and a referral to an outside agency."

"Counseling?" Why hadn't she thought of counseling? She was a psych major, for goodness sake. Counseling helped people recover from trauma. Janie didn't let other people in. Not close friends and especially not strangers. She would never have it. Katie accepted the card. "I'll see she gets it."

Mrs. James left the room and Katie turned her gaze to Janie, and squeezed her friend's hand.

One of Janie's eyes peeked open and she returned Katie's squeeze.

"Hi," Katie said.

"Hi, yourself." Janie looked gray and thinner than ever. Her voice was weak and tinny.

"I'm so glad you're awake. We've been so worried. How do you feel?"

"Like I've been run over by a garbage truck."

Katie hesitated for a moment, but then asked, "What happened?"

"How the hell do I know?"

"You don't remember?"

"The last thing I remember, I was walking down Ann Street. Heading to Jim's."

"Then what?"

"Then I woke up here. Some guy in a white coat was flashing a light in my eyes."

Katie winced. Mrs. James was right. Janie blocked out everything. "You were attacked, Janie."

Janie shook her head. "They said that, but I don't think so."

"No, this is serious. You were drugged. Tied up. Left by the water tower. You're dehydrated. That's why you have an IV. You have some wounds around your eyes. I guess they were taped shut."

Janie ran her fingers along the scraped skin and winced. "Not possible."

Katie rubbed her arm. "Honey, it's true. Don't worry about it now. The important thing is that you're all right.

Whoever did this to you didn't rape or kill you and you're going to heal. Just remember I'm here for you. If you want to talk about anything, I'm right here."

"I don't need to talk."

"I know," Katie said. "But just in case you change your mind, I've got a card for you from a social worker."

"I won't change my mind."

Katie stroked the top of Janie's hand.

"It's not your fault," Janie said.

"It is my fault. If I hadn't lost it, you wouldn't have left."

"Let it go, idiot," Janie whispered.

"Listen to me. I know you. I know you don't want to dwell on things, don't want anything to be a big deal. But you don't need to do this alone. For once, Janie, let me in."

Janie's eyes looked sad and tired. "Same goes for you."

Katie nodded.

"We're more alike than you want to admit," Janie said. "Whether or not you recognize it, we're the same. We're both loners. We both like to think we don't need anybody else."

Katie smiled as she touched her friend's cheek. "But we have each other."

Janie's eyes closed and her lips curved into a smile. "Always."

Katie waited until she was sure Janie was asleep, kissed her forehead, and went to find Bobby and Jim. She spotted Bobby sitting on the couch facing the lounge entrance, sat down beside him, and rested her head on his shoulder. "Where's Jim?"

"He went to find a nurse," Bobby said. "He wants to know when Janie will be released."

"She seems good. I talked to her."

Bobby nodded. "I saw her for a few minutes when she woke up. She asked for you."

"I wish I would have been here."

"She was only with it for a few minutes. She doesn't remember."

Katie half-heartedly agreed. "Is Jim okay?"

"I think I calmed him down."

"That's good."

"Hungry?" Bobby asked. Katie nodded and they headed to the cafeteria for a bite to eat. Through her exhaustion, she forced down half a tuna sandwich. Then they went to find Jim. He sat next to Janie's bed dishing mashed potatoes into her mouth.

"See, you're on the mend," Katie said.

"I feel like a sack of shit," Janie answered.

"And you look like one, too," Katie sang. "What's the word?"

"They say I'm good to go soon, but they look at me like I've got the plague."

"They're just concerned," Katie assured her.

"I'm fucking fine. I want to get the hell out of here."

"When are they going to release you?"

Jim spooned more potatoes into Janie's mouth and she had to swallow before answering. "After the doctor shows up."

On cue, a nurse marched in and announced, "You visitors need to step out." She started to pull the curtain around Janie's bed and barked, "Skedaddle."

Jim fisted his hands on his hips, facing her down. "When can we come back?"

"We're going to give her a shower and let her rest until the doctor arrives. Check back in an hour."

Katie snuck to Janie's side of the bed and gave her a quick peck on the cheek. "We'll be back later, when the Gestapo is through with you."

The three of them returned to the lounge. Katie broke the silence. "She seems more like herself."

Jim wrung his hands. "It's how she handles a crisis."

"You're right," Katie admitted. "Her typical, 'And other than that Mrs. Lincoln, how did you like the play?'"

"Exactly."

Three hours later Katie spotted Janie's dad in the doorway. She approached him and asked, "Have you spoken with Janie?"

"Just the doctors," Mr. McCormick replied.

"She's awake," Katie said softly, silently pleading with him to visit her. She couldn't read his mood. Is he just worried, she wondered? He kept his eyes straight ahead; he wouldn't look at her. "They'll release her soon."

"I'm aware," Mr. McCormick said. "I'd like you accompany me when I drive her home."

"Of course. When you need me, I'll be here, or in Janie's room."

Janie's dad turned abruptly and left the lounge.

Darkness soon fell. Bobby and Jim stepped outside to stretch. Katie waited until the doctor left Janie's room to speak with Mr. McCormick, then snuck into see her friend. Janie slept and soon Katie fell asleep in the visitor's chair. Before long it seemed, the morning nurse bustled in and opened the blinds. They both woke, blinking at the bright sunshine.

"Time to get ready to go home, young lady," the nurse said.

"Thank you, Jesus."

Katie stuck her ribs with a gentle poke. "See? You are religious!"

Janie grinned and Katie smiled back at her.

"Lie back. They'll bring a wheelchair when they're ready."

Janie laid her head on the pillow, closed her eyes, and fell back asleep in an instant.

Katie thanked God. After two endless days, police interviews, physical exams and tests, Janie would be going home. A novelty—Janie McCormick—the girl who survived.

An hour later, the nurse showed up with a wheelchair. Together, they helped Janie into the chair and wheeled her to her dad's car. Pale and weak, like a fragile shell, she climbed into the back seat and lay sideways on the bench. In virtual silence, her dad drove them back to the dorm. Katie led the way upstairs, unlocked the door, and Mr. McCormick guided Janie to the desk chair. Janie propped her head on her hand, wobbling. Her dad made a quick return trip to his car to retrieve the bouquet of flowers her stepmother had sent. Out of duty, no doubt. Dad seemed anxious to leave and dropped five twenty-dollar bills on the dresser. He kissed Janie on the forehead, and instructed Katie as he headed out, "Take good care of her, young lady. I'll call later to see how she's doing."

Katie ushered him out and the phone rang. She muttered, "shit."

Janie grabbed a nickel off the desk, shuffled to the swearing jar, and dropped the coin inside. She looked tinier than ever—like she would fade away.

Katie answered the phone, spoke a few simple words and hung up. "Jim said he'd be here soon, sweetie."

Janie offered a sliver of a smile. "It's good to be home."

"Let's get you into bed."

Janie snuggled up against the daisy-covered pillowcase. She appeared more doped up than earlier that morning. Katie pulled the matching comforter over her roomie's shoulders and tucked her inside. She plucked her favorite floppy-eared stuffed dog from the top of her bed, and shoved it under Janie's chin. "Here, I'll even let you have Fluffy."

"Wow, I must rate."

Katie fought back tears. "You sure do."

"Listen stupid," Janie said, "I know you think this is your fault. It's not. I'm okay. The bastard didn't knock me off. You're stuck with me."

"Sleep, silly goose. Sleep."

Janie nodded off within seconds. Katie sat nearby, watchful and brooding, confused by Mr. McCormick's abrupt departure. How could he leave her now, when she needed him more than ever? No matter what his personal issues, he should be able to set them aside and be there for Janie. He was the parent, not Janie, or her for that matter. Why couldn't he care for his daughter?

Chapter 20

ONE STEP AT A TIME

May 1970

Katie locked the door behind her. The doctor had sent home a healthy supply of sedatives and recommended plenty of rest, so she expected Janie to doze for hours. As she rounded the corner, she spotted Bobby and Jim waiting in the third floor lounge. She walked in and sat down next to Bobby. "She's asleep."

"The cops and docs agree, right?" Bobby answered his own question. "She doesn't remember much. Good thing. Saw the same in 'Nam. The body goes into shock. Shuts down. Mind does the same thing."

"If those kids hadn't discovered her when they did... we have so much to be thankful for. She's home, safe, and fairly sound."

Jim seemed lost in thought—he stared out the window.

Katie leaned forward and touched his arm. "You hangin' in?"

"I'm going to find the bastard and kill him."

"Right now Janie is our priority. We need you here, not behind bars because you went on some vengeful rampage. It's odd, isn't it? The last thing she remembers is heading down the street to your apartment. She won't be able to help us, unless by some miracle, she remembers. Selective amnesia."

Jim growled under his breath. "The mother fucker kept her so full of drugs she has nothing to remember."

"Either way, it could be so much worse. He didn't rape or beat her. She'll be all right, in time." Katie looked to Bobby. "What do the cops think? Have you heard anything?"

"They still believe Collins is their guy. Best guess? Janie's abduction is a copycat. Some kook seeking fifteen minutes of fame. It casts suspicion on the cops and John Norman Collins, but they have too much evidence against Collins for this to affect their case."

Katie shook her head in disbelief. "Don't you think it's odd?"

For a brief moment, Jim's anger turned to logic. "If it's a copycat, why did he let her live? Why didn't he hurt her? Rape her? Beat her?"

Bobby shot a warning look at Jim.

"I'm not trying to make trouble. Trust me, I'm glad she's in one piece. I'm just thinking out loud. If they think it's a copycat, are they even going to look for the bastard? If not, I'll fucking find the guy…"

Bobby interrupted, "Stop thinking you're going to figure this out. Let the cops handle it. Just because they don't have any leads right now doesn't mean they won't. Janie's abduction is different. First of all, they found her alive. Consider, too, the MO didn't match."

"Hell, they're going to blow the whole thing off. Since Janie's okay, they'll say some stupid, wigged-out maniac did it just to see if he could, but won't strike again. It's all hush-hush, too. Did you notice? Since the first report, there's been nothing on the news or in the *Eastern Echo.* You'd think they'd send out a warning."

"They're playing it close to the vest," Bobby acknowledged. "No one's come forward with any information—doesn't mean they aren't working on it."

"I know all about the system. After my dad died, it took over a year to get the life insurance company to rule it an accident and not a suicide. Tell me how you force a fucking tractor to flip on top of you!"

I can't listen to this right now, Katie thought. Anger welled inside, and she couldn't pinpoint why. "You two are making me crazy. I can't take it. Janie's safe and you're going ape shit about every damn thing. Maybe you should leave."

Bobby zoomed in on Katie's sudden outburst and his antenna kicked onto full alert. He reached out and touched her arm. "Are you all right?"

She needed to distract him. "Can you run to K-Mart?"

"What do you need?"

"Hold on." She tiptoed back into the room and grabbed the swearing jar. She toted the container back to the lounge and dumped the coins onto the table. She counted $7.50. "There's enough. Buy Janie the Barbra Streisand *Funny Girl* album. In stereo. She's wanted it forever. It'll cheer her up."

Bobby looked confused as he left her off at her door. "Um. . .okay, we'll give you a break."

She hadn't fooled him. Katie shuffled back to the room. Tired as she felt, she couldn't slow her thoughts. Bobby was right. This was different. And like Jim, she wondered, why hadn't this supposed copycat raped or beaten Janie? Or killed her? Maybe the guy was interrupted. Why else would he drug her and then leave her tied up beneath the water tower?

Studying Janie's angelic face, peaceful with sleep, she sighed. Seeing her roommate so serene made her all the more grateful Janie hadn't been more seriously hurt. Her throat swelled with tears, and she swallowed hard. Was the bad stuff ever going to end?

Katie changed and climbed into bed. She remembered the sun-filled morning two long days ago when she made one of the biggest and most important decisions of her life—to trust Janie with the truth about what happened with Mark. She couldn't tell her now. It would be like saying, "I'm more important than you. Your stuff is incidental. I'm the one with the bigger problem." Katie swiped at her tears. No, she thought, I need to be her rock. Maybe I should just give in and tell Bobby. But I can't risk losing him.

She listened to Janie's breath—it almost hummed—and at last Katie was lulled to sleep.

Two hours later, Bobby phoned from the front desk. Katie rolled over and reached for the receiver. "Hello?"

"Hi, it's me. I'm downstairs. Is she awake yet?"

"No. I don't think so."

"Jim bought some beer and headed to his apartment. We can order pizza. You guys need to eat, and a distraction might be good for Janie. Whadda ya' think? You up for it?"

"I'll need a few minutes. She's out cold. I don't even know if I should wake her. She was pretty doped up when we got back."

"It's your call," Bobby said.

"Hold on." She leaned over and shook Janie awake. "Sweetie, can you wake up?"

Janie opened one eye. "What?"

"The guys are ordering pizza. At Jim's. Do you want to go?"

Janie propped herself on her pillow, rubbed her eyes, and nodded.

"We'll be down in five," Katie said before hanging up the phone.

"Just leave your pajamas on," she whispered to Janie. "Here, I'll help you." She pulled a sweatshirt over Janie's head. In the bathroom, she sat Janie on the toilet, splashed water on her face, helped her pull on jeans and a t-shirt, and brushed her hair. After Katie dressed herself, she led Janie down the hall and into the elevator.

"We'll be downstairs before you know it." A twinge of guilt plagued Katie as they rode down. She needed a break from this crisis for her own good rather than for Janie's.

Bobby smiled as they entered the hall. "Let's head out, ladies."

Katie scrambled into the back seat, leaving Janie the front, making it easier for her to climb in and out. Three minutes later, they drove into the parking lot of Jim's apartment complex.

"I feel like I'm on another planet," Janie rambled as they exited the car, "but you'd probably say that's normal, wouldn't you?"

Katie agreed. "I've always said you need to be locked up. If you're sealed away, the aliens won't mistake you for one of their own and haul you off in a spaceship."

"C'mon, let's eat," Bobby chimed in.

In the doorway of Jim's apartment, he greeted them with a wide smile, took Janie's hand, and led her to the couch. "You don't want a beer, do you?"

"Are you kidding? The Pope's still Catholic, isn't he? Just give me a slice of pizza, a beer, and a Coke chaser. And I'll need to bum a smoke." She sat cross-legged on the sofa, and Jim wrapped a blanket around her shoulders. In spite of her good humor, Janie shook like a dry leaf on an October afternoon.

Bobby set out paper plates and napkins, cold cans of Coke and bottles of Stroh's. He popped a beer, took a long draw, and served pizza all around. Katie sat on the floor in front of the coffee table. She pulled the pepperoni off her pizza and saved it for last. Bobby plopped down on the floor next to her, picked the pepperoni off her plate, and popped it into his mouth. She slapped his hand and smiled. Jim put Janie's new album on the turntable and scooted close to her.

Katie swallowed a bite of pizza. "Feels great, doesn't it?"

"Feels like it's supposed to," Janie answered.

Jim suggested the girls spend the night. They passed a knowing glance between them. Janie, much more awake now, thanked him for the offer, and asked if she could see how she felt in an hour. Katie knew that look. Clearly, she wanted a chance to put her head together with her roommate.

An hour later, she followed Katie into the bathroom and asked, "What do you want to do?"

"Whatever you want, kiddo. It's your decision."

"Part of me knows it's stupid, 'cause after all, they're just guys. It's not like they can save us if the Big Bad Wolf shows up."

"There's strength in numbers, and even though they're just guys, they're bigger than us. If it makes you feel better, then it's the right thing to do."

"Yeah, I want to stay here. Mostly I just want the four of us to be together."

"Me, too."

Janie rested a hand on Katie's shoulder and laughed. "I know you've never spent the night with Bobby. Remember the old rule. Keep your shoes on."

"Remember my rule," Katie added. "Keep every zipper fastened, every button closed, every snap shut. It's the Catholic creed."

They laughed. Like old times.

Katie wrapped her arms around Janie and squeezed. "I love you so much."

"No shit, Sherlock. Now knock it off or you'll make me blubber, and you know how I feel about blubber."

Katie's nerves caused a sudden panic, and she felt her breath catch in her chest. "Where will we sleep? Maybe we could have the boys sleep in Jim's room and you and I can sleep in the extra bedroom."

Janie snorted. "Yeah, I'm sure that's what the guys had in mind."

"I'll go tell them what we've decided."

"Let's go. I can't wait to see this."

Jim's roommate, Chuck Parker, spent the summer with his folks, working construction, so his bedroom, equipped with a double bed, was available.

Katie tried to act nonchalant. "Short of having you guys sleep in Jim's bedroom and us in Chuck's, do you have any suggestions?"

Jim snuggled up next to Janie and nuzzled her neck. "Just the obvious."

"Not a night for romance, dip stick," she piped up.

"Hey, you can't blame a guy for trying," he said.

Katie wagged her finger. "You gentlemen know this isn't the time."

"Killjoy," they answered in unison.

"It's a night for cuddling and nothing more."

Bobby and Jim acquiesced and raised their glasses in some kind of hidden male bonding moment.

Bobby and Katie left the living room and headed to Jim's extra bedroom. Bobby plunked down on the edge of the bed and kicked off his shoes. He reached out to Katie and she joined him. He took her face in his hands and kissed her, gently brushing her lips with his.

She sat in a slice of moonlight and gazed into Bobby's eyes. Bobby wanted more from her, and she couldn't keep the truth from him any longer. He deserved to know. No more secrets. But when she looked into his sweet, trusting eyes, she hesitated.

"What is it? You nervous? I thought we already established you weren't going to let me."

"We need to talk."

He sat at attention, as if readying himself for a fall.

"No, it's nothing like that," she said. She threw her hands up in frustration. "I don't know what I'm saying. It's just," she stumbled, "it's just…there's something you should know."

Bobby held his breath. "Before you start, I need to say one thing," he paused, ran his finger along the side of her face, and said, "I want to be with you—forever. I know things have been tough. But I feel the same way about you that I always have. I love you."

A chill ran down her arms and she huddled them around her ribs. "Wait, please." Tears slid down her cheeks.

He laughed nervously. "Not quite the reaction I hoped for."

"You may change your mind after you hear what I have to say."

He tipped his head down, as if readying himself for bad news. "Go ahead."

"When I went home for Mark's dad's funeral, something happened." The words caught in her throat. "This is so hard."

Uneasiness bubbled from his chest. "Just tell me," he said.

"It's not what you think."

"Tell me."

Katie inhaled a deep breath. "Mark drove me home from the funeral home. My mom took the car, and it was dark and a long walk. Since the riots…" she trailed off, shook her head and continued, "He stopped the car. He… he forced himself on me."

"That son of a…"

"Stop. Listen. I need to tell you all of it. It's coming between us. I can't stand it anymore."

The muscles in Bobby's neck tensed and bulged. Then, in a moment, a softness overcame him and he placed a gentle arm around Katie's waist. "It's okay. It's gonna be all right."

Katie's words burst out in choked sobs. "He ripped off...my underwear...put his hands all up me. He…hit... me."

Bobby stood and pounded his fist on the window jamb. "Your eye. Why didn't you tell me?"

"I was a...fraid you'd be mad...at me. Because I didn't…fight hard enough. Afraid you wouldn't ever… want me."

Bobby rushed to her and gathered her in his arms. "I'm not mad at you, lady. This is not your fault." He caressed her shoulder and pulled her into his chest. "He raped you?"

"He got close," she choked. "I was able to break away."

"Thank God."

She crumpled into Bobby's arms.

He settled a pillow beneath her head and pulled a blanket over her. "Shhh. It's all right." He climbed in next to her, fully clothed, spooned himself around her, and hushed her to sleep.

The next morning, Bobby's arm still enshrouding her, they woke slowly. He stroked her shoulder, kissed her forehead, ran his fingers through her hair, and traced the silky strands down past her shoulders and onto her chest. "Can I ask you something?"

"Sure."

"Who is this guy?"

"What guy?"

"Mark."

"What do you mean?"

"What kind of guy would do this to you?"

"I'm not sure what you're asking."

He propped up on his arm and gazed down at her. "What do you know about him?"

She rolled onto her back and stared at the ceiling. "You mean did I have any clue he would hurt me?"

Bobby nodded.

Katie closed her eyes and shook her head. "No, not really. My brother Tom never liked Mark. In fact, there were rumors floating around that Mark beat the crap out of this guy after a wrestling meet during our junior year."

"No way."

"I don't know for sure. Tom just said Mark told off some kid during a meet. Some kind of fistfight in the locker room afterward. A couple of days later, Tom heard the guy wound up in the hospital with a broken nose, a concussion, and a dislocated shoulder."

"Do you think Mark did it?"

"If you believe the rumors, he did." It's all…what's the expression...smoke and mirrors, she thought. Mark. Janie's dad. No one is who they should be.

Bobby turned cop. "Did you ever ask him about it?"

"What do you think? Of course I asked him. I couldn't date a guy who pounded on everyone just because they made him angry."

"Well," he paused, "what did he say?"

"Bobby, are you even listening to me? I checked it out. He blew me off. Laughed about it and told me not to believe everything I heard. I understand why you're questioning my judgment, but…"

"Did you believe him?"

"Look, I'm not sure." Her cheeks warmed and she sat on the edge of the bed, pulling away from him. "Stop being a cop. Be my boyfriend. I told myself to keep my eyes and ears open. I never heard anything like it again, and I wanted to believe him, so I thought everything was cool. All right?"

"You're right. I'm sorry." Bobby folded his hands in his lap. "You know what really matters?"

Katie inhaled a sharp breath. "No, what really matters?"

Bobby stared at her, his eyes contrite. "What really matters is you're okay, and you're here with me."

She exhaled and cuddled into him.

Chapter 21

TAKING CHARGE

May 1970

Katie, Janie, Gwen, and Cynthia camped out in their dorm room the next night. They donned their pjs early, and fired up some Jiffy Pop on Gwen's hot plate. Cynthia contributed a homemade sweet potato pie, and for Janie, a six pack of Vernors, Detroit's official get well ginger ale.

In a secret bathroom confab, Cynthia, Katie, and Gwen agreed to treat Janie as if she were sick. They would nurse her back to health with the mothering she had missed out on as a child. Hovering like guardian angels, they checked her every move. "Do you need anything? Can I plump your pillow? How 'bout a drink?"

Janie had raised herself, as she often said, and had never been this pampered, ever. She lapped up the attention like a feral kitten.

Katie smiled. It was just like old times. At the end of the evening, she climbed into bed and reached for the lamp switch.

"Janie?"

"What, idiot?"

"Just thinking."

Janie giggled. "How fun for you."

"Maybe there's something you'll remember."

"Huh?"

"Maybe, over time, something will come back to you...about the guy."

Janie shifted in bed. "Wouldn't that be nice."

"Actually, it would. If you felt like you could help the cops find the guy, I think you'd feel better." *We would all feel better.*

"Hey, asshole, I hear what you're saying, but I'm trying to fall asleep here. Nice time to bring this up. What, you want me to have more nightmares than I'm already having?"

"No. Sorry." Katie crawled out of bed and threaded the Mama's & the Papa's album onto the spindle of the turntable. Janie loved their mellow music. "Better?"

"Thanks. Now shut up."

Katie lay awake for hours, her stomach flip-flopping along with her restless thoughts. If someone appeared weak, through bad posture or a look of vulnerability, whatever the hell that meant, they were more likely to be the victim of a crime. Janie's brassy. Confident. And a fighter. But she's encountered loss in her life. Serious loss and pain. Could someone who didn't know her, someone just walking on the street, see that? Picture her as a victim?

Take a step back, Katie. It's a puzzle. Just a puzzle. Figure out the motivation of the perpetrator. What would cause someone to kidnap a young girl? Why did he allow her to live? Maybe because Janie couldn't identify him? But why take her at all? If he didn't sexually assault her, was it a simple attempted robbery? That didn't make sense. Why would he have bound her? What did that mean?

She decided to try easing some information out of Bobby. He knew the cops' thinking these days. Even though they had a suspect behind bars, they also knew the one who'd assaulted Janie still roamed the streets. They couldn't be so stuck on making Collins the right guy that they made him the only guy, could they?

If she started her own search she could make things right for Janie by helping the cops. She vowed when she woke up in the morning, she would figure out how to solve this crime.

Katie woke up three hours later unable to quell her spinning thoughts. She grabbed a pocket–sized notebook and a pencil stub. Starting at square one, she flipped on a night light while Janie slept, tilted the light toward the cave she made under her covers, and scribbled down notes.

Janie disappeared the night of May 15th. The kids found her the following night, almost exactly twenty-four hours later, still dressed in her original clothing. Her hands were bound with thin leather straps, and her mouth gagged with a bandana.

Janie had been drugged. Maybe Janie remembered a needle prick, a voice, or a smell. Bad people had a special smell, didn't they? They must smell dangerous. Probably a putrid smell, like spoiled milk, or old sweat. She wrinkled her nose at the thought as she wrote furiously on her note pad.

Maybe the drugs smelled. Like antiseptic, or alcohol. Maybe the guy had a medical background. Did he swab her with an alcohol pad before he shot her up? Quivering at the thought, she kept writing. He could be a drug addict, she decided. Made sense. If he were some screwed-up degenerate, it would make more sense; he would be on drugs himself.

Possibly she could help Janie remember the guy's clothing. He could have rubbed up against her. Maybe she felt the hair on his arms, the roughness of denim or softness of a cotton t-shirt. Katie couldn't see a maniac wearing a plain old t-shirt—then again, maybe she could.

Adrenalin pumped through her veins. She closed the cover on her spiral, set the pencil on the bed stand and, knowing she had a plan, fell asleep.

Katie reported to work at eleven the next morning. She walked through the cafeteria then perched on the stool near the cash register. The small spiral notebook sat firmly tucked in her skirt pocket, and she kept her eye out for suspicious characters. At first she felt silly, like some ridiculous impostor. *Cafeteria cashier turned spy.* She envisioned the fumbling TV Detective Colombo in his ratty raincoat. She thought people could tell just by looking at her she was trying to be something she wasn't—an older Nancy Drew—sleuth extraordinaire.

The cops, always visible at the Union, sauntered in and out, touching base with their university contacts.

They were everywhere. Part of Katie's new job would be to keep track of them—hidden in plain sight at her lookout post.

No one knew her. No one knew Janie. And no one knew how much Katie loved to eavesdrop. If she simply did her job and paid attention, she told herself, a clue would fall into her lap. Staff buzzed about the abduction of another coed and gossiped about how lucky Jane McCormick was to be alive. Katie committed their words to memory, ready to record them at the first opportunity.

"Kathleen Hayes?"

Preoccupied with her own thoughts, Katie missed the unfamiliar face snaking through her line. Dressed in a suit, out of character for the usual cardigan-clad professor in her line, she chastised herself for overlooking him.

"Yes?"

He flashed his badge. Detective Wyatt. Now that she looked closer, she recognized him from the precinct when she visited Bobby there some time ago. "I wonder if I might have a word with you."

"I'm working right now. I'm the only one scheduled who can operate the register. We can talk right here. It'll quiet down in about three minutes."

"You could come down to the station."

"No, sir, it's all right." Katie tried matching his professional demeanor with her own. "We can talk now."

After making change and helping the next few customers, she slipped down off her stool, and smoothed her uniform skirt. She turned away from the register and asked, "What do you need to know?"

Detective Wyatt sipped his coffee as if it remained his chief reason for being there. "Tell me a little more about your roommate."

"Janie?"

"Yes."

"She's a great girl. Smart and funny. She's my best friend."

"We've heard she's a risk taker. She likes being the center of attention."

"Well, yes, I guess you could say so."

"We have reports she does outrageous things."

"Janie? She likes to have fun, sure, but outrageous?" *What the hell does he really want?* An uneasy feeling crept over Katie.

"Did you know she laid on the runway at Metro airport to watch planes land?"

"Oh, that. Janie talks big. She likes to get a rise out of people."

The detective locked eyes with her, like he'd made an impressive point. "I see."

"No, you don't." Katie refused to be intimidated by this jackass. "So, you think Janie set this whole kidnapping up? Not possible." She shook her head. "She left the dorm because I made her mad and she went for a walk—to cool off. I can assure you, she did not plan this." *What a prick. Janie's a victim.*

"We have to check into every possibility, miss. There's nothing to get riled up about." He sipped his coffee, looking smug. "I'll get back to you if I think of anything else."

Can't wait.

He turned and walked away. She felt the steam spewing out of her ears. A long line formed behind her register. Katie glanced up at the clock. Sure enough. The lunch crowd had arrived. *Shit.*

She fumed through the rest of her shift and hoped stupid Detective Wyatt hadn't gone to the dorm to confront Janie. She seemed so fragile lately. The way she sponged up attention, the way her tough exterior crumbled, and the way she trusted them to take care of her. How on earth could anyone accuse Janie of staging this?

The clock finally read two, and she left her register and walked to the back room to punch out. She removed her apron and hung it on a hook.

"You look disgusted," her co-worker, Dave, said.

"Because I am!"

"Anything I can do?"

"No, thanks."

Just what she needed. Dave. The guy gave her the creeps. On a slow day a couple of weeks ago, the boss made Katie stay back and help load the dishes before the lunch crowd arrived. The way Dave stared at her made her feel like she couldn't breathe.

"I'd do anything in the world to make you feel better, Katie."

She cringed. Her instincts warned her to stay away from him. How could she recognize this Dave creep from miles away when she had grown up with Mark, for years, no less, and hadn't seen what he was capable of? She felt that horrid "bugs crawling over her skin" feeling and turned and walked away, ignoring Dave and heading straight for the phone. She dialed Bobby at work.

"Campus Police," he answered.

"Bobby, it's me. You'll never guess what happened at work today."

Chapter 22

NOT MY GIRL, YOU DON'T

May 1970

Bobby's Chevy sat parked in front of a meter just outside the dorm. Katie opened the passenger door and hopped in.

"You can file charges," Bobby said.

"What are you talking about?"

"Against Mark."

"I can't."

"What he did to you…it's a crime."

Katie closed her eyes and swallowed hard. "I need time."

"Time?"

"To decide," Katie said. "It's too much to deal with, especially now."

Bobby grasped her hand and sighed. "I'm supposed to be the guy who takes care of you. I should have figured out that something happened between you and Mark. I let you down. Shit, I can't even keep the cops from bugging you about Janie's disappearance. I'm pretty much locked out of the investigation. I'm an across-the-board failure these days. Can you forgive me?" He shook his head in disgust.

"This is not your fault, Bobby. None of it. In a way, we're both victims of Mark. He hurt me, he hurt you, he hurt us. I'm pissed, but I refuse to be a victim. We're survivors you and me. As far as Janie's disappearance, we did what we needed to do."

Bobby shrugged. "Yeah, maybe. Meanwhile, I called Joe Smokovich. Remember, Joe and I served in 'Nam together."

She studied him. He was coming undone. "Of course, I remember Joe."

"We met at Ted's, the bar across from campus, on Cross Street a block or so from the Water Tower."

"I know where Ted's is."

"I made sure to sit in a booth at the back so no one could overhear us. Then he asks me, 'what's up,' like we're two guys getting together for a beer. I demanded to know what the hell was going on. He acted clueless, like he had no idea what I meant, so I told him his guys were bugging you at work, and it pissed me off."

The muscles in Katie's neck tightened. "What did he say?"

"First he ordered a beer and lit a cigarette. He acted cocky, like he had something on me."

"Do you think it means something?"

"He thought about playing me."

She folded her hands in her lap and tried to create a sense of calm within herself and for Bobby. She wasn't used to seeing him this wound up. "Go on."

"He really started acting like an idiot, saying how good you look. I told him to quit wasting his time being an asshole. Next, he leaned back, took a long drag on his smoke and chugged his beer like he's a big man."

"Your blood pressure is rising just talking about it." She took his hand, brought it to her lips, kissed it, and held it. "It's okay. Everything is going to be all right."

Bobby, oblivious to her overtures, continued. "He says they have to check every avenue and they've heard some pretty wild stuff about Janie. I tried getting him to let me in, but he wouldn't."

"Nothing?"

"He said there's nothing to worry about it. Just making sure Janie's abduction wasn't a hoax. Evidently, the police chief is pretty upset a new girl disappeared just as they are about to go to trial with Collins. There's pressure from the top. The press is crawling up their butts, the mayor, the university president—they are all on their asses to close this one up. I told him they can't wrap it up by making up shit, and this is making up shit."

Katie patted his hand in another futile attempt to cool him down. "It's all right."

Bobby reached inside his glove box for a cigarette. He inhaled a long drag and sat back, resting his head on the driver's seat, and blowing out a puff of smoke.

"Where did the two of you wind up?"

"I apologized. Told him I'm pretty darned protective when it comes to you. I don't like them questioning you. I know they have to talk to everyone, but they could have given me a heads up, you know?"

"I understand."

"Joe says they can't. He appreciated my feelings, but I'm an employee, not a cop. He said I already hear a lot of privileged stuff, and he's right. Anyway, he told me to watch my step. Keep my nose where it belongs. He's afraid it'll cost me if I don't."

"It's okay." She rested her hand on his chest. "Relax."

Bobby finally took a deep breath. "I ended up losing my temper. I said, 'I like you, Joe. I consider you a friend. But I gotta tell you, if you go after an innocent nineteen year old girl, and imply she set up her own abduction just to get some sort of sick attention, you're barking up the wrong tree.' I told him Janie isn't a fruitcake. This really happened. I admitted I'm too close to the situation, but he should listen to me all the more. I know Janie. She wouldn't make this up. Meanwhile, the pervert is still out there running around."

"I know you're angry, but listen to Joe. The last thing I want is for you to lose your job over this. You're the one who told Jim to let the cops do their job. Follow your own advice. It'll be okay. You're not responsible for any of this."

Bobby took Katie in his arms. "I'm beat."

"I know. I woke up today thinking I would figure out who did this to Janie, and instead the police are accusing her of faking the whole thing."

He bounced his palm against the steering wheel. "My family is on vacation. How about we go back to my house and pretend we have a normal life."

"You mean play house? Sounds like a plan to me." She snuggled next to him, pressed her head into his shoulder, and he backed out of the lot.

Katie loved the drive to his parents' place. Peaceful fields and farms dotted the landscape of US 12, and the recent spring rains added depth to the fresh greens of the trees and grass. Bobby pulled off the two-lane highway and dashed into the Beer Depot. She rolled down her window while she waited for him, smelled the fresh air, enjoyed the lingering evening breeze, and grinned when he returned with a six-pack.

Bobby handed her the carton and started up the engine. She left her window open and let her hair blow in the breeze. He looked over at her and smiled, grasping her hand and squeezing it. Her unfocused panic vanished, and she attributed it to his firm grip.

Within fifteen minutes, they arrived at the Kirsch home. Small, neat, and homey, it reminded her a little of being at her own house, but free of the excess emotional baggage. The front room felt lived in—a crocheted afghan tossed haphazardly across the back of the couch, newspapers stacked in a loose pile on the step stool next to the well-worn rocking chair. The late day sun poured through the fingerprinted picture window. Its light cast shimmery rainbows on the hardwood floors.

When she looked up, a wicked ray of sun hit her right between the eyes. A sudden knot gripped her. Nerves? Katie escaped to the bathroom, sat down on the toilet seat and took a deep breath. This evening had potential—that was the cause of the dryness in her throat. She pressed her hand to her stomach, and tried to calm its flipping.

Am I really ready to make love with Bobby? What if I don't know what to do? How to act? Janie says relax and it'll happen. Another deep breath. *Okay, I'm relaxed. No, I'm not.*

Why do I think I'm ready? Is it because I want to be? I'm nineteen, for God's sake. I can make my own decisions. Why don't I know what I want? I want Bobby. But do I want him because I hope it will wipe away what Mark has done to me? Or do I want him because I love him?

A groan escaped her lips, and she chuckled, the irony of her situation becoming crystal clear.

I'm making a major life decision while sitting on a toilet seat. And on a hunch or an instinct.

She removed a brush from her handbag and smoothed her hair, touched up her blush, and smiled in the mirror. Staring back at her, she saw a pretty young woman, content with her decision. She walked down the short hallway and found Bobby tidying up the kitchen, wiping the counters with a sudsy dishrag. She pulled up to the maple table in a ladder back chair.

"Drink?" he asked.

"I'd love a beer."

He popped the cap off a tall cold brew and handed her the bottle. She smiled as she took him in. Strong and sturdy, he looked dashing—like a military man with his sandy hair trimmed short in conformance to a soldier's standards. He smiled back at her, then opened a bottle for himself, and leaned against the cupboards, crossing his long legs. His elbows rested on the black and white ceramic tile counter; he seemed relaxed and composed.

"What are you looking at?"

"You," he replied.

"Feel better?"

"Much. Glad to put that day behind me."

"Me too. It probably doesn't sound right, but I'm glad Janie doesn't need me tonight. I've been so busy taking care of her, it feels good to just hang out."

Bobby nodded. "She went to her folks, right?"

"Yeah, not ideal, I know, but Jim's with her."

"And the cops will leave her alone. If they look for her, they'll be looking on campus." He took a swig of his beer. "Feel like food?"

"Maybe later."

She rose and wandered over to him. Against the backdrop of a fiery sunset, she wrapped her arms around his waist and pressed herself against him. He placed his hands on her cheeks, tipped her head up and kissed her—a long, gentle, lingering kiss.

"Mmm," she moaned. "Did you mess my hair?"

He stepped back a bit to check. "I'm afraid so."

She giggled into his chest. "Do it again."

He clasped her hand and led her down the short hallway to his bedroom. The room held a single four-poster bed, covered by a hand-sewn quilt with squares of blue. Blue plaid curtains warmed the room. She sat on the bed and watched as Bobby pulled down the roller shades on the two windows.

He sat next to her and tipped her back so they lay side by side on the narrow mattress. She cuddled into him, took a deep breath, and filled her senses with his smell. His spicy scent soothed and calmed her.

He caressed her head, rubbing her scalp.

"You have magic fingers," she said.

"You think?"

He kissed her face, her cheeks, her nose, her chin.

Katie leaned over top of him and kissed him, their tongues probing and teasing. They moaned and giggled.

"I love you," she whispered.

His fingers skimmed Katie's shoulders and arms, his hand traveling to the bottom of her shirt. He lifted it with a single finger and stroked the skin beneath.

She surrendered to him, overpowered by her wanting. Leaning into him, her own hand under his shirt, she traveled the smooth silk on his back and waist.

They played with each other, searching new crevices. Bobby released the clasp on her bra and her breath quickened. He cupped her breast and toyed with her nipple. Her groan became an invitation.

She lifted the end of his belt, undoing the buckle and releasing it. He helped, unbuttoning his pants and sliding them down his legs and onto the floor. She wriggled and kicked off her Levis, giggling and moaning the entire time. She was hungry for him. Shirts flew off, one tossed over a chair, the other in a single heap on the rag rug in the middle of the room.

Limbs tangled, tongues flirted, and fingers teased. They made love. Long and unadulterated. Then lingered in ecstasy, meshed together by love and contentment.

"Wow," Bobby whispered.

"Hmmm," she replied.

"Are you okay?"

She propped her head on her hand, gazed at him, and smiled. "I believe I've never been better."

"You look radiant, but I want to be sure. I want our lovemaking to be perfect for you. This wasn't exactly the time and the place I planned."

"C'mon," she teased. "What did you think we'd be doing in here? Folding socks?"

"Not exactly," he admitted.

She rested her head on his shoulder.

"Can I get you anything?

"As a matter of fact, yes." She kissed him and they made love once more. When they finished, she nuzzled her head in the hollow of his shoulder and they slept.

Sunshine flooded Bobby's room in spite of the drawn shades. Katie peered at him, dreamy-eyed and still flushed from last evening's love fest.

He peeked at her with one eye. "Are you looking at me again?"

She grinned. "I am."

"Are you hungry?"

"Starved."

"Why don't you get a shower and I'll whip us up some eggs."

"Sounds great."

Bobby kissed her on the cheek as she grabbed the quilt from his bed and wrapped it around her. She leaned over and ran her hand through the silky pelt on his chest, kissed him on the cheek, and trotted out of the room.

Unbelievable. Amazing. No wonder everyone makes such a fuss. It was special because I was with Bobby, and no one can ever take that away from me. Not even Mark. Katie stuck her tongue out at her reflection in the mirror. "Nanananana," she sang out loud. "That's for you, Mark."

She stepped into the shower, and sang out clear and strong. She washed her hair, donned yesterday's clothes, and joined Bobby in the kitchen. His chest was still bare, and she snuggled her head into it, drank in his spicy scent, and grinned.

"You look happy."

"Oh, this is way more than happy."

"What every man longs to hear." He dished up eggs. "Your timing's perfect. Let's eat before it gets cold."

Chapter 23

OVERDONE

May 1970

By eleven, Bobby dropped off a love struck Katie at the dorm. They agreed she would catch up on some studying while he worked his four-hour shift. At least that's what she told him. In truth, she had other ideas—finding Janie's attacker.

Donning a light jacket, she grabbed a textbook and spiral notebook for cover. She climbed the steep hill to the library as sunshine spilled on the sidewalk path, leaving her feeling warm and invigorated.

Inside, she headed to the second floor to pore over psychology articles related to kidnappers and their victims. Two hours later, she couldn't decide whether her mind was clearer or more muddled than ever. Most articles involved famous people who had been kidnapped. Janie wasn't famous and her family didn't have serious money. She hadn't been held for ransom. None of the cases Katie found were in any way similar to Janie's abduction. Reading about the Lindbergh case and the

Thorne kidnapping were different animals altogether. They both involved children. The only others she found involved kidnapped Mafia crime leaders. None of her research helped.

Next, she tried to find a profile for kidnappers. No information there. In her frustration, Katie turned to typical aggressor profiles. A few characteristics stood out:

Short-tempered

Fights or reacts impulsively

Lacks social skills

Struggles with attentiveness

Tries to bully people who are weaker than themselves

May have been bullied themselves

She made furious scribbles, then turned to typical victim profiles and noted:

Have low self esteem or feelings of inferiority

Are afraid others will hurt them

Lack athleticism

This is bunk. Either she needed a hell of a lot more time for research, or her psych degree, pronto. Back to the drawing board. On second thought, maybe she should pull out a new drawing board. She packed up her few notes, headed down the hill, and back to her room.

Half an hour after she settled in at the dorm, Janie showed up, duffle bag in tow.

Katie asked, "How'd it go?"

"Jim picked me up at six and took me to my dad's for the night."

Katie rested her hand on Janie's shoulder, concerned she forgot their talk. "I know. Remember, we talked before you went."

"I wasn't up to driving home alone, and Dad didn't want to come here."

Big surprise, Katie thought. "It was a good idea to go home."

"Jim wouldn't let me go by myself. He wanted to be sure the witch didn't beat me up too bad, and he didn't want me driving."

"Both good reasons for him to go along."

"It was embarrassing."

"Why on earth?"

Janie wandered across the room, sat cross-legged on her bed, and held her head in cupped hands. Katie sat at her desk and assumed a therapist pose, worried and concerned.

"Jim acted really sweet on the way there. He just stayed quiet and held my hand."

She peered into Janie's eyes, trying to see inside her heart. Her roomie looked unusually tired today and her round, alabaster face appeared drawn and gray. "He has a good bedside manner."

"He was afraid the cops might show up here and want to talk to me again."

Katie nodded. She knew far more than Janie did about this. She had shared the detective's visit to the cafeteria with Jim. In fact, she had advised him to hustle Janie out of town.

"When we got to the restaurant," Janie continued, "I went to the john to freshen up. By the time I came out, Dad and Betty had arrived. Jim stood next to them looking like a cornered animal."

"I'm sure he did fine."

Janie began to laugh.

"What's so funny?"

"At dinner, Betty asked me if I'm having any nightmares or if I've remembered anything."

"From what you've said, it sounds like Betty. Just what you want to talk about at dinner, huh?"

"Right in the middle of it, Jim looks over at my dad and says, 'How about them Tigers?'"

Katie laughed. "You gotta love Jim. Master of distraction."

"Get this. When we went back to the house, they wanted to play cards." Janie paused to chuckle. "Betty's still wearing heels and touching her bouffant hairstyle to make sure the tresses are all in place. Shit, she sprays it with shellac! What's she worried about? Jim keeps kicking me under the table. He wasn't prepared for the helmet hairdo, or her fox wrap with the beady little eye."

Katie choked on her drink and sprayed a fine mist of carbonation out of her nose. "She did not wear that! When I was a kid, I used to sit behind a lady in church who wore one of those. I had this fantasy the critter would come to life right in the middle of Mass and bite her neck."

Janie snorted. "It gets better. After we're done playing cards, Dad decides it's a good time to discuss sleeping arrangements."

"This is gonna be rich."

"He looks at Jim and tells him he will be staying in the guest room, and I will be *staying* in my room. Then he adds, 'no funny business.' Both Jim and I lost it. Dad starts up again, telling us he's serious. I started chewing ice just to aggravate him. He hates it when I crunch ice."

"You are so bad."

"You should have seen the look on Betty's face. I thought she might reach out and choke me with those witchy nails of hers. Dad says he's just trying to cover all the bases. I told him if Jim hit a home run, he'd be the first to know."

They laughed uncontrollably, coughing and hyperventilating.

"Sounds like a great visit."

"We went to bed, woke up, ate breakfast as fast as we could, and headed back here."

"Hysterical. And hilarious."

Janie rubbed her belly. "Speaking of food, I'm starving. Let's go to lunch."

"I wonder what delicacies are being served."

After lunch, the girls headed back to their room.

The phone jingled as they walked in the door and Janie grabbed the receiver.

"Hello? Oh, hi, Jim. Tonight? Yeah, we can come. Hot dogs on the hibachi? Sounds delish. Got any relish? We'll pick up some snacks, too. See ya."

"What's up?"

"Jim wants us to come over for a barbecue later. He already talked to Bobby. We need provisions."

"Whenever you're ready."

Janie tossed her keys to Katie. "Let's boogie. You're driving."

They headed outside into the bright May sunshine. Janie linked her arm in Katie's and rested her head on her roommate's shoulder. Katie narrowed her eyes. "You feeling okay?"

"I'm fine."

Katie checked out Janie's eyes. Still sunken and gray. No sparkle. "I'm worried about you."

"I know, Mom."

Seated behind the wheel of the Pinto, Katie shifted into reverse. She yanked the wheel to negotiate the sharp turn out of the tiny space. "Where to?"

"How about K-Mart, then the grocery store? Jim gave me a list."

"Typical. He asks us over and expects us to bring everything."

Two hours later, they pulled into the apartment complex toting umpteen bags of goodies. Jim stood at the top of the stairs, smiled and watched the two of them struggle with the goods. "Need help?"

Janie stuck out her tongue. "What does it look like, Bozo?"

Jim and Katie passed a knowing glance. Slowly, ever so slowly, the old life appeared to be sparking in Janie.

"Bobby called." Jim raced down the steps to help with the bags. "He's running late."

Katie nodded, then headed to the kitchen. She chuckled to herself. Ten months ago, she would never have considered choosing beer over a soft drink. She leaned against the kitchen counter and thought back on the past year. Her life had taken some huge turns. Not all of them good, either.

Of all the things, she knew the incident with Mark packed the greatest impact. Funny, she thought, how the bad stuff sticks with you. *Here, I should be grateful—to have Bobby in my life and Janie alive, and yet the first thing I ever think about is Mark's hands on me.* She drank a slug of beer. *Some days it's easier than others to play pretend.*

Katie felt so much better since she'd told Bobby about Mark. Relieved, in fact, bordering on peaceful. Her psych reading explained she would have scars from the trauma for a while, but she was hopeful. She could push past this with Bobby at her side, she just had to give it time.

They were closer now than ever. Focus on that, she told herself. The rest will fall away.

Jim loaded the charcoal bricks in the hibachi and doused them with lighter fluid. He lit the briquettes and the three of them sat in folding porch chairs, their feet perched on the balcony railing, drinking up both the beer and the sunshine, waiting for the fire to heat up.

Janie guzzled a beer. "This feels great!"

"Better than great," Katie added.

Jim lit a cigarette and passed it to Janie. She inhaled a long, slow drag and passed it back to him. They seemed tight. Janie relaxed around him, wore less of her happy-all-the-time mask, and Jim guarded her like one of Liz Taylor's diamonds. Katie hadn't imagined Janie would finally feel her mother's love in the form of a loyal and devoted boyfriend. *Sometimes I really am stupid. Some psychologist I'll make.*

"Can I bum a smoke, Jim?"

"Oh, boy," Janie said. "Here we go."

Katie laughed. "Whatever do you mean?"

Janie chuckled. "You're coming over to the dark side. You know, your mom is going to blame this on me, too." She exchanged a knowing look with Jim.

Katie lit her cigarette, coughed, and sputtered.

"It's like swearing," Janie said, "it takes practice."

"Shit, I guess so. It might not be worth it."

"Personally, I'm proud of myself," Janie answered. "You came to college Miss Goody-Two-Shoes, and now you swear, drink, smoke cigarettes, *and* have sex."

Katie began to gag. "What?"

"I know you spent the night with Bobby. The after-glow is blinding."

Jim's eyes widened and he jumped up like the fire had spread to his chair. "I'll give you ladies a few minutes." He hurriedly stubbed out his cigarette. "I'll grab the dogs and buns." He squeezed Janie's shoulder as he made his way past them and into the apartment.

Katie scrunched her eyebrows. "I'm sorry. Please don't hate me. I wanted to tell you, it just didn't seem like the right time when you came back from your dad's."

"I'm not mad, goofball. I just want details."

"It wasn't at all what I'd imagined. I thought I'd be scared and embarrassed for him to see me naked. But it seemed natural."

"Were you drunk?"

She giggled. "No! But I did have one beer right before."

"Probably helped," Janie mused.

"Yeah, right. One sip and I relax." Katie paused and sipped another drink from her beer. She wasn't sure she wanted to share this, even with Janie. It was personal, and between her and Bobby, but at the same time she could hardly contain herself. "We were at Bobby's house. His family was Up North so we were alone. We made love in his bedroom."

Katie's eyes traveled upward to a fluffy cloud, then she continued. "The blue patchwork quilt on his bed, the way his muscles flexed when he pulled down the window shades, the smell of his pillow."

"Now you're getting all dreamy on me. I want details. Did it hurt?"

"No. Not at all. It was romantic. The right place and the right time. And now I feel like a different person. You'll think I'm silly, but I feel complete."

Janie nodded. "He's the right guy."

"Absolutely the right guy."

As if on cue, the right guy appeared.

Bobby leaned over and gave Katie a peck on the cheek. "Hey, you two, whatcha talking about?"

"About what a hunka-hunka burning love you are," Janie said.

Katie kicked her in the shin, and Janie yelped.

"As long as it's all good, I don't mind." He chuckled and popped a beer. "Anybody up for a refill?"

The girls nodded in unison. "The sky is still blue, isn't it?"

He left to fetch drinks.

"Hey," Janie said.

"What?"

"I'm glad it was good for you, honey. Before my disappearing act, you were a real bitch. I still think something happened between you and Mark, but I won't bug you about it. I'm just glad things are different for you now."

"They are different. It's official. Bobby and I are in love. I'm happier than ever. If I can just find the guy who hurt you, and not let them hurt anyone else, I'll be totally content."

Katie slipped inside to the bathroom. She overheard the guys talking in the kitchen and bided her time, curious to hear if Bobby shared their news with Jim.

Jim spoke first. "They still jawing about what a love machine you are?"

Bobby chuckled, sounding embarrassed. "Help with the food?"

"You can stick spoons in the salads. Salads. As if I'll ever be caught eating a salad."

She missed what Bobby said.

"I've seen the guy a couple of times," Jim said. "Outside the dorm. He drives an old clunker—a black rusted-out Mustang. It's a '64. The guy's a serious long-hair. I was tempted to tap on his window and ask him what the hell he was doing. Something about the guy makes me nervous."

"Is it a hunch or the fact he's a creep?" Bobby asked.

"Both. I mean, what's he doing sitting outside the girls' dorm? Not jumping out of his car and going in to pick someone up, just sitting there. And he's parked in the metered section. I literally saw the guy step out of his car and put more change in the meter. Something's screwed up, don't you think?"

Katie made mental notes. She intended to find out who Jim was talking about. A longhair in a black rusted-out Mustang. Shouldn't be too hard to find him if Jim spotted him more than once, and at her dorm.

Bobby's voice reentered her thoughts. "Keep your eyes open. Don't intervene on your own. In fact, if you see the guy again, get his plate number and I'll run it through the DMV."

"We'd better get outside before the girls wonder what we're up to," Jim said.

Katie flushed the toilet, washed up, and joined them out on the balcony. *If only I can find the rat who did this to Janie. It will make everything better.*

Later, on the drive back to the dorm with Bobby, emboldened by the evening's drinks, Katie piped up. "I'm going to find who did this to Janie."

He humored her with a smile and squeezed her arm. "You think so? What's your plan?"

"Investigative procedures."

"How about we work together? Have any ideas where to start?"

"I know some of the girls arranged rides off the board."

Ride boards, posted in every dorm, at the library, in the lecture halls, at the Union, at the bookstores—allowed students hook ups for rides home or to the nearby U of M. Tear-off strips of paper with phone numbers on them were cut into the actual message and allowed those interested to take one. The rider simply arranged to wait at the designated pick-up spot and kicked in money for gas.

"Yeah," Bobby said. "I've heard some of them used the boards."

"But Janie was just walking down the street."

He parked, stepped out, then walked her to the door. "We'll make a plan tomorrow. For now, go inside and get some rest." He smiled and kissed her on the cheek.

She rifled through her purse for her room key.

"Here, let me help you." He took her purse and propped her against the door while he peered inside. "Here you go."

She smiled up at him. "Love you."

"Love you, too."

Chapter 24

INTERLUDE

May 1970

Just a tad hung-over, Katie woke at 8:00 a.m. She had a full day ahead of her. The first of her three-hour spring classes, Abnormal Psychology, met in four hours and she still needed to read fifty pages of text. She lazed in bed thinking about Alka-Seltzer, and sang the song in her head. *Plop-plop, fizz-fizz, oh what a relief it is.* Without question, she needed relief. When she finally wrenched herself out of bed and wandered in to the bathroom, she plopped two tablets into a glass of water. The world came more clearly into view, and she eavesdropped as Cynthia chatted on the phone in the adjoining room.

"Yeah, we'll see you tonight. Everyone is showing up at seven. Come to the room and then we'll head down. We reserved The Grill from eight 'til eleven."

The fog cleared and Katie remembered. Tonight was Gwen's graduation party. Gwen wanted a celebration her family could attend, and she wanted it on campus. Underneath her worldly exterior, she was a sentimental slob. She tried to keep it a secret, but her time spent at Eastern meant the world to her.

Cynthia had rented out The Grill. Gwen and her entire family planned to drive from Detroit for the evening's festivities. Gwen's family would supply the food, and The Grill furnished tableware and soft drinks. Cynthia sang in a local band and they would provide the entertainment.

The invitation to a black person's party and one held right on campus was out of the ordinary. Way out. Katie and Janie felt honored.

Katie stepped back into the room, searched for Janie, and spotted her head stuffed beneath her pillow.

"Janie," she called. "Wake up."

"Hmmm," Janie moaned.

"Wake up. Tonight's Gwen's party, remember?"

"So?"

"We promised we'd help decorate."

"Later," Janie moaned again. "I just went to bed an hour ago."

Katie turned on the water in the shower, allowing the spray to warm up while she brushed her teeth. Getting some of the decorating done before class would help. She decided to skim the fifty pages rather than study them, and hope for the best.

Cynthia walked in and joined her at the sinks. "Morning," she said.

"Are you excited about Gwen's party?"

"I can't wait. Glenda called. She's coming early to help."

"When do you want to set things up? Maybe we should decorate this morning and then we can just hang out."

"They won't let us in 'til after the lunch and afternoon crowd. We can't get in before six."

"I guess I have no excuse then. Time to finish my Psych homework."

"Sorry."

"Yeah, what a bummer."

Katie hopped in the shower, made quick work of her morning routine, and high-tailed it to the library before class. She arrived back at the dorm at two o'clock and found Janie still asleep. "Hey, goofball, are you going to wake up today?"

"I'm awake." Janie threw off the covers, fully dressed beneath them. "I'm just laying here. Hiding."

"Are you okay?"

"The world's too much."

Katie sat down on the edge of Janie's bed. "You mean like everyday?"

"Every fucking day."

"We have to hustle and help set up for the party. What are you wearing?"

"My pink hot pants and my white boots."

"Are you trying to shock the blacks? I don't know how much they can take of your skinny white legs."

"Exactly my point."

Janie sat up and slugged Katie in the arm.

"Ouch! You seem like you're getting back to your old self."

"Hey, there's no other way. I have to toss all the bad shit behind me and move on."

Katie knew all about it. She stood and walked to her desk to check her mail. Janie jumped up from bed and smoothed her blankets.

"What about you?"

"I'm still high on love. I can't wait until Gwen's party tonight. I'm wearing my favorite dress. Maybe I'll wear my boots, too, so we'll both be the height of fashion."

"Style queens."

Cynthia poked her head in the door. "You guys want to go pick up the streamers and party stuff with me?"

Katie looked to Janie and they smiled at each other and nodded.

"Let's go." Light reflected off of Cynthia's ring finger.

"Whoa," Janie said. "Who turned your finger into a lighthouse?"

"William."

"Let's see!" Katie and Janie took turns holding Cynthia's hand and turning it to catch the light.

"It's beautiful," Katie said.

"Thanks."

"Did you set a date?"

"Not a firm one, but we're thinking about next June. Once I finish this last class, I'm going to start sending out my resume and transcripts. Hopefully, I can land a teaching job by September. Then, we can save money and have some time to plan. I'm so excited." Cynthia raised her spindly arms in jubilation.

Katie hugged her. "Are we bridesmaids?"

"I'm not sure my neighborhood is ready for your pale asses, but you're definitely invited to the wedding."

"Hot damn." Janie ran over to the window, ripped down the drapes, wrapped them around her, and assumed the role of blushing bride. Picking up her hairbrush from her desk, she used it as her bouquet, and hummed "Here Comes the Bride" as she double-stepped across the room.

After an early dinner and a stop at K-Mart, they decked out The Grill with crepe paper streamers and cardboard cutouts of graduation caps. The room looked festive. Gwen showed up in a pencil skirt, a form-fitting sweater, and platform heels. With Marcus on her arm, she looked as if she owned the place. Her people filed through the door, forming a double-line behind her. Her aunts cut a wall of middle-aged elegance, clad in their fancy dresses as they congregated outside the restaurant.

"I guess we don't know her after all." Katie felt disappointed that she hadn't guessed Gwen came from such a huge family.

Janie slugged her in the arm. "You're just mad you didn't figure it out."

"I like knowing who people are."

Janie snickered. "Now there's a news flash."

As Cynthia's band set up their equipment, Motown sounds played on the jukebox. The roommates made themselves useful by setting out the food—casserole dishes, pies, cakes, and every other possible confection.

Katie turned to her roommate. "Do you like doing this?"

"What else are we going to do? We don't know anyone."

Fifteen minutes later, once Gwen's guests filtered inside, Cynthia tapped on the microphone.

"Hello, everyone! We would like to welcome all of you here this evening, to celebrate a tremendous accomplishment. Gwen Brown, my roommate and friend, has graduated."

Cheers rose from the crowd.

"Please help yourselves to food and punch. The entertainment will begin shortly."

Janie elbowed Katie in the ribs. "Damn it. There's no real beverages. Want me to run upstairs and get some vodka?"

"Not for me. But then again, I'm sure Gwen will spike the punch. It's her party, remember?"

"I'm going to ask her." Janie flitted through the crowd as she yelled for Gwen.

Cynthia thumped on the microphone again. "I'd like to ask Katie Hayes to join us for a Supremes' song, our first number this evening."

Surprised as anyone, Katie made her way to the makeshift bandstand. "What the heck?"

"C'mon, girl, get your fanny up here."

"Oh my God." Janie darted to the bandstand. "Can you believe it? You're going to be famous. The first white girl to sing with a black band on EMU's campus!"

Katie watched Janie's eyes fill with tears. "Since when are you so sentimental?"

Drums and piano began the intro, and Janie pushed Katie forward. She stood center stage in front of the microphone. Dressed in an empire waist mini-dress with bell sleeves, her long hair flowing in curls around her shoulders, she smiled over at Cynthia, and they began to sing.

"Baby, Baby, where did our love go?"

The back-up musicians sported matching Afros and outfits, black dress shirts over apple-red slim cut poplin pants. Katie stuck out like the runt of the litter. In spite of this, a new peace flooded her. Here she was, a white girl in 1970, singing with an all black band, three short years after riots shook the nation. Maybe this is what Cynthia tried telling me about, she thought. I'm coming into my own.

Chapter 25

DETECTIVE HAYES

May 1970

Two weeks later, Katie, dressed in her brown cafeteria uniform, scaled the hill to the Union for her eleven o'clock shift. Leaves bloomed as the flowering dogwoods petered out, but their sweetness lingered. Still smiling, her hips swayed a bit more than a couple of weeks ago. Her long hair swung freely as she walked—she hadn't pulled it into the regulation knot at the nape of her neck yet. She wasn't in a hurry either. Out of the corner of her eye she caught a glimpse of a Mustang keeping pace with her as she walked. Was he following her?

Plenty of people milled around. Not the normal crowd one would see during the regular school year, but a good sampling of spring semester attendees. Katie slowed a bit, looking for places to duck inside if the car indeed trailed her. As she slowed, the car did, too. Her heart raced, and her hands turned clammy in an instant. Too much coincidence for her liking—Jim mentioned a Mustang and now she saw it—she fought conflicting urges—the desire to spin around and confront the driver, and the longing to run like hell.

A car horn blared and she jumped like Jack from out of the box. As she turned, she spotted Jim's souped-up Trans Am slowing nearby, breathed a sigh of relief, and relaxed.

She leaned into the open window. "I'm so glad it's you."

"Need a lift?"

"Normally no, but today I'll let you drop me off." She hopped into the passenger seat. "What are you doing on campus at this time of day? I never see you here." Katie figured he must have been following the Mustang, but she didn't want him to know she had overheard him and Bobby talking. She drummed her fingers on the door handle, anxious to hear his reply.

"Just running up to the bookstore."

Seemed like a pretty lame excuse. Classes started three weeks ago. She breathed a silent harrumph and prided herself on her newly honed detective skills. Jim had tracked down the guy and followed him.

As he pulled back onto the road, the Mustang sped ahead, peeling rubber and leaving them in its wake.

Katie's stomach tightened. "I wonder what his problem is."

Jim shrugged as he pulled into the parking lot next to the Union. "Who knows?"

"Thanks for the lift," she said. "See 'ya later."

"Yeah, don't sweat it." He watched her stroll inside then drove off.

She wished she had been able to steal a look at the guy in the Mustang. The back door of the kitchen swung closed behind her and she placed her time card under the punch clock. It made a heavy cut into her card and the clunky noise of the machine made her jump. She still felt uneasy after the walk on the hill and spotting the Mustang at her side. Was this the guy who snatched Janie? She was determined to find out, but how?

As she reached back to grasp her hair into a ponytail, she felt hot breath on her neck and shrieked. "Dave, oh my God, you scared the living daylights out of me."

He smiled. "Hi, Katie. Whatcha doin'?"

"Punching in, what does it look like?"

"Geez, don't be mad."

"You scared me half to death. Don't ever do that again."

Dave's head fell. "Sorry."

Some kind of creepy guy like Dave grabbed Janie. But way worse. Dave, obnoxious in a personal space kind of way, in a not the brightest bulb in the pack kind of way, didn't seem dangerous. Not really.

He stepped back a few feet and wound his long, frizzy hair into a tie at the base of his neck. She groaned, shook her head, and walked away.

After work, she decided she'd talk to Bobby and see if he knew anything about the guy in the Mustang. Maybe Jim called in the plate number by now, and maybe Bobby had run it through the DMV.

Her mind wouldn't leave it alone. The Mustang dude could be a big clue. She dashed from her station at precisely three o'clock and raced over to the Campus Police station, still in her cafeteria garb.

Out of breath and sweaty, she hurried to the desk and asked Bobby, "Any news yet?"

"Not much." He looked perplexed. "Wait a minute. What are you doing here? And what do you mean?"

"About the guy, the guy in the Mustang."

Bobby laughed. "You are a quick study. How'd you hear?" He leaned across the counter and kissed her cheek.

"I overheard you and Jim talking at his apartment. Did you get the plate number?"

"Slow down." He smiled and shook his head. "Yes. I ran him through the DMV. He came back fairly clean—just a couple of speeding tickets. The guy is Robert D. Wilson. From Toledo, Ohio. Twenty years old."

"You're right. Not much information. Maybe we should keep an eye on him."

"I'm thinking I shouldn't let you out of my sight."

She smiled coyly. "Why not?"

"Because, you're trying to do detective work. You're supposed to be a psych major."

"Aw, c'mon. By nature psychologists and cops are curious. We both want to know what makes people tick."

"Yeah, well, I think I mentioned a long time ago, you need to be careful. You and Jim both seem to want to get involved in cop business. Relax. Let us do our jobs."

She frowned and pursed her lips. "Spoil sport."

"If this Robert Wilson guy turns out to be shady, at least you won't wind up alone with him."

"You can't follow me around each and every minute."

"I want you safe."

"I can take care of myself."

"I'm aware. I don't know how the hell I'll pull it off, but I'm going to keep track of you."

As he spoke, she busied herself and came up with some plans of her own. Robert David Wilson. She committed the name to memory. He could be a student at the college. At work, there was a binder with all the staff and student names and numbers. If someone forgot their code, she could search the database and find it for them. Maybe she could find this guy's name in the files.

One of Bobby's supervisors appeared and she decided to make herself scarce. He had been scrutinized enough since Janie's kidnapping. She also knew not to mention the DMV search in front of this guy. Surely, Bobby's search occurred outside of his jurisdiction as an employee.

"I'm off in ten minutes," he muttered.

"I'll wait outside for you."

"Sure. Meet you out there."

Ten minutes later, the two of them laughed all the way to the car. "What do you feel like doing?"

Bobby raised his eyebrows.

"I wish you had your own place."

"Just thinking the same thing."

—

They planned a picnic. First, the girls drove to Jim's apartment to bake a tin of brownies and assemble sandwiches, fruit, and potato salads. Katie, Janie, and Jim then met on the north edge of campus. A small grove of trees stood on a grassy knoll and the fragrance of blooming lilacs filled the air—a perfect place to enjoy an afternoon of sunshine.

Katie felt happy and light, as if nothing could deflate her. On the surface, Janie seemed back to her ornery old self. She gave everyone a hard time and teased them nonstop.

Katie spread out a blanket as Janie served three lemonades spiked with vodka. Jim stretched out his legs on the blanket and leaned back on his elbows with his drink and his usual smoke. Janie curled up alongside him and he lit her cigarette, her hand cupped around his. They acted like they would be together for a very long time.

Katie took a seat on the picnic table bench, stretched her neck, and turned her face to the sky to drink in the warm rays. Her mind wandered. She hadn't imagined Janie would ever be this close to anyone. Katie hadn't imagined she would be right here, this minute, feeling so satisfied with her life. True, her life hadn't been all berries and cream since she left home and come to college, but somehow today, things were different. Better.

She replayed making love with Bobby for the millionth time, seeing the breadth of his shoulders, feeling the soft, gentle touch of his chest hair against her breasts. A tingle traveled up her legs. Without meaning to, a hum escaped her lips.

Janie frowned. "What the hell is wrong with you?"

Katie flushed. "Nothing." She lightly tossed her head. "Pass me a cigarette, Jim."

"Here we go again."

"What?"

Katie didn't cough or sputter this time.

Bobby sauntered down the curved sidewalk from the commuter lot. She smiled and jumped up, ran to him and gave him a deep and lingering kiss.

"Hello to you, too." He grinned at her and kissed her again.

Jim turned toward Bobby. "You'll never believe this. I forgot the playing cards. We want to play cards later, right? Take a drive to the apartment with me and we'll grab them. A ball and a couple of mitts, too."

"Sure." Bobby smiled and leaned down to kiss Katie one more time.

Janie watched the guys walk away. "You really are in love with him, aren't you?"

"He's the most loving, tender man I've ever known."

"Like out of how many?" Janie asked.

"I know, it's not like I have 'experience' but I'll tell you something. If he's all I ever have, in my entire lifetime, it will be enough." She curled her legs under the blanket. "What about you? Is Jim the one?"

"I'm not sure. I'm letting myself get close to him, probably closer than ever, but I'm not comfortable with it at the same time, you know?"

"It's scary for you to get close to people because you lost your mom."

"Thank you, Dr. Hayes."

"You know I'm right."

"I hear you."

Katie opened a bag of chips and they both snacked, the silence broken only by their crunching.

The guys' faces popped over the hill and the girls folded the top over on the bag, securing it with a clothespin.

Bobby and Katie passed a glance and she served him a drink. He touched the glass to his lips and sipped. "Pardon me, miss, do I feel my brain softening a bit with a touch of this liquid? We are on campus, you know, and drinking on campus is illegal, a punishable misdemeanor." He hauled out his badge and held it up to his chest like a sworn officer.

"Sit your ass down and shut up," Janie said.

He laughed and pulled the cards out of the deck. "My partner and I…" he patted Katie's thigh, "are gonna beat the pants off you."

He dealt and they won the first three hands of pinochle.

"Enough of this nonsense," Janie said.

Katie pulled out the food from the Styrofoam cooler and set out paper plates and napkins. Janie sliced off slivers of brownie and shoved them into her mouth.

Katie tossed back her head and chuckled. "You seem hungry."

"I'm starving." She held her mouth open like a baby bird.

Jim broke off a bite of his tuna salad sandwich and fed it to her. Janie made loud smacking noises and banged her knees together under the table.

The breeze picked up and on its heels, in the distance, sirens sounded, ordinary at first, as if a lone fire-engine passed down Cross Street. Then, more sirens wailed and police unit lights, flashing from the back edge of campus, came into view from Ann Street off to their east. They, too, headed south.

Bobby paused mid-bite and began to pace. "What the hell is going on?"

"Stop playing cop," Katie said. "You're off the clock."

Janie piped up too. "You can't jump at every flashing light, Bozo."

"I know," Bobby admitted. "But I've got cop in my blood. It's hard to turn it off."

They finished eating, lost in conversation, and dealt out the cards again. Bobby and Katie won every hand. Pinochle aficionados, they claimed. A glance toward Janie confirmed her exhaustion. They packed up and headed for home. It had been a full day.

Chapter 26

ANOTHER GIRL

June 1970

The phone rang early the next morning. Katie picked up and answered with a groggy hello.

"Hi, it's me," Bobby said.

"Hi." She rubbed her eyes, shaking off sleep. "What's wrong?" It was way too early for Bobby to call.

"It's bad news."

She bolted upright. "What? Is it Janie?"

"No, she should be right there with you."

Katie glanced over at Janie's bed and spotted the telltale bump under the covers. "You're right. She's here." She inhaled and tried to calm her jackrabbit heartbeat. Still, the hair on her arms shot up. "Just tell me. What is it?"

"Come downstairs."

"You're here?"

"Come right now, please."

She threw on a pair of jeans under her nightshirt and grabbed a t-shirt from the drawer. After she brushed her teeth, she ran a comb through her hair. As she paused to look in the mirror, she wondered what on earth could be wrong. Janie's here, she reassured herself, and her family must be safe. If they weren't, it wouldn't be Bobby who would deliver the news. Still, him showing up so early meant something major had happened.

She rushed out the door, and paused to lock it behind her. Racing downstairs, she rounded the corner, and spotted Bobby pacing a strip of tile.

She ran up to him. Her hands held his forearms and she immediately panicked as she looked into his tear-ridden eyes. "What, what is it?"

"It's Cynthia."

Goosebumps rose on her arms and a lump formed in her throat. "What?"

"They found her early this morning. Under the water tower. Bound and gagged."

"Oh my God, is she going to be all right?"

His head fell. "No. I'm so sorry, Katie. Cynthia was strangled."

She dropped his arms, ran to the restroom across from the cafeteria, lifted the toilet seat, and vomited. Bobby followed her into the public ladies' room, wet a paper-towel and wiped her mouth.

She slumped on the floor. He kneeled behind her and wrapped his arms around her shoulders. She sobbed, shaking with shock. "Are you sure?"

"I'm afraid so."

"How do you know?"

"The department discovered her purse nearby...during the night sometime. Some fraternity brothers were headed back from a party, drunk and falling all over each other. One of them stumbled over Cynthia's body."

The same spot as Janie, Katie thought. "Maybe it wasn't her. Maybe there's some mistake."

Tears flowed down his cheeks. She gulped air and he held her. "Probably not."

"What do we do?"

He shook his head and Katie realized all the color had drained from his face. "I don't know."

"Do you know anything else?"

"I've heard some stuff this morning."

"Tell me," she said.

"She was partially nude, so probably raped."

Katie wailed and held her head in her hands. "Oh my God." She choked over the phlegm in her throat. "She's so tiny, she could hardly put up a fight." Racked by chills, she rubbed her arms.

"The cops are still at the scene. They're looking for evidence, securing the location, talking to witnesses."

"How did you hear?"

"I went into work at the regular time. You could almost feel the buzz. At first, I overheard another girl had been discovered, but I couldn't catch the victim's name." He stopped and shook his head again, as if he couldn't believe his own words. "The frat rats found her about two in the morning. When I showed up at six, all the departments, the Ypsilanti police, EMU campus cops, and the state troopers were still there. The fire departments, too."

"I can't believe it."

"The Ann Arbor cops might have been around, too." Bobby appeared lost in rehashing the sequence of events.

"Initially, no one knew if she was a girl from campus or not. Once they found the purse, they used her driver's license picture and matched it with the body."

"I can't think of her lying there, her hands tied, her mouth gagged. Oh my God."

"We should get out of here," he muttered.

"Why?"

"I just need to move." Bobby stood and began wandering in circles. She pulled herself up and walked over to the sink, pulling her hair back with one hand and splashing cold water on her face with the other. He lit a cigarette.

"Can I have one of those?"

He handed her one and lit it.

They sat back down on the floor, neither one of them able to stand, and flicked their ashes into the toilet.

"Has anyone called her family?"

"I'm not sure. I imagine they sent an officer to the house."

Cynthia was the oldest girl in a family of four siblings. Best friends with her mom, and constant tease of her dad. Not in a bad way, but in a fun way. She worshipped her parents, and even sadder, they worshipped her. Cynthia's brothers adored her.

Katie recalled a trip to Cynthia's house one weekend, a novelty of sorts, going to a black person's house, she'd felt stupid for imagining their life any different from hers. It wasn't. They drove up to the brick bungalow on the tree-lined street and the family came running out, as anxious to meet her and see their daughter as Katie's parents when she went home. Mr. and Mrs. Jackson held their daughter at arm's length and looked at her as if they hadn't seen her in years, instead of just a few short weeks. Each of them held her tight and long. She remembered Cynthia's brothers and how they jumped up and down waiting for a hug. Her brothers, skinny and scrawny, just like Cynthia, sported big brown eyes and soft little ringlets. One of Katie's biggest surprises was the softness of their hair. She welled up again thinking about Cynthia's family.

"I have no idea what to do."

Chapter 27

TELLING JANIE

June 1970

The police were waiting for Katie and Bobby as they exited the restroom. Two campus officers and the housemother, Sue Hutchinson, confirmed Cynthia's death and walked Katie over to the couch. Still in shock, tears spilled down her cheeks. She ceased wiping them, couldn't answer the police officer's questions, and someone wrapped a blanket around her shivering shoulders. In the dorm lounge, people milled about, their voices hushed.

Somehow she pulled herself together, and the cops allowed her to go upstairs and wake Janie. They talked to Bobby and gathered information from other coeds who knew Cynthia personally.

Katie didn't want Janie finding out from anyone else. After Janie's recent ordeal, it all seemed surreal. Too much. She couldn't imagine Janie weathering this. To hear Cynthia would never be coming back...

"Come with me, sweetie," she told Janie. Still half-asleep, Janie tumbled from her bed. Katie led her through the bathroom and sat her down on Cynthia's bed. She sat next to her and held her hand.

She choked back sobs. "I have the worst news."

"Hasn't enough happened lately? There's a fucking storm cloud hanging over us," Janie mumbled.

"Shhh," she whispered. "Can you feel Cynthia in here?"

"You've lost your marbles, haven't you?"

"Cynthia is dead, Janie."

Janie knew. Katie could tell. As if some sixth sense kicked in, the realization crept into her eyes. Janie knew Katie held back after Mark tried to rape her, and she knew when her grandma died two years ago, before anyone gave her the news.

They sat shocked, taking in their surroundings.

Everything sat right where Cynthia had left it. Her rattail comb stuck out of her make-up bag. The round 4" mirror stood propped on her desktop, and her chair sat at a forty-five degree angle as if she had just pushed it out and stood up to get dressed. Cynthia's trademark housecoat, short, puffy-sleeved and floral, lay draped over the back of her chair.

The air smelled of her cologne, a soft flowery fragrance. The room remained neat and tidy, with textbooks stacked on the desk next to an 8" x 10" glossy photo of William. Cynthia's high school graduation tassel hung from the frame. Tears washed down both of their cheeks, and they clung to each other.

"How?"

Katie wrestled with how much to tell Janie and sobbed as she recalled what she overheard someone telling Bobby. The bindings around Cynthia's wrists were the same as the ones found in Janie's abduction—leather shoestrings.

"Like you, sweetie, he duct taped her eyes shut, and used a bandana and leather shoestrings as restraints."

Janie reached up and touched the skin around her eyes. "I have to remember something."

Katie heard the conviction in her voice, but she also heard exhaustion and defeat. "I know, honey, but you can't force it."

"Why did he let me live and not Cynthia?" Janie asked.

Katie worried. Janie had enough to deal with. Survivor's guilt, too? "I don't know."

Janie stood and walked out, slamming the door leading through to the bathroom to their room. Katie heard the other door slam too. Then she heard crashing. Glass breaking, heavy objects striking the doors and walls with thumps and thuds.

She rushed to Janie. Their room resembled a battlefield. Lamps lay smashed on the floor, photos, books, Katie's Smith-Corona typewriter, and the trashcan... Janie had tossed and tumbled everything.

Katie wrestled Janie onto her bed. "Stop," she soothed. "Stop."

Janie struggled. Finally, after what seemed like an eternity, Janie fell to the floor and sobbed. Katie rifled under Janie's bed and blind-searched for cold metal. The flask was hidden inside a pillowcase amongst the dirty clothes. After she pulled it out, she unscrewed the top and offered it to Janie, who took a deep slug and handed it back to Katie, who loosely screwed the cap back in place. The desk drawer stood half-open and she reached inside and found the sedatives Janie had brought home from the hospital. They tumbled out onto the desktop, and she picked up one. She handed the pill and the flask to Janie.

Wordlessly, she placed the tablet in her mouth, took the flask from Katie's hand and washed down the medication. Then she curled up in a ball and Katie pulled the covers up around her. She closed the curtains, turned out the lights, locked the door, and stumbled downstairs in a stupor.

The place still streamed with cops, university personnel, and frantic, weeping coeds. The mood remained somber and surreal, as if the world had stopped. Cynthia had headed to the bus stop a little after nine o'clock after her shift at Winkleman's, a women's clothing store at the Arborland Mall on Washtenaw Avenue. Passengers reported seeing her exit at the Cross Street stop about 9:45 p.m.

Until a month ago, William met her at the bus stop on a regular basis and accompanied her back to the dorm when she worked late. No one had scheduled to meet her there last night, no one waited for her when she exited the bus.

By afternoon, the *Ann Arbor News* as well as the *Detroit News* ran headlines flashing the death of yet another coed. Katie read on. John Norman Collins' lawyer screamed foul—you've got the wrong guy. That fact that Collins was arrested and charged with only one of the murders while the others remained open, begged new questions. How could they really think they had the right guy? Only enough evidence existed to charge him with one of the crimes.

Katie recalled her trip to the library a few weeks ago. She wished she had located more research on serial killers. A smaller article on the front page of the news printed only a brief description. A serial killer is one who kills more than three people in a short period of time. How short, she wondered. Most often, the victims are not related to each other and are unknown to the killer.

This was different. Janie and Cynthia did know each other.

Back to reading the background on John Norman Collins, Katie cringed when she found he worked at McKenny Union as a clerk—the same location where she worked as a cashier. His trial now in full swing, witnesses for the prosecution and old girlfriends reported Collins acted surly most of the time, and was sexually aggressive.

Also, Collins held a petty criminal record for stealing.

Cynthia's death provided his defense counsel the perfect opportunity to ask for a dismissal of the charges. The prosecutor's office wouldn't budge though—pointing out this was the first girl to have been murdered in almost a year, the last having occurred the previous July. Also, Cynthia's skin color differed from the other victims who were all Caucasian. They didn't think they held the wrong guy, but they did think there was another guy. Some kind of copycat.

Bobby, Jim, Janie, and Katie, dressed in their Sunday best, climbed into Bobby's Chevy Bel-Air. Riding to the funeral together kept them from falling apart. At least partly. The first twenty minutes of the hour long ride remained completely silent. They stared blankly ahead. Bobby turned to look over his shoulder and broke the hush. "Did the cops seem suspicious of you, Jim?"

"They still think I did this to Janie," he said sarcastically.

"The only evidence they have is what we already know. The duct tape, the leather shoestring ligatures. Same stuff he used on Janie."

"Thanks for the reminder," Janie said.

Since Cynthia's murder, the cops had interviewed each of them. Katie and Janie were too strung out to care—nothing mattered anymore. For the past two days, Katie had skipped work and neither of them attended class. In fact, they barely got out of bed, showered, or ate.

The night before they visited the funeral home was beyond difficult. But today, there was no way to prepare to say a final goodbye.

As soon as Katie walked into the funeral home, she noticed Cynthia's parents both appeared to be on sedatives—to keep them insulated from the brutality of their daughter's passing. Even for her, seeing Cynthia dressed in her finest and lying in a casket felt surreal. She kissed her friend, and momentarily imagined her cheek feeling warm. It was impossible to let go of Cynthia's hand, but Bobby ushered her away from the casket, reminding her other friends and family needed a turn to say goodbye.

Jim held Janie up. Literally. Feeble, as if she could barely stand on her own two legs, she sobbed as Jim led her to Cynthia's casket. Katie and Bobby followed again, giving Cynthia one last kiss before the casket was closed and the huge procession followed the hearse the few miles to the church. The service lasted for two solid hours with readings from the bible and eulogies from Cynthia's family. Gwen spoke, her mellow voice breaking as she tried to read a farewell message to her four-year friend and confidant. Cynthia's cousin sang, her voice reminding them all of Cynthia's own. The tears wouldn't stop flowing; the agony seemed endless.

Cynthia's parents led the procession out of the church, her little brothers blindly following as Janie must have done at her own mother's funeral, and Jim at his father's. The mourners filed behind Cynthia's body, wailing and moaning as the entire world stopped.

The four friends followed the motorcade to the cemetery. They watched as the pallbearers, William included, marched Cynthia's body to the gravesite and set it on the unearthed ground. William looked lost, his eyes welling with tears as his body loomed over the other pallbearers. At almost six-five, everyone had always laughed at he and Cynthia. Here she was, this little wisp of a girl, and her one and only was a towering gentle giant. He stared into the crowd, as if hoping she would appear any moment, alive and well.

Lowering her body into the grave left the mourners numb. Like robots, they tossed dozens of roses on her final resting place.

They joined the family and other friends back in the church basement for a luncheon; they couldn't eat, or make light conversation, and made excuses for an early exit.

Neither Katie nor Janie could escape it. News reporters from the local press wanted to speak with them—to gain the inside story of Cynthia's life, under the pretext of keeping interest in the story alive until the killer was found. Human interest, they called it.

Terror grew. Cynthia's death meant another killer remained at large. Reporters accosted Janie, hounded her to remember details. Janie, forever flippant, became even more silent and morose. Katie's heart broke. She felt helpless to protect Janie. Helpless and hopeless.

The phone rang constantly. Katie decided they would only use it for outgoing calls. No longer worth the aggravation of answering it, they became desperate and removed the receiver from the hook, covering it with towels so the constant beeping sound alerting the disconnected device became muffled, until the bleeping finally stopped.

The foursome spent less and less time together. For all of them, time together equaled pain—a reminder of what they shared. Old times became buried times, and new times appeared impossible to create.

We're falling apart.

Chapter 28

THE PACKAGE

June 1970

The next week was a nonstop blur. Katie felt grouchy each minute of every day, and the cops continued to anger her. Individual law enforcement agencies sent representatives to see if Janie remembered anything about her abductor or the series of events before, during, or after her kidnapping, which caused her already impossible struggle with a hefty case of survival's guilt to heighten. She kept herself medicated with a steady dose of Stroh's beer and spent more and more time at Jim's. Her hideaway. Katie tried but she couldn't seem to say anything right. Everything she said, everything she did, pissed off Janie.

Katie verified her alibi for the night Cynthia was murdered about five thousand seven hundred and twelve times. Her life felt like someone else's. Bobby continued to feel the cops suspected the four of them might have been involved in Cynthia's death. None of it made sense.

They had lost a dear friend, continued to deal with Janie's ordeal, and endured repeated badgering. The victim had become the accused. Katie wanted to scream.

Bobby was frustrated too. He became less privy to the investigation, and the department cut his hours. His co-workers sneered at him. He hated it. Not only was he unable prevent Cynthia's murder, he got pushed to the outside at work. He no longer felt like one of the gang, and said the department was chomping at the bit to fire him.

"I'm not sure what it is, but the mood has shifted. Nobody wants me to hear a word. If I walk into a room, all conversation stops. It's like I have a disease or something."

His mood grew even more somber; he was no longer the happy, even-tempered guy Katie fell in love with last September.

They set a date for the following night. Check that. They agreed to have dinner at The Grill. Katie recalled their first date—the excitement, hope, and newfound possibilities—the tone felt much different now. Bystanders whispered about them, pointing them out as friends of Cynthia's and singled Katie out as the roommate of the girl who had been kidnapped.

"I'm going to figure this out."

Bobby pushed his food around his plate. "Figure out what?"

"Who did this to Cynthia."

"Can't you just let it go?"

"No, I can't."

"Just what I need. Having to worry about you on top of everything else. You don't know what you're doing. Let the cops do their job."

"Bobby, I'm worried about you. You're not yourself."

He nibbled a bite of his burger, tossed it aside on his plate, and pinched his lips together. "I don't know how you can expect me to be myself. I feel responsible. You've lost Cynthia. Janie's still recovering. I'm in jeopardy of losing my job—maybe my entire chance at a career."

"Do you think it's *my* fault?"

He stayed quiet.

A knot formed in her chest. "So, sort of, is that what you're saying?"

"Just drop it."

"Great, so now you're going to tell me what we can and can't talk about."

Bobby stood and brushed the crumbs off his lap. He glared at her. "You know what? This was a bad idea. I'm not hungry. I'm heading home."

Katie's face reddened. "Fine."

She headed upstairs to her room, tumbled the dead bolt closed behind her, sat on her bed in the dark, then rolled over onto her side, jumping as the edge of a sharp object poked her. Reaching for her nightlight, she flipped the switch, picked up a little box, and turned it over.

The small package had arrived in the mail, and she assumed Janie had set in on her bed. Katie's grandma often sent little gifts, a package of candy with a five-dollar bill tucked inside, a cheery card, but there wasn't a return address on the box. Not a huge deal, just a little unusual.

When she peeled back the edge of the parcel and the locket tumbled into her lap, she froze. Cynthia wore a gold heart on a gold chain just like this, every single day for as long as Katie had known her. The locket held a tiny photo of her precious William on the left side of the heart, and one of her parents on the right.

Katie jumped off the bed as if on fire, and paced the floor as she stared at the locket. Maybe I'm wrong, she thought. Maybe it belongs to someone else. She lifted it gingerly between her thumb and index finger, and turned it over in her hand, running her thumb over the metal and fingering the engraving. Next, she walked into the bathroom and held it up to the bright light. CAJ. Katie stared at it. CAJ. Cynthia Ann Jackson. Her first instinct, to drop, throw, or deny the existence of this memento, passed as she forced herself to control her breathing. She held the necklace up to the light again and slipped her nails between the two halves of the heart. The locket dropped open. William's image stared back at her, and Cynthia's parents beamed with pride.

It didn't seem real. Katie still expected Cynthia to walk in the room at any moment. Was this some kind of sick joke? She slumped against the wall as the room spun. Deep choking sobs racked her body. She couldn't comprehend what this meant. Someone had targeted *her* friends. Why?

Her head ached like a jackhammer pummeled right between her eyes. One deep breath, then another, she fought to halt the flood of feelings. Keep it simple, she thought. *Simple.*

Maybe the locket is somehow related to the crimes. Janie wore one. Wait a minute, does she still have hers? I don't remember seeing it in her bag when we brought her home from the hospital. That's silly. Lots of girls have lockets; they're all the rage. How can I make a big deal about a single piece of jewelry when everyone has one? It's not about lockets.

Reality hit her right between the eyes. The killer hadn't been after Cynthia, or even Janie. He was after her. Why else would he send the locket to her? The killer was sending her a message. Who could be doing this? Who wanted to hurt her? Mark? No. He had assaulted her, but he wasn't capable of murder! Who else? It could be some nut, some creep she didn't know. *Think, Katie, think*. Dishwasher Dave—the creep from work? No, he was a mouse. *Think*.

She plucked the notebook and pencil from her bag, turned to a fresh page and wrote "MARK." On the next page, "DAVE." Her hand began to shake. Just write down the words, she told herself. Just do the work. "JIM" she wrote. Her hand still quivered as she flipped to the next page and wrote "BOBBY." Her entire body wanted to convulse and she wrapped herself in a blanket. She couldn't be sure of anything anymore. The ground under her feet became unstable, like walking on wet ice.

She knew one thing for certain—Janie's kidnapping and Cynthia's murder—both were her fault. But how? Somehow these horrific events all circled back—back to her.

Katie began to pace. Decision time. Should she go to the cops with the locket? They might not believe she received the necklace in the mail. She might complicate things for Bobby; they knew she was his girlfriend. He already blamed this whole mess on her. Did she have any real proof that the killer sent this evidence to her? The stupid little box showed up out of nowhere. She could hardly believe it! Would they? If she told Bobby, his knowing might jeopardize his job even further. And what if the cops thought *he* stole the necklace and tried to cover his tracks? Or what if they thought she grabbed the locket from Cynthia's room and used it to gain attention? No, she needed to keep this to herself. She'd figure out the mystery on her own.

After inching over to the bed, she lifted the box again, turned it upside down and shook it, hoping for a clue. *Let there be a message.*

She picked up and fingered the locket, and said her first prayer in a very long time. *God, put an end to this madness. Protect us. Keep us free from evil. Bring us back to each other.*

Lost, alone, and sad beyond measure, she wanted to give up. Would her life ever be the same? Since coming to college, aside from Bobby, her life had turned to shit. And now, their connection had disintegrated, too.

Maybe she should give up, go home. Maybe if she weren't around, bad things would quit happening.

Maybe she should run. Maybe she should hide.

She washed her face and noticed deep, dark circles under her eyes. Her hair stuck to her head—no shine or body. Totally unmanageable, like the rest of her life. Shocked by her reflection, she stepped in the shower and lingered under the stream of hot water. *How do I make the bad stuff stop?* As she scrubbed her head more and more ferociously, she thought there must be some possibility she hadn't considered. How the hell could she figure this out and keep everyone alive? Keep herself alive.

Gwen? Could it be about Gwen? Dripping wet, she rushed over to her notepad. G-W-E-N she wrote, watermarks dotting the page.

As she toweled off, she glanced at the door to Gwen and Cynthia's room. Maybe the crimes didn't have anything to do with her after all. What if the victim was meant to be Cynthia all along? Maybe he nabbed Janie by mistake. Granted the two girls were different as night and day—Janie with her snow-white complexion and yellow hair, Cynthia with her dark skin and ebony Afro. But their body sizes, especially after dark, were almost interchangeable.

Maybe she needed to go into her suitemate's room and hunt for clues. The cops had already conducted their search for evidence, so she wouldn't be treading on their territory. Cynthia's family hadn't come to gather her belongings yet and Gwen had removed her possessions when she left. It's possible, Katie thought, some bit of evidence could still be lying there—a piece of paper with a phone number, a calendar note with a date or meeting time.

She hadn't been inside the room since she first told Janie about Cynthia's death. The time still didn't feel right. She dried her hair and tossed in some electric rollers. While she waited for them to cool, she applied foundation, blush, and a dash of mascara. Clean jeans and a freshly laundered blouse left her staring in the mirror at an improved version of herself.

Who am I kidding? This is about me. He sent me the locket, didn't he? He's after me.

Chapter 29

KATIE GOES EXPLORING

June 1970

Her attitude shifted. Katie decided to walk downtown to Bimbo's and sit at the bar. *To hell with Janie, Jim, and Bobby.* Their disapproval made her blood boil. Having a beer, all by herself, would help her clear her mind and make some firm decisions about what she wanted to do with her life. While she knew going home wasn't an option, staying stuck in the dorm with this shade pulled over her head wasn't reasonable either. *Fuck this guy, this asshole who thinks he can control my life.*

She laced her shoes, pulled on a lightweight jacket, and stuffed a five-dollar bill and some loose change in her pocket. Keys in hand, she marched through the door and locked it. At the last minute, she thought about leaving a note for Janie. *Screw it. I'll be back long before she knows I'm gone.*

Finally, she thought, I feel like a human being again, being out by myself, on my own. Her steps lightened.

The painted graffiti on Pray-Harold, the undergraduate classroom building, with the huge white peace symbols, stood out in the darkness. Whistle in hand, its place on her key ring firmly established, she strolled up the hill to the edge of campus, and began to sing "Eli's Coming."

She startled when a familiar voice came out of nowhere.

"Hey, Katie, how you doin'?"

She turned toward the shadow and gripped her keys tighter, confused by the familiar voice and the panic causing her stomach to churn.

"Mark," she suddenly registered. "What are you doing here?"

"Just came up to campus to visit a friend. Small world, huh?"

"Evidently," she answered, perturbed but unafraid. Mark couldn't touch her now.

"Where are you off to?" he asked, joining her stride by stride.

She tossed her hair off her shoulder. "Somewhere."

"You can tell me. What is it, are you off to meet lover boy?"

"No, as a matter of fact, I'm not. It would be best if you just backed away. I don't want to have to call the cops on you."

"Why would want to do that?"

"Mark, stop being an ass. Get the hell away from me."

Mark clucked his tongue. "Katie, Katie, Katie."

Oh shit. What if it is Mark? What if he's here right now to kill me? Control yourself. Don't let him see you're afraid.

"Katie?"

It took her a moment to realize she heard another voice, one other than Mark's. Unsure which way to turn, she swallowed, scrambling to regain her bearings.

Mark turned with her. He heard the voice, too.

"Dave, hi." What the hell is he doing here, she thought? She glanced from him to Mark, then at the sky. With her luck a meteor would strike any minute.

"Just left work. Going out for a beer. You and your friend want to join me?"

"Um, no, I don't think so. Mark's just leaving. Can you direct him to the commuter lot? I'm off to meet a friend. Sorry, running late."

"Far out. I'd love to help out."

Oh my God, it is freak night, she thought. "See you two later."

She dashed into Brown-Munson Residence Hall, slipped into a stall in the main bathroom, and locked the door. She drew her knees up onto the toilet seat, and sat in the dark. The tile floors and walls added to the chill crawling through her. *Goddamn him showing up. Just what I need.*

She imagined herself as a strong and powerful warrior, complete with sword and shield. Joan of Arc, persecuted for pursuing what she believed in, but fearless and ready to face whatever the world threw at her. Joan was nineteen, like me, when she was burned at the stake,

Katie thought. *Maybe Mark is my cross to bear. But for me, burning at the stake is not an option.*

I am strong and fearless, too. Mark will not rule my life, nor will Bobby or Janie, with their ideas of who I should be or who I should become. I will not give in to my fears. I will find Janie and Cynthia's assailant. I'll show them all.

She unfolded her legs and stood. With her keys strategically placed between her fingers, she ventured back into the night, hurrying down the lighted campus path, and through the city blocks to Bimbo's door. She strode inside, assumed a seat at the bar, and ordered a draft beer. Then, as an afterthought, she marched over to the cigarette machine, plunked three quarters into the change slot and pulled the round metal knob, waiting as a pack fell to the bottom tray.

Her beer in its frosty mug sat frothy and amber-colored in front of her. She grabbed a book of matches from the bar counter, struck one of them, and lit her first cigarette of the night. Bobby couldn't tell her what to do. Fact is, she thought, he doesn't recognize I'm the one the killer wants. Both Janie and Cynthia were close to her, and the killer sent *her* the necklace. The package was addressed to her, not Janie, not Gwen. Who wanted her? Why?

She needed to approach this in an organized fashion. Mark first. M-A-R-K. Although violent enough to have tried to rape her, she couldn't imagine he would kill anyone. His seemed a crime of passion; he wanted to have sex with her. The violence, his hitting her, came from her lack of cooperation. As hastily as she came to this conclusion, she dismissed it. Mark could have done this. She remembered what her brother Tom said about him.

Is it just me, hoping Mark couldn't be capable of this kind of brutality? I can't dismiss what I know about him. Just because my mom doesn't like him, and I hate her opinions about my life, especially correct ones, I can't disregard them. I have to quit acting naive about people, and stop being such a pushover. He showed up tonight. He taunted me—let me know he's still out there, haunting me.

She shuddered and took another long swallow of beer.

Mark.

The beer slid down her throat, and the cigarettes, as she smoked one after the other, delivered confidence and courage. She peered through the smoke as it swirled around her head. It's like my ideas, she thought, thick.

It could be someone other than Mark. What about Dave? Was he after her? Had he been following her, or like he said, just leaving work?

The nametag on the bartender's shirt said "Bill."

"Excuse me, Bill," she said. "Do you have a pen, or a pencil?"

"Sure." He handed her a pencil.

She grabbed a cocktail napkin from the stack on the bar, and jotted down some notes:

> What time does the cafeteria close on Friday night?
>
> Check work schedule. Dave.
>
> No sign of Mark for months. Why now?

Someone bumped her elbow, and she quickly balled up the napkin and stuffed it in her pocket.

"Hi," Joe said. "I'm Bobby's friend, Joe."

Katie peered at him. *Unbelievable.* "I remember."

Bartender Bill arrived and took Joe's order. "You're friend finally showed up, huh?"

"Oh, no," she answered. "He's not my friend."

Joe smiled and crossed his arms. "What? We're not friends? Any friend of Bobby's is a friend of mine."

She stared straight ahead, sipped her beer, and tapped another cigarette out of her pack. Joe's lighter appeared and he flicked the flame in front of her, ready to assist. Damn it, she thought, is there a full moon tonight? *What's the best way to handle this?*

"Nice night, huh?"

She regrouped and nodded.

"Where's Bobby?"

Her voice broke. "I'm...not sure."

"You guys aren't having trouble, are you?"

"Of course not." She remembered what Bobby said about Joe, how he made a comment about liking her looks. It ruffled her. As a cop, he had no business making that remark. What went on between her and Bobby was private. She noticed Joe's sports coat, and looked him straight in the eye. "Are you just finishing up a shift?"

"I finished at nine, completed some paperwork, and stopped off here. It's close to the post."

Katie nodded. "How's the investigation going? Have you made any progress?"

He ignored her question. "I'm awful sorry about your friend. I know this has been hard on you. I had no choice but to interrogate you. That was business. But know that I understand losing a friend is never easy, especially at this age."

She couldn't decide if he was patronizing her or not, so she studied his face. He seemed older than Bobby, with a heavier beard; his eyes a deep brown, like black coffee. He wore his hair cropped short, a crew cut. Dark, like his eyes. Not a bad looking guy, not good-looking necessarily, but not so bad either. "How old are you?"

"Turned the 'big three-o' last month," he said.

"You and Bobby served in 'Nam together."

"Right."

"But you didn't know each other well over there."

"No, I served in the infantry, Bobby served as an M.P."

She averted his gaze. "I know what Bobby did." Then rethinking her acerbity, she turned to him and smiled.

"Yeah, sure," he said.

"Are you married?"

"Not yet. This summer. July."

She offered congratulations.

"Thanks." He quieted for a moment.

"Be right back." Katie slid off the stool and as she made her way to the restroom, tried to decide her next move. *If I leave now, out the back, I won't have to try to think of what to say. I shouldn't drink more. I don't want to slip up and tell him what's going on. On the other hand, if I disappear, maybe he'll become all the more suspicious.*

She assumed her place in line, waiting for a stall to open. None of the other girls looked familiar, and she inhaled a deep breath. I want to be invisible for a while, she thought.

She finished in the restroom and calmed her breathing. Joe Smokovich's arrival provided an opportunity, she decided, a chance for her to garner some information. She tossed her hair off her shoulder and strolled back to the bar. Joe scooted her stool back for her and she climbed up and smiled at him. "It must be fascinating… being a detective."

"It can be. Most days it's pretty frustrating."

"I'm sure. Especially now, when you thought this string of killings seemed all sorted out."

Joe nodded and gazed into his mug.

"I respect what you do," Katie said. "I hope you don't think because my friends and I are upset there's been no arrest yet, and because we spout off sometimes, we don't appreciate your efforts."

"Thanks."

Mostly, she meant the words. But buttering up people worked for her in the past, and she might as well lay it on thick now. There was so much at stake.

"This really throws you guys off, doesn't it? Thinking Collins committed the murders, and now this new one comes along."

"Actually, it's nothing short of infuriating. Trust me. We want to catch this guy as much as you want us to. The fact that someone else is out there, another goddamn lunatic, it's maddening as all get out."

"I'm sorry."

Joc looked puzzled.

"I am. This is horrible for everyone." She closed her eyes and sipped her beer.

Joe lit a cigarette. "I've seen a lot. 'Nam is the worst place on the planet. But seeing a young girl murdered, seeing more than one, it does things to me."

"Like what?"

"It makes me sick, sad, and angry."

"Same way it makes me feel," Katie said. "Exactly the same. When Janie disappeared, I was scared. Petrified is more like it. But once they found her and I knew she would be all right, I took a deep breath, even though I still felt sick to my stomach. And you're right, the sadness gripped me soon after. It's a normal progression from sadness to anger. I'm furious about Janie's abduction. When I think about Cynthia, it's different. I'm still in the sick, sad stage."

"You're a psych major, right?"

"How'd you guess?"

"Bobby mentioned it. But you sound like one, too."

She smiled, secretly patting herself on the back. Joining Joe at the bar made tons of sense. Colluding with the enemy. The rest of her beer slid down, and she pulled another cigarette from her pack. "How do you feel about the investigation so far? Do you see any similarities between Janie's abduction and Cynthia's death?" Immediately, she kicked herself—*no way would he divulge information, especially to her.*

"Do you?"

"A few," Katie said. "It's obvious they were both recovered in exactly the same spot. And the duct tape and the bindings appear similar. Looks like comparable crimes to me, but I'm just a layperson, not a detective."

Joe tilted his head back. "We'll figure it out. Hopefully, soon. What about you? What will you be doing all summer?"

"I'm going to stay here. I'm done with home."

"Any special reason?"

While Joe waited for her answer, he flashed two fingers at Bartender Bill and two freshly-filled frosty mugs arrived a minute later.

"It hard to go home once you've been away. But you know all about those things. You're full grown, as my baby brother would say."

He nodded. "Grown and almost married."

"You seem a tad undecided about the married part."

"It's a big decision. But we've been together a long time, and she waited for me to get back from 'Nam. Seems like the next logical step."

"What's she like? What does she do?"

"Peggy? She's a great girl. A nurse at the U."

She smiled. "Really? A cop marrying a nurse. She'll be able to take care of you if you get hurt on the job."

"Good point."

"You'd better be absolutely sure," she said. "Not fair to either one of you if you're having more than the usual nerves."

He slugged down his beer, set his mug on the bar with a thud, and stood. "You ready to get out of here?"

"Me?" She looked startled. "No, no. I'm fine. You go ahead."

"How are you getting home?"

"Walking."

"I don't think so." The breath huffed out of him. "Unbelievable. You'd walk home, by yourself, after what's happened to both your roommate and suitemate? C'mon, I'll give you a lift."

She obediently hopped off her stool and rubbed her hands on the tops of her pants, grabbing her cigarettes from the bar, and stuffing them into her pocket. Then she scooted in behind him, sized up the evening, and decided it couldn't have gone any better.

A cop. She couldn't have a safer escort. Still, she weaved her keys between her fingers, just in case the situation called for a quick defense. They walked the side street to the back parking lot, bright city streetlights paving their way. He held the door of his '69 Mustang for her.

"Nice ride," she said.

"Thanks. My gift to myself for having lived through 'Nam."

She climbed in. "Seems like you deserved it."

He sat behind the wheel and closed the door. "You have no idea."

"You seem pretty comfortable talking about 'Nam. Bobby avoids the topic."

"Different strokes is all."

"I guess." She looked at him in the glow of the dash lights. This guy *is* all grown up. In spite of herself, she felt a stir of attraction. An older, settled guy. One with a real job, a career, and goals in life. A guy with an honorable purpose and limitless possibilities.

He brought her back from her thoughts. "Putnam Hall, right?"

"Right." They rode in silence, but she noticed him glancing at her every few seconds. Not as if he was trying to read her thoughts, but as if he was attracted to her. Was she imagining this?

Joe parked in front of the dorm entrance and laid a hand on her thigh. "Here you are, then."

No, she wasn't delusional. She dipped her head and murmured, "Thanks for the ride."

"My pleasure."

Chapter 30

ON THE HUNT

June 1970

The next morning, Katie searched for the napkin she'd been writing on at Bimbo's. She read her notes and set up the day's plan. First, she needed to check on the Friday night cafeteria hours. It didn't make much sense it would be open late on a Friday during Spring Semester, but she could be wrong Then, she thought, I should head into work and find some time alone with the schedule board.

She jotted a simple note for Janie. "At work."

Dressed in jeans and a light t-shirt, she scaled the hill for the umpteenth time this year. The temperature climbed and a trickle of sweat snaked down her back as she mounted the steep grade. Nervous jitters infested her stomach and she supposed heightened adrenalin would be the norm for a while. Until she solved these crimes, there would be no peace.

The outside of McKenny Union resembled a post-card. Sun reflected off the wall of plate glass windows framing the cafeteria, and petunias, her favorite, spilled out of the brick flowerbeds. Reality hit her as she approached the entrance. She imagined John Norman Collins reporting for work as she did on countless days, just an ordinary guy coming in to clerk at the bookstore, unnoticeable and unremarkable. She shivered.

The metal handle of the cafeteria door stuck, and as she tugged, she paused to read the posted hours. Monday through Friday the sign read, open 11:00 a.m. to 9:00 p.m. The hours Dave mentioned checked out. She walked to the back of the food line. Still early, hardly anyone milled around. Double doors led into the kitchen. A lone, oversized desk, complete with a black desk-model phone, sat in the back. On the wall in front of the desk, the weekly schedule was thumbtacked to the corkboard. To the right of the bulletin board, the heavy-duty punch clock hung on the wall, along with employee time cards.

She skimmed the cards. Dave. Dave what? She realized she didn't know any of her co-workers last names. Stupid. Katie knew the order of the cards; they were organized by last name, a comma, and then a first initial. Find the D's, she decided, and go from there. Two names appeared with the first initial D. One Baxter, the other Murray. Baxter's name appeared on the Saturday schedule. Not Wilson.

Wait a minute, she thought. Friday. I need Friday, not Saturday. Time ticked on—someone would interrupt her soon. Her hands trembled as she looked again. Friday. Both Baxter and Wilson's names appeared on the Friday schedule. According to the list, they both worked from four o'clock 'til close. Katie needed confirmation. She'd check the punch cards. At least that would confirm either

'D's actual presence during their scheduled hours. She would verify Dave's last name the next time she saw him.

She located Baxter's card. First name Doug. Next she skimmed Wilson's card from the slot. Robert. Robert Wilson. It sounded familiar. Robert D. Wilson. The guy in the Mustang. She smacked her forehead. Dave Wilson. How could she have missed this?

"Hi, Katie! What are you doing here?"

The voice sounded behind her. Marilyn Jacobs, her shift manager.

"Oh, hi. I just came in to check my schedule for next week. I thought it might be changing with spring semester wrapping up."

"Did you turn in a shift change request?"

"No, not yet."

"Honey, if you haven't turned in a change, you're stuck with the old schedule for at least a week. I'm swamped with meetings."

"It's not a problem."

"Oh dear, I'm sorry. How thoughtless of me. You lost your friend, didn't you?"

Katie's throat welled with tears. "I'm afraid so."

"Tell you what. If you need some time off, just let me know."

"No, no. It's fine. I've taken enough time. I just thought...I forgot about the schedule change forms. My mistake. Sorry."

Marilyn patted her on the back. "It's okay, hon. None of us can think straight."

At a loss for words, Katie couldn't think of a good reason to stand around. "I'll be heading out then."

"Have a good weekend. We'll see you Monday, right?"

"Yep. See you then."

She walked inside the cafeteria, filled a Styrofoam cup with coffee, and popped a lid on top. After dropping some coins in the square leather box next to the register, she headed back outside to a wooden bench under a large oak tree. Shaded and shadowed, she sat alone, thinking.

Mark. *I have to set him up. Call him, tell him I want to see him. Just to talk, to work things out.* He'd bite, for sure. It gave her the willies, the mere thought of it—having to see him, meet him, talk to him. *Set the meeting in a public place. Maybe Bimbo's, right there at the bar.*

But she'd need a witness. Bobby. No, it couldn't be Bobby. It would have to be a cop. A real cop. But then she would have to explain. Heck, Joe wouldn't even let her walk home alone. He certainly wouldn't let her do anything as dangerous as meeting Mark. Then again, would Joe even believe her? She'd come up with some cockamamie idea her former boyfriend murdered girls in his spare time—seemed farfetched even to her.

An idea sparked. She would invite Joe to Bimbo's on the night she arranged a meeting with Mark, and call him to meet her a few minutes after she knew Mark would be there. It would have to be on a weeknight—a slow night where he could overhear their conversation.

Who was she kidding? Mark wasn't going to admit he kidnapped Janie and killed Cynthia in public, but he would love the idea of having her alone. She could imagine sitting in his car, just the two of them. Vomit rose from the back of her throat, just like it did that night.

She needed to be brave, to summon courage from the depths of her soul.

If she told Bobby, and then he told Joe, the two of them could come together and keep watch. They could station themselves outside Mark's car, sneak up on it. She could crack the window, and when Mark spilled the beans, they would come into view, guns blazing, and place him under arrest before he knew what hit him.

Only on television did it work out that perfectly. Suddenly chilled, she sipped her coffee.

I need to move, she thought, and chase away the fear for a few minutes. Find a distraction. She traipsed back to the dorm, kept her head down, and focused on the cracks in the sidewalk. Letting out all her breath, she counted the lines, being careful not to step on them. *Step on a crack, break your mother's back.* Quelling her racing heart proved impossible. She needed to regain command of her emotions. In Mark's presence, she'd better be able to control her fear. Act, not react.

She glanced up, hoping to spot a familiar face, smile at a friend, feel comfortable again and put herself in a manageable place. Once she entered Putnam, she stopped at the front desk, and dialed her room. It rang three times before Janie picked up.

"Hello?"

"Hi, it's me."

"What'd 'ya want?"

"I miss you. Come down for lunch."

"Gimme five."

"Okay." Katie hung up the phone and the breath washed out of her. She sat on the orange vinyl couch, the one with the perfect view of the hallway Janie would waltz down in a few minutes.

As Janie rounded the corner, looking coy, she smiled. Katie stood and they hugged—a long tight hug.

"I've missed you."

Janie smiled. "Yeah, me too."

"Let's go eat weird stuff."

"I hope it's rainbow-colored and rubbery."

They headed into the cafeteria where they each grabbed a gray plastic tray and filled it with cheap industrial silverware and a paper napkin. After the hair-netted cafeteria lady filled their melamine plates with mashed potatoes and fried chicken, they stopped off at the soft drink stand and filled up their large cups with ice and soda. They sought out their corner, trotted over to their table, and chatted all the while.

Janie hooted. "Girl, you are in so much trouble."

"What? What did I do?"

"Joe told Bobby you went to Bimbo's last night, and he called Jim. I heard them talking and I asked Jim about it. Bobby was P-I-S-S-E-D."

"Why? He was the one who wanted to go home after dinner. He's all bent outta shape about how he might lose his job, like it's the end of the world."

"God, Katie. What's gotten into you? His job is important. I love you, but you're out of your gourd on this one."

"What makes you say that?"

"Two good reasons. He's on the GI Bill, right? One, he needs the money. The other, he wants to be a cop. He's like an intern now, right? If he loses his job, he'll be selling himself down the river, screwing up his career."

Katie cocked her head and looked at Janie, ashamed of herself for being so thoughtless and selfish. "Oh my God, you're right. I'm a total ass."

Janie leaned back and nodded.

"You're a lot smarter than you look," Katie said.

Janie smirked. "I know."

"Okay, he's upset about his job. He's entitled, you're right. But I can still go to the bar by myself, can't I?"

"You know who you're talking to. I ain't gonna stop you. But by yourself? You'd have my ass casted and fixed if I pulled a stunt like that. You know you would."

"Damn it," Katie said.

"What?"

She reached out and grabbed her friend's hand. "You're right about everything. Thanks."

Janie dipped her head. "You're welcome."

Katie ate a bite of her overdone chicken and sighed. "I'm really lucky, you know?"

"To have a friend like me? Yep, you sure are."

"No. Not that. I'm lucky my parents are Up North for the summer. No newspapers. No phone. If they knew about Cynthia's death, and about what happened to you, they'd never let me stay here."

"You have a good point."

"Even if they drive into town for something, they wouldn't hear anything. They don't even have a TV."

Janie scratched her head. "Really? No television?"

"No reception. My grandpa has a TV but you can't tune in a station to save your life."

"Perfect."

"It's kind of weird, really."

"What?"

Katie furrowed her brow. "That my folks let me stay. Surprising."

"Did you want them to make you come with them?"

"No, not exactly. It's just a little strange. I never thought being on my own would happen this way, this quick."

"Better now than when you were six," Janie replied.

Katie rolled her eyes. "Do you think we'll be friends forever? Do you think God brought us here, to this campus, this year, for a reason?"

"You're the smart one."

"I wonder sometimes. There has to be a reason for everything, even if we don't understand it."

"Like some big cosmic energy that keeps the world spinning?"

Katie bit her lip. "Sort of. I wonder if someday, years from now, the two of us will look back and laugh about all of this."

"Probably not."

"I said it wrong. Of course we won't laugh. But will we get over this? Survive it? Learn from it? Rise above it?"

Janie shook her head. "I don't know. What do you think?"

"Of course. You and me? We're survivors."

Chapter 31

TAKING CHARGE

June 1970

Katie picked up the phone after a lazy afternoon with Janie. Bobby should be about finished with his shift. Rather than wait for him to come to her about her night at Bimbo's, she'd call him first. Maybe she could distract him by letting him know what she uncovered about Dave.

"Campus Police, how may I direct your call?"

Katie recognized Bobby's voice. "Hi, feel like coming over after work?"

"I've got some errands to run, and I'm overdue on a paper about violence in society."

"Yikes," she said, "seems strange to be taking a class about violence right now."

Bobby chuckled, putting her at ease. They hadn't spoken since the incident at the Grill.

"I miss you," she said.

"Gotcha."

Katie heard his voice soften and asked, "Well? What do you think?"

"Feel like going out?"

"Totally."

"Give me an hour or so. I'll come by and pick you up."

She said goodbye, kicked her feet up on her bed, and laid back on her pillow.

Janie sat on her bed watching. "I detect a smile."

"Feels better talking to him."

"See? Sometimes I'm right."

Katie smiled at her roommate, and Janie stood and walked over to the turntable. "I'd better start getting ready."

"Why? What are you up to?"

"Going over to Jim's." She headed toward the bathroom. "You know what's really weird?"

"What?"

"Every time I round the corner I expect to see skinny old Cynthia standing there with a pick sticking out of her fuzzy head."

"I do the same thing. I can't imagine we will ever look at it any other way. It's good, though. It means we aren't forgetting her."

"Still, it feels unreal. It shouldn't be this way."

"It shouldn't."

Janie closed the bathroom door and turned on the shower. Katie closed her eyes and mentally picked out an outfit for her date with Bobby in an attempt to clear her head of everything else. If she didn't take a break every now and then, she would wear herself out.

Janie sauntered out of the bathroom in her terry cloth robe. "All done."

Katie slipped around her and traded spots. "My turn."

After her shower, she rejoined Janie in the room. She sat down at her desk, dried her hair, and wound it in electric rollers.

"Going for the curly look, tonight?"

"I need to be as pretty as possible. It might distract him from memories of his bitchy girlfriend."

"You can always hope," Janie said. She painted on some lipstick and blotted it with a tissue. "I'm outta here."

"Have fun."

"You, too." Janie swung her handbag over her shoulder and slipped out of the room.

Katie unrolled the curlers and picked up her make-up bag as the phone rang. "Hello?"

"Is this Katie?"

"Yes," she answered, trying to place the voice.

"This is Dave. From work."

"Oh, hi."

"Would you like to do something tonight? I know its last minute, but I just thought, after running in to you last night, it might be fun to get together. Outside of work."

Her breathing halted. "I'm busy tonight." An opportunity, she told herself. This is an opportunity.

"Oh." He sounded sad and dejected.

"But thanks for the call. And thanks for helping Mark back to the parking lot."

"I didn't. After you left, he said he remembered another stop he wanted to make."

Goosebumps rose on her flesh. "Really?"

"Yeah. He seems to like you a lot."

She winced and bile filled her throat. "Thanks for calling. I guess I'll see you at work next week."

Blood drained from her veins. She turned to the page entitled "DAVE" in her notebook, and wrote:

Dave called me in dorm room–7 p.m.
Wanted to get together
Said Mark liked me a lot—Dave and Mark talked about me
Dave is Robert D. Wilson

After a solid thirty seconds, she inhaled. *Finish getting ready. Go out with Bobby. Have fun.*

The temperature seemed ten degrees warmer than five minutes ago. She reapplied deodorant and decided on a lighter sweater than the one she originally picked out. She couldn't wait to apologize to Bobby, kiss, and make up. Katie grabbed her purse and headed downstairs to wait.

He opened the heavy entrance doors and she smiled; he looked brighter today. They strolled outside into the bright sunshine, the sun just beginning to ease its way to earth.

Bobby wrapped his arm around her. "Want to walk over to the Wooden Nickel for a beer?"

"I've never been there. Have you?"

"A couple of times."

She hooked her arm around his waist and rested her head on his shoulder. "Let's try it."

They sauntered down Ann St. to Huron and entered the darkened space, picking a corner table carved with lover's initials and messages. Make Love Not War. Bobby retrieved a pitcher of beer and two frosty mugs from the bar. He filled them and lifted his glass. "To a better day."

Katie dropped her chin to her chest. "I'm sorry about our fight. I should have been more understanding. Instead of listening to you, I couldn't stop trying to figure out Cynthia's murder."

He fingered the handle on his mug, pursed his lips, and nodded. "We all need a mission right now. If we figure out who did this it will keep the pain from setting in. I get it. I know how it works."

She studied him. He did know all about it.

"You've never told me much about 'Nam."

He reached into his shirt pocket for his cigarettes, tapped one out of the pack, lit it, inhaled, and then blew out a puff of smoke. "Most M.P.'s don't see much action. But my battalion offered support to a tactical zone once. That day, we secured perimeters, set up roadblocks. A buddy of mine from high school served in the infantry there. Anyway, I ran into him. We talked for about two minutes, said we'd catch up after we wiped their asses. Fifteen minutes later, I found him dead. The Vietcong caught us by surprise. The one day I showed up to help protect fighting infantrymen, I couldn't."

Katie wanted to look away—it hurt to see Bobby in this much pain. "I'm so sorry. I didn't know."

"I saw death, bodies maimed and gutted. It's worse somehow when it's someone you know—more real, and it hurts a helluva lot more. The guilt, the helplessness, it was all I could do to get through the days. I couldn't even attend his funeral or offer my condolences to his family."

"You could go now," she said.

He blinked and nodded. "I guess I could."

His clear blue eyes shone, even in the smoke-filled darkness. "My point is this. I understand your need to figure this out. I'm a selfish asshole, too, worried about my job when you're suffering the largest loss of your life."

"We're both sorry."

"Even Steven."

"Now tell me why the hell you went to Bimbo's by yourself." He didn't sound pissed, he sounded concerned.

"I understand you're worried about my safety, but I can do whatever I want." She sipped her beer and then took his hand. Should she tell him about her plan to frame Mark? About her concerns regarding Dave? It didn't serve any real purpose for him to know about any of those things. If he knew, he'd be all the more protective, and she didn't want him to stifle her mission.

He rubbed his thumb on the top of her hand. "I love you. I want you safe."

"I needed to clear my head is all," she said, "that's why I went to the bar."

"I understand, trust me, but it's not safe out there." He nodded toward the doorway. "Think about it. Whoever did this targeted Janie and then Cynthia. It's too close to home. It could be about you, and it scares the hell out of me to even think about it."

Katie's stomach flipped. "You think so, too?"

"We have to consider all possibilities."

A longer draw of beer traveled down her throat. "I'm scared."

"You should be." He shook his head. "You need to be more careful than you've ever been. You can't let down your guard." He sat silent, thinking. "Is there any chance Mark could be responsible for all of this?"

She shivered and tears rimmed her eyelids. "I don't know. I don't think so. I've played it over and over in my mind. He did unspeakable things to me, I can't deny it. I never would have guessed him capable of rape. If I hadn't stopped him, there is no doubt in my mind what would have happened. But murder?" She shook her head. "I just can't see it."

"I know. It's a far cry from attempted rape to murder." He locked eyes with her. "You know some criminals escalate."

"I've researched."

"Would he despise you enough to hurt the people closest to you?"

"No way."

"The cops aren't stupid. They're going to come to the same conclusion we have. It's likely they're keeping a close eye on you, on all of us. They figure it's someone close to you, or even Jim, or me."

She'd been over it a thousand times. While it didn't seem probable, she realized that she had to keep every possibility in mind.

"I did figure out one thing." She hoped Bobby wouldn't be too upset with her.

"What?"

"Robert D. Wilson works in the cafeteria with me."

"What? How?"

"By chance, I looked for a Wilson. Turns out he goes by Dave."

"This is big," Bobby said.

Katie told him how she pieced the puzzle together.

"I need to fill the guys in on this."

"Right this minute? He's just a creep, Bobby. I'm sure it's nothing more. Let's have another beer." She reached over and grabbed his cigarettes from his shirt pocket. "And let's change the subject. I've got the willies."

"Fair enough," he said. "I'll be right back."

Katie spotted him in the phone booth, and it was a good ten minutes before he returned with refills, sat down, and kissed her.

Chapter 32

UNLIKELY PARISHIONER

June 1970

The next morning, Katie decided she needed to spend some time at church. She stepped into a skirt and some skimmers, left Janie a note on the desk, and slipped out the door. Walking in broad daylight must be safe, she reasoned. And the chapel was only two short blocks away.

A small congregation of worshippers stood outside Holy Trinity, the eight o'clock mass having just let out. She slipped by the gathering and through the double doors into the cozy space. The perfectly ordered pews with their straight, thickly lacquered backs glinted in the stain-glassed rainbow of sunlight.

Immediately, she calmed. She questioned why she had stayed away so long. God had been her mainstay for all her early years—the years of confusion when she first noticed other moms were different from hers—she witnessed other moms bouncing a child on their knee, wiping noses, and caressing their youngsters soft, shiny hair while guiding their reading by pointing to the appropriate spot in their Missal.

Her mom kept herself busy singing and fluffing her hair while Katie searched frantically in her pocket for tissues, mopped noses, and shushed the boys when they began to whimper from boredom. It seemed like a lifetime ago, and she yearned for her mom in a way she hadn't for a very long time.

Lost in her own private pain, she prayed for hope, for peace, and for protection. For Janie first, then for Cynthia's family, and for her own. She'd been out of touch with her parents, her brothers, and her grandma for more than a month; she was unexpectedly lonely.

Lord, give me strength. Keep me safe from whoever is out there. Let me keep my wits about me. Help me to see this through, find whoever has done this, and bring him to justice. Make me the smarter one. Help me not to be foolish but to be measured in my thinking. Let me outsmart him, trick him, instead of him being the one to deceive and destroy.

Katie's mind whirred. He'd snuck up on Janie without warning; otherwise she would have remembered something. What happened to Cynthia? She could have been overcome without warning as she stepped off of the bus, or she could have been coerced, especially by someone like Mark. Maybe he claimed to be Katie's friend and said Katie was in trouble. Under those circumstances, Cynthia would have gone with him. Maybe she saw her abductor's face. Maybe that's why she wound up dead.

Katie knew Mark could be manipulative. He twisted things. He tried to make people feel sorry for him, or use them to get what he wanted. But Mark didn't know anything about her relationship with Cynthia. It didn't make sense.

Organ music filled the chapel, and she rose along with the other worshippers, opened her hymnal, and began to sing "Holy God We Praise Thy Name." Her back straightened as her courage returned, if only for a moment.

Bobby. He would never hurt her. And she trusted Jim, too. Nancy Drew would have considered them though, and the police would do the same. But they would quickly be eliminated as suspects. Neither Bobby nor Jim ever demonstrated, even in the slightest, a tendency or desire hurt women for the sheer pleasure of it. Plus, they had alibis. The four of them had been together picnicking.

Mark on the other hand, possessed all kinds of motivation. A man scorned by his mother, then by his father, and lastly by his girl—Katie. His history, at least rumors of it, suggested violence. Katie remembered his quick trigger and victim personality. *Nobody understands me, nobody respects me.* She recalled Mark's mantra, his husky voice ranting about some guy being out of line and how he would love to give him a piece of his mind, no, make that a piece of his muscle. Mark fought to be the best at everything he did. If not, he blamed someone else. In wrestling matches, if he lost, which hardly ever happened, he would blame it on a bad call or an injury. There was always an excuse.

More and more she became convinced.

Stop. Slow down. Don't get ahead of yourself. The hair on her neck stood at attention whenever she came within two feet of Dave. And he had certainly been stalking the dorm. Maybe even her.

"From darkness to life," Fr. Greg's sermon continued.

How apropos, she thought, her stomach twisting. She tried refocusing on the message, then contemplated her next move.

As the crowd filtered row by row to communion, she stood, waiting for the coed in front of her to inch ahead. An usher backed up to indicate her pew's turn to file forward, and she looked up. Joe Smokovich smiled at her. She flushed, then reverently tipped her head toward her chest and folded her hands in prayer as she followed the line to the front.

Could this be sheer coincidence? His showing up here? It's not like he could just show up and step into the usher role, she told herself. The way it worked, he would have been scheduled. She forced her shoulders to relax, received communion, crossed herself, and walked back to her pew. She knelt and said a simple prayer. *Good Lord, help me to make sense of all of this.*

Katie picked up her hymnal, joined in the communion hymn, and furtively searched for Joe. She couldn't spot him. He must be at the back of the church. After the mediation hymn, the worshippers assumed their seats, soothed by the gentle strains of an acoustic guitar and a Bob Dylan sound-alike singing "Put A Little Love in Your Heart." During her high school years, Katie performed as a folk singer at her church back home. Again, a twinge of homesickness gripped her.

She decided once she arrived back at the dorm, she would find her stationery and write a few letters. Maybe ask Mom to have the boys write. It might make sense to plan a visit—she could always take a weekend. The drive to Caseville, only two and a half hours away, could provide a much-needed getaway for her and Janie.

At the priest's request, the congregation stood for the final blessing and Katie returned to the present. In spite of her frenzied thinking, she felt relaxed and renewed. She nodded hello to a few familiar faces, slowly weaved her way through the intimate crowd and out the back doors of the church. Joe stood at the door, holding it open as he passed out the weekly bulletin. He smiled as he handed her a copy. "Hi, Katie, I didn't know you attended Holy Trinity."

She blushed, toying with the heart charm on her necklace. "Obviously not as often as I should."

"Beautiful day."

"It really is."

"Do you have plans?"

Katie squinted at him. "What do you mean?"

"Breakfast. I'm not on duty till noon. There's a little diner around the corner from the post. Serves a great breakfast special. What do you say? You up for it?"

She tried to size him up. Why would he be interested in having breakfast with her? He was engaged. It must be something else. He must be trying to pump her for information. "No, I don't think so."

He laid a hand on her arm. "It's just breakfast. Broad daylight and all. And I'm a cop. You'll be safe."

She couldn't help but snicker. He did have a way about him.

"Okay," she agreed. "But it'll have to be quick. I have a ton of studying to finish."

They strolled down the narrow sidewalk to the tiny parking lot sitting at the north end of the chapel. Katie spotted his police cruiser. "I've never ridden in a police car." She threw up her hands and waved them with feigned excitement.

"I'll turn on the siren for you and flash the lights, if you'd like."

"No, no. Not necessary. In my book, the less attention the better."

"You don't feel funny about this, do you? Do you think Bobby will mind?"

"No, not at all," she lied. "He's totally cool. What about Peggy?"

"Peggy? Peggy knows she's the girl for me."

Katie arched her brows. "Then why aren't you taking her to breakfast?"

"She's working this morning."

"Oh." Katie felt a bit foolish.

Joe pulled onto Hamilton and then left onto Michigan Ave. The diner stood around the corner, like he said. He parked, they climbed out, walked inside, and took the last two available seats at the counter. Every other Sunday churchgoer had decided to frequent the place, too.

"So, studying today?"

"First I need to send a letter off to the family. Then, yes, catching up on my reading. I have to make it up to the rehearsal halls, too. I've let my voice practice fall to the wayside…all year it seems, kind of like church. I'm resting on my God given talent and it's beginning to show. I need to polish my technique."

Joe nodded, then asked, "How do you feel about Jim?"

The question came from out of the blue. "Jimmy? Why do you ask?"

"Just wondering."

Katie narrowed her eyes and pursed her lips; she couldn't hide her irritation. "I thought you invited me to breakfast, but now it seems like you're pumping me for information. Is this an interview?"

"Sorry. You're right, I did say breakfast."

He seemed disappointed he hadn't asked her for more than breakfast.

The waitress leaned over the counter and poured steamy coffee into white ceramic mugs. Joe paused and waited for Katie to order.

"I'll have blueberry pancakes, crisp bacon, and maple syrup," she said. Joe ordered eggs over easy, an extra side of bacon, and white toast.

Katie smiled to herself. Some things remained predictable.

The stub of a pencil stuck out like an antenna from behind the server's ear, her kinky curls barely contained under her brown hair net, and her apron strings hugged her waist like an old friend. The way she flipped over her order book and tucked the cardboard flap between tickets, so the carbon would produce the receipt—she performed the expert move like a seasoned quarterback making a routine pass. It looked as though she had worked this short order job her whole life, almost as if she had been born to fling plates.

"She's good," Katie remarked.

Joe's eyes followed Katie's to the waitress, and he nodded. "Truthfully, I'm as interested in catching this guy as you are. Just trying to do my job. I'm paying for breakfast, so look at it this way. A little conversation for me, breakfast for you. It's a nice day, and we'll both walk away with full stomachs."

She added a long dribble of cream to her coffee, picked up her mug, and sipped. "I guess there's no harm in talking about Jim. He's a good guy. True, he'll get bent out of shape when things don't go according to plan, but not dramatically so." She paused to thank the waitress for delivering her meal, and placed her napkin in her lap. "When Janie went missing, he panicked. Just wanted to find her. We all did. I know it upset him, your interviewing him. But mostly he felt guilty he couldn't keep Janie safe from harm. Trust me, you can eliminate Jim as a suspect. He wouldn't swat a mosquito."

Joe nodded as he dipped a slice of toast in his egg yolk and sopped the golden liquid onto his bread. "Okay, so if we dismiss him as a suspect, who's left?"

We, he said. Did he really think of them as team? "I'm not sure. You're the cop. What do you think?"

"We have to look at everyone who's close to you girls. It has to be someone who knows all of you. We're checking on Cynthia's friends and acquaintances, but it seems more likely it's someone who knows you...or Gwen...or maybe Janie."

"I hear you, but I'm not sure why you believe that, and I don't know how I can help you. I can't imagine who would have done this." The ease with which the lie fell from her lips surprised her, and she couldn't put her finger on her reasoning either. Except maybe she was an idiot. Or too invested in solving this herself to elicit help.

Suddenly famished and anxious to escape from Joe, she quickly devoured her meal, making light conversation. She didn't know for sure if Bobby had told him about Robert D. Wilson. It wasn't her place either.

When she finished eating, she glanced at her watch. "Thanks a lot for breakfast. It really hit the spot. Do you mind dropping me off? I need to study."

She hopped down from her stool and hurried outside while he threw a few bills on the counter. He joined her in the car, started up the engine, and dropped her off at the dorm.

Katie let herself out of the car. "Thanks again."

"My pleasure," he said.

She stood back and eyed the clearly marked vehicle. Shit, she thought. I bet everyone on earth saw him drop me off. Double shit.

Chapter 33

RETURN OF THE DEMON

June 1970

Moments later, Katie spotted a familiar vehicle model, with the engine in the rear of the car, backed into a parking space. She knew only one person who drove a Corvair. Her hair stood on end as she stepped from the parking lot to the dorm; she thought she spotted Mark. She squeezed between two closely parked cars and tried to keep her gaze inconspicuous. Her full view of him was obstructed by an open trunk, yet she recognized his imposing build.

Katie fumed. The nerve of him to show up at her dorm. She quickly glanced at her wrist and checked her Timex. 11:30 a.m. The hell with it, she thought. She decided to face her demon headfirst.

She scanned the landscape. Things looked quiet. Most of her dormmates spent Sundays recovering from weekend partying, and summer semester proved even quieter with attendance so skeletal. Right now, she wished for anyone else's presence—anyone but Mark's.

"Mark," she called out and walked directly toward him, careful to keep a safe distance.

He turned toward her and smiled.

"Katie! Gosh, it's great to see you. I told you I have friends on campus. I thought while I visited, I'd stop by and say hello."

"We have nothing to say to each other. I thought you understood."

He stepped closer and reached out to touch her arm.

She backed away.

"Katie." He shook his head. "You know I would never hurt you."

"You did hurt me. I'm smart enough to know it's best to stay away from those who cause me harm."

"It's one of the reasons I wanted to talk to you. I'm really sorry about what happened. You can't blame me for being distraught. My dad just died."

"Don't kid yourself. Nobody does what you did because their dad just died."

Katie wished she could mace him. She remembered the canister sat tucked in her purse on her key ring, and she hoped she could inconspicuously rifle her bag and grab her keys. She reminded herself—we're standing in broad daylight. *I'm safe.* Mark wouldn't grab her here.

"By the way, I have something for you." He reached into the trunk, then paused and rubbed his chin as he peered into her eyes. "Really, I just came to apologize and let you know how truly sorry I am. I can't stop thinking about you. It's been months and I can't get you out of my mind. See? I really mean it." His eyes begged her to believe him.

"You've lost your mind. You tried to rape me. Then you had the gall to call me and send a letter. Don't you get it? I didn't answer you because I'm not interested in anything you have to say."

"You're losing your cool, Katie. How unlike you."

Her eyes narrowed. "You're darned right I'm losing my cool. You are a filthy bastard. Stay away from me. I want nothing to do with you."

Even as she said this she wrestled with herself. *I'm supposed to be trapping him, getting him to agree to see me so I can confront him about Janie and Cynthia. I'm blowing it.*

"I know you don't mean it. God says we should forgive each other. Remember St. Peter? He asked Jesus how many times he should forgive his brother. The Lord answered, 'I tell you not seven times, but seventy-seven times.' Surely you can forgive me this once."

He stepped toward her and Katie rushed to back away. Her foot caught on the curb and she tumbled backwards. She lay on the sidewalk helpless, as helpless as she had been in his car the night of his attack. In an instant, Mark knelt on the ground next to her.

"Get away from me!"

"I'd never hurt you, Katie. I'm here to help you." Mark's voice sounded different—like the night he attacked her.

The flashback enveloped her and she screamed.

A voice boomed from above. "Everything all right here?"

It took her a moment to recognize the voice and take a breath. She looked up, choked in the middle of a scream. She saw Bobby and calmed.

"It's fine, Officer," Mark said. "This young lady tripped. I'm simply trying to help her up. I guess she panicked."

Bobby approached Katie as he would a stranger and placed his hand on her shoulder. "Are you all right, miss?" She played along, surmising that Bobby wanted to appear professional with her while he was on the job.

"Yes, thank you."

"Let me help you." Bobby placed his hand under her elbow and gently helped her stand. All the while he kept his eyes fixed on Mark. Katie brushed herself off.

"It's time for you to leave," Bobby told Mark.

Mark smiled and tried to come between her and Bobby. "Katie's a friend of mine."

Bobby lifted his head in a just-try-me-buddy challenge and clenched his jaw. "Take off."

"Hold on for a minute. I have something for her. Let me grab it. It's in my trunk." Mark walked the few steps over to the open trunk. Bobby's hand gripped his Billy club. "Get down," he murmured. Katie crouched in front of the car.

As Mark reached inside, Bobby poised himself. Mark came out with a long narrow jeweler's box. Bobby motioned to her, implying safety as Mark stepped forward and offered a small package to Katie. "Here, this is for you."

"I don't want anything from you."

Bobby's hand maintained a firm grasp on his nightstick. "The lady indicated she's not interested. Beat it."

Mark stooped down and set the box on the pavement in front of Katie. "Back off man, I'm leaving. But seriously, Katie, I want you to have this. It's yours."

He turned, climbed into his vehicle, revved the engine, and screeched his tires on the way out of the parking lot.

Bobby wrapped his arm around Katie. "You okay?"

She nodded as she tried to stop her knees from hammering together. "Fine."

"Cup of coffee?"

"A Coke would be good," Katie said.

Bobby led her towards The Grill. She studied him with clearer eyes and backed away. "You're on duty. You shouldn't have your arm around me."

"Is that all you can think about right now?"

"It's not all I'm thinking about, it's just a good distraction."

She looped her arm through his and they descended the steps and entered The Grill. They claimed their spot—the one they had occupied on their first date. "I'll get your drink," Bobby said.

Katie plopped down and inhaled a big breath. She gazed at Bobby as he stood in line with their beverages. He looked so handsome in his uniform. Her knight in shining armor, he had saved the day. As he walked toward her, he smiled. It made her feel warm inside, and safe.

Bobby sat down beside her and patted her thigh. "So, you want to talk about it?"

"I'm okay now," she said. "Fine, in fact."

"Good." Suddenly, a look of recognition crossed his face. "Shit, that was Mark, wasn't it? I blew it."

Katie confirmed his suspicions with a nod. "Bobby, let it go."

"Just so you know? If I would have been smart, I'd have taken him out."

"I appreciate the thought."

The narrow black jewelry box remained on the pavement, tucked between two parked cars, perfectly placed on the yellow line.

Chapter 34

THE BEST LAID PLANS

June 1970

They sat silent for a while, sipping their respective drinks, searching each other's gaze now and then, smiling, and lacing their fingers together. Bobby sat, waiting. Katie loved so much about him—his patience, his passion, his intelligence, and his humanity. She loved how much he loved her. And she loved him back in the same way. If only the timing were better. If only it were time to settle down, time to get married. But she knew it would be a while. She said a silent prayer they would last long enough.

A sudden urge crept through her; she'd held out far too long. "I think it's him."

Bobby's eyes narrowed, and Katie witnessed his wheels turning. "What do you mean?"

"Mark. He's the one who kidnapped Janie. He's the one who killed Cynthia."

"What? But why?"

"To hurt me—to get back at me for dropping him."

"Seems a little drastic, doesn't it?" Bobby's voice sounded even and controlled in spite of his furrowed brow.

"I received a package. I should have told you right away, but I chickened out. I didn't want to jeopardize your job, or us, or anything. And I kept thinking...trying to reason it out." She watched him, waiting for a reaction.

His hand moved from her fingers to his chin. He tapped his upper lip with his index finger. "What kind of package?"

"A locket. Cynthia's locket."

He closed his eyes and blew out a puff of air. "When?"

"Right after she died. In the mail, in a box, addressed to me."

Bobby shook his head. "You should have told me. It's evidence."

"I know."

"You have to turn it in."

Tears welled in Katie's eyes. "I wanted to figure this out myself, not cause anyone any more problems, keep everyone safe—keep you from losing your job, keep anyone else from dying. He's after me, you see? It's me he wants."

"He wants you enough to kill your friend?"

In spite of the fact that she knew how impossible it sounded, a new realization engulfed her. "Oh my God! The package, he tried to hand me a package. I've suspected him for a while, but it's this, now, this is how I know..."

Katie bounded out the door and raced to the parking lot, her drink tumbling from her hands. Bobby didn't miss a beat; he was hot on her heels. Her eyes searched the ground between and beneath the cars. It must still be here.

For a second, the air rushed out of her—maybe the box had vanished. Then, from between the two vehicles where Mark had parked just thirty minutes ago, she spotted the corner of a black box. She reached out for it, then stopped. But then Katie leaned forward, then picked up and pushed back the top of the spring-loaded box. Inside, she found a fine-linked gold chain with a gold heart-shaped locket.

Katie flipped it closed, as if she'd be stricken dead if she stared at it a moment longer. Bobby, standing across from her, hadn't seen the contents.

"What is it? You look like you've seen a ghost."

"It's a locket…a plain heart-shaped locket."

"Let me see."

Katie handed the box to Bobby and watched as he pulled it open and peered inside. He grabbed an ink pen from his pocket and flipped the locket over.

"It's engraved," he said.

Katie peeked over Bobby's forearm and read the inscription.

Katie
My Life
My Love
My Forever
Mark

Her throat closed, her breathing becoming so shallow, it almost stopped. She swallowed. "Oh, no, I'm right, aren't I?"

"I'm not sure. I need to rush this over to the precinct and talk to Joe. The cops will pull Mark in for questioning. Go upstairs and stay put. You'll be safe in your room. Is Janie home?"

"I'm not sure. I've been gone all morning. She spent the night at Jim's, but she could be back by now."

"Go upstairs. If she isn't there, call Jim's and have the two of them come and stay with you."

"I want to come with you." Katie intertwined her fingers in his, squeezing with all her might. He lifted her hand to his mouth and kissed it.

"Not yet. I'll call you as soon as I know something. Go to your room and be sure to bolt the door. You'll be safe there."

"Okay," Katie said. "But I'd feel better if I could do something."

Bobby held her close for a brief moment. "Staying safe is doing something."

"Call me as soon as you figure out what to do."

"I will." He squeezed her shoulders and kissed her forehead. "Now go, I'll watch 'til you get inside."

She inhaled a deep breath and nodded again for added strength, and then headed inside the dorm. Eerie quiet greeted her as she heaved open the weighty glass door and slipped into the entryway.

On Sundays, it sometimes stayed quiet all day. It's not like there are a million people around during summer term, she told herself. *I'm just upset about Mark*. Still, she caught herself moving with caution and uncertainty as she walked through the lounge hallway to the opposite side of the dorm. *Dammit. I forgot to give Bobby Cynthia's locket.*

A cheerful female voice interrupted her fears. "Katie?"

She froze. "Huh?"

"Hi!"

Mary, her best friend from high school, stood in front of her, grinning broadly. She turned and hugged her friend tight. What a relief to see a familiar and welcoming face right now! Like an angel, Katie thought.

"Mary! What are you doing here?"

"I got a lift over from the U to meet up with a ride home."

"Who are you riding with?"

"I'm not sure. Some friend of a friend. A girl named Cheryl Stevens."

Katie nodded. "I know her. She's an upperclassman who lives on the first floor. She grew up in the Cooley High neighborhood. Want me to take you to her room?"

"I told her I'd wait for her in the lounge. We're meeting in five minutes."

"Too bad you aren't going to be here longer. I'd love to catch up."

"Me, too. How'd your year end up?"

"Great." Katie didn't waver when she lied. "I love it here. The Profs are great and I love my job."

"How's the guy?"

A huge smile enveloped her face. "He's the best."

Cheryl walked around the corner and Katie rushed through more hugs and goodbyes. They promised to get together soon.

Katie turned the corner to the elevator and pushed the round call button as she thought about Mary, and how they'd been friends since the fifth grade. Then her thoughts turned to Cynthia's locket. She decided to run the necklace over to Bobby.

The elevator doors opened and she rushed in. The doors closed and darkness surrounded her; the light must have burnt out. A gloved hand clamped over her mouth. She tried screaming, but the cloth over her face stifled all sound.

Her legs collapsed and the world turned black.

Chapter 35

CAPTURED

June 1970

A cool, damp breeze stirred Katie to wakefulness. She slowly lifted from the depths of a deep, murky haze, and as she became more aware, her lashes fluttered against a binding. As hard as she searched for light, darkness shrouded her. Her body, stiff and sore, shivered against the swelling chill—her breath coming in short, staggered gasps as she struggled to move. Her hands, individually bound behind her, pressed against something hard, and she began to twist her neck and shoulders; she fought to move her elbows from behind her—in order to free herself. Impossible. Her hands were secured in a vice-like grip, seized and immobilized. She squirmed in protest, but soon understood her efforts proved futile. Her breath caught in her throat.

I'm going to die. I'M GOING TO DIE!

Breathe. Get your bearings.

After numerous interminable moments, she began taking inventory. *There's a cold hard surface beneath me…I'm sitting.* She wriggled again. *I'm tied at my hands and my feet, even at my knees. Tied to a chair. Blindfolded.* The cloth over her eyes felt smoother than she would have imagined… freakily smooth and soft. *I'm gagged.* The binding around her mouth was rough, and she explored it lightly with her tongue. The cloth pilled on her taste buds, causing her to retch and choke. She inhaled through her nose and tried to speak, but could not. She gulped again, trying to quell the overwhelming nausea.

Shivering. Cold. Freezing. God help me, I'm naked. Try not to freak out, Katie. You're going to be all right. She squeezed back the tears. *No crying allowed.*

She struggled to scoot her chair forward. It creaked, but wouldn't budge. *It must be secured to the floor.* In an odd, unimaginable flash, the sign above her desk zipped through her mind. *Don't Panic. Breathe. Think. Pray.*

The urge to surrender gripped her. *Just let me die. Let this be over. NO! THINK. Knowledge is power. Where are you?* She forced her bare toes to search the floor. Cold. Smooth. As much as she wanted to pull away, she continued to explore. Concrete—a concrete floor. A sharp sliver pierced her toe, and she curled it back and inhaled a long breath in a feeble attempt to calm herself. A smell traveled on the breeze—one with a musty tail. She added the clues: inside + cold + dark + damp.

In the blink of an eye, she remembered the night she had peered through the broken window into the basement of the farmhouse where she, Bobby, and Jim had searched for Janie.

It's my turn. He's brought me here—to the farmhouse.

His voice entered the darkness, hushed, yet clear and familiar. "You awake?" It was a casual question. *Was this real, or a terrible nightmare?*

"Mark," she mumbled his name around the binding covering her mouth. She couldn't speak clearly.

"I knew you would come," he said.

Her mind raced. He's deranged, she thought. *I didn't come, you brought me here.* She reminded herself: He abducted Janie. He killed Cynthia.

Stay sane. Be the voice of reason. It was her only chance, but she couldn't form words or think of what to say. She breathed in through her nose, squeezed her eyes shut beneath her blindfold, and prayed. A moment later, she made soft sounds rather than crying out or protesting, hoping Mark would be interested enough in a conversation that he would remove the gag. Her body shook, racked with a bone deep chill, and she fought the impulse to leave her body, the horror of this place, and Mark.

Another swift blast of air, and something blew up and settled over her; it enveloped her from head to foot. *What was he doing? Wrapping her body in order to move her?*

Her mind raced and tears welled in her throat. Mark had wanted her all along. Now he had her. She prayed: *Let Bobby find me. Please God, let him figure it out.*

A scratching sound entered her awareness. What on earth could he be doing? She cringed as the sound came closer. The object stopped next to her and then she felt a hand on her blanketed leg.

"There now, don't you feel better?"

Katie willed herself not to flinch or react. "Thank you," she mumbled. She hoped her tone would soothe him, like when she used to pacify her brothers in the colicky days of their infancies. They couldn't understand her words, but the melody of her voice calmed them. On the outside, she sat stone still and waited. Inwardly, she prayed for a miracle.

"It's not like I wanted to do any of this, you know. First that Janie friend of yours; she kicked and screamed. I had no choice but to drug her. I had to keep her quiet. I didn't even want her," he spat out. "I wanted you, Katie. Just you. Always you. If you would have answered my phone calls, my letters, none of this would have happened."

A wave of anger seized her, but Mark only saw her nodding head, and heard her soothing voice. As she nodded, the blanket slid down, revealing her shoulders. The edge of the covering caught on the chair, so while her head remained exposed, the rest of her body stayed somewhat protected and warm. Maybe it helped that he could see her face; it would make her more real. She wished he would sense her faked calm and not her abject fear.

He kept talking. "I didn't mean to hurt your other friend. She kept fighting. I tried keeping her still…and…I didn't know my own strength."

Katie's throat closed, her breathing coming in short spurts. Mark raped Cynthia! He beat her. He was a madman. *Don't go there. Keep your head. It's your ticket out. Back to Bobby.*

Mark's voice choked on his confession. "I...j...ust wanted...you."

Katie nodded again. "I know," she said. "You didn't mean to hurt anyone. You wanted me to love you." Even though she recognized that Mark might not be able to decipher her words, she prayed he would feel that she understood him.

Mark's hand moved up her thigh. She cringed and clenched her jaw.

His endless confession continued. Katie wished she could block her ears; she didn't want to hear a word of this. Tears flooded the inside of her blindfold, and soon panic stole her ability to hear. She couldn't take any more. In spite of the blanket's warmth, she began to shake. Inexplicably, Mark noticed and reacted. He lifted the blanket from her. She shook violently, as much from fear and shame as the icy air. He placed it back around her, cocooning her. Her uncontrollable shaking continued.

"I'm sorry. Look at you. You're trembling. Poor Katie."

Never had she felt hate like this. She muttered continuously, praying under her breath. *God, help me. Bobby, save me.*

She felt Mark's hands move behind her head and resisted the urge to pull away. He undid the knot, pulled the gag from around her face and sat down next to her again, replacing his hand on her thigh.

"There," he said.

She inhaled a jagged breath, sniffed back tears, and summoned courage from some unfamiliar depth of her soul. "I know you didn't mean to harm those girls. I know you love me. I've thought about it. Everything you did was out of love. I see it clearly now."

Please God, let me say the right things.

She envisioned Janie in Mark's clutches. He'd drugged her, meant to kill her, and then brutally assaulted and murdered Cynthia. *Just keep talking. Don't think about it.*

Mark wailed. "I need you."

Shivers rose up her spine, but she ignored them. "I know."

"If we could just go away together. Just the two of us. I know I can make you see."

Katie plugged in the listening skills she learned in Psych 101 and reflected Mark's words back to him. "If we could be alone, we could be close.

"If we got into the car right now, we could be at my parent's cottage in a few hours," she said. "We could be alone there. We could be safe."

Katie knew enough to keep him here—not let him take her anywhere. She needed another plan, needed to buy some time. She willed her body to stop shaking. "I need to use the bathroom, Mark. Can you just untie me for a minute?"

Although her eyes remained covered, Katie had gained a little control with the gag removed; she could talk to him, try to reason with him. She hoped he would leave her blindfold in place. If he couldn't read her expression, he might not be able to read her thoughts. If she could just trick him into releasing her hands, she could get away.

"You're trying to work me," he said.

"No, I'm not. Honestly, think about it. How long have I been here?"

"See, you are trying to trick me. To find out what time it is…"

Katie spoke calmly, but with authority. "Does it really matter what time it is? You've taken my clothes. I'm embarrassed and humiliated. If I have an accident sitting in this chair, I'll be mortified." She paused and added, "If we're going to be together, you have to trust me."

His fingertips traveled the length of her arm and fear gripped her like the jaws of a tiger. "You're beautiful, Katie. I love your body. If you're naked, it will keep you from running away from me. No," he said, a sudden anger spewing from his lips, "if you really have to pee, go ahead."

"If we're going to drive Up North, I have to dress. Please, let me go to the bathroom first. I want to come with you, Mark. You're right. We need to get away…have time to talk…and think…and plan."

He relented. "I'll untie your feet and legs. Walk to the next room, squat and pee in the corner. I'm not untying your hands."

"Thank you."

Mark released her feet, legs, and hands from their bindings, then retied her hands. In front of her this time.

She stood and realized how weak she had become in what she imagined was a very short time. Certainly, Bobby would have discovered her missing by now. Mark held her arm above the elbow.

"There's glass on the floor. Please, can I have my shoes?"

Mark seated her back in the chair and slid her feet, one by one, into her shoes. Then, he tied the laces together. She cursed silently. He pulled her up and led her into a narrow passageway.

"There," he said. "I'll turn away. Pee. Right here."

As Katie squatted, she realized she could reach her feet, and even with her wrists bound, untie the laces through her legs. Once she untied them, she would have to shuffle her feet as if her shoelaces remained knotted, and she hoped darkness would obscure her break for freedom. *Find the light.* Katie tipped her head and attempted to peer from beneath her blindfold. She couldn't remove it; Mark might retaliate.

She stood, scuffed her shoes along the floor to alert Mark that she had finished. He stood some distance away from her. "Come toward my voice," he called. She followed orders, her hands cupped and outstretched to protect herself from bumping into a wall. All the while, she moved with painstakingly slow steps, planning her escape.

Finally, she reached Mark, and he grabbed her roughly above the elbow.

"You're hurting me!"

"You'll be fine," he barked.

She summoned her high school acting skills. "Why are you mad?"

"You're trying to get away."

"I'm not. Now, give me my clothes. I'll dress and we can go."

"I'll give you something to wear, but I'm staying right here to watch you." He reached down and she felt him touch her shoes. He growled, then slapped her face, hard.

Katie screamed, cowered, and pleaded with him.

"They came loose when I moved. You have to believe me."

Shuffling sounds startled her.

"Mark, where are you going? You can't leave me here." *Why did I say that?*

Katie felt a rush of air, a swoosh. Her pants. She sighed in relief.

"Thank you." She slid off her shoes, and in spite of her bound hands, slid her legs into her pants as hurriedly as possible, slipping them up over her hips. Imagining she could remove the blindfold with a quick flash of her hands to her face, she knew the timing must be perfect. As soon as he saw her do this, he would freak out, and stop her from making another move.

Again she heard a noise, just a dull scraping this time, before he flung another item at her. Her t-shirt. She dropped it and scrambled to the floor, fumbling. Somehow, she retrieved the shirt, inched it up on the inside, located the neck hole, and pulled it over her head. The shirt trapped her inside. She used her elbows to angle the shirt down toward her waist.

"Let's go," he growled. He reached out and tugged at her arm under her shirt, pinching her. Katie winced and cried out in pain.

"You have to untie me. At least let me put my shirt on. Then, you can tie me up again if you want."

"You're trying to get away."

"I said I'll come with you and I will. Please be reasonable, let me get dressed."

Mark sliced away the bindings. Katie pushed her arms through her sleeves and rubbed her wrists. He grabbed one of her arms, turning her toward him.

She couldn't risk being his next victim. *This is my chance.* She had to run—fight for her life—try to break free. Breaking his grasp, she gouged at him. Her fingernails became weapons, clawing blindly at his face. She kicked him and screamed as she yanked the blindfold free. Pitch black, like being in a cold, lightless cave, her eyes did not adjust. At the same time she turned away from him, hoping the way out would be behind her, in the opposite direction from where he stood.

She reached through the darkness like a cornered animal. Her hands and feet finally free, she twisted, hoping for one of two things—a weapon, or a way out. Her hand landed and fit around a slim, rough pole. Frantic, she let her hand travel its length. It must be a rail, she thought, it's angled up. Stairs? As soon as she grabbed hold and moved her foot forward to search out a step, Mark's fingers gripped her arm.

A blow to the back of her head left her dizzy. *Fight.*

With her free hand, Katie groped for the handrail again and her eyes began to adjust. She caught shadows in the dark. Mark pulled her back as she locked her grip on the handrail. She dragged herself up two steps, and her surroundings came into view. At the very top of the stairs, a sliver of light poked through the darkness. He yanked her arm, and then she turned, let go, and kicked with her right foot. Hard. It landed square on his nose, like she'd hit a bull's eye. He released her as his hands flew to his face and he doubled over in pain. She scrambled to the stairs, and lost her footing on the rickety steps, slamming to her knees, and scraping and skinning herself.

Mark lunged after her, his hands clutching her ankle in the narrow staircase. She battled with all her might. He would never come as close to her again as he did the night of his father's wake.

Suddenly, light filled the space above and voices boomed.

"Stop where you are! Put your hands in the air!"

Mark's body rose above her, and his kneecap planted her face on the stairs. While she couldn't see who'd come to her rescue, she recognized the voice. Her eyes squeezed shut in thanks and relief, praying her terror would soon be over.

"Put your hands over your head."

Mark's forearm forcibly coiled around Katie's throat, and he yanked her to her feet, flanking her in front of him like a shield. He backed away and dragged her down the steps, back into the cellar. The lead officer, the one shining the flashlight, pointed the beam onto Mark's face.

Mark snarled. "You want her dead, keep comin' after me."

The officers kept their guns poised and targeted him with hawk-like eyes. Deafening silence filled the space.

Shrieks of laughter haunted the basement. Mark cackled in disbelief, as if reality eluded his awareness—almost as if the cops weren't real—as if they didn't understand his power and invincibility.

Katie's eyes searched for Bobby. There he stood, at the top of the stairs, behind Joe, nodding at her, reassuring her she'd be all right.

Mark's grip tightened around her throat, and he squeezed. Katie choked and sputtered.

Suddenly, Katie heard a click from behind her head. It registered. The cock of a gun. She froze. Her breathing stopped. As if she watched the whole scene unfold like a slow-motion movie, she glimpsed the muzzle of a snub-nosed revolver from behind her left shoulder. Her knees weakened. Mark's grasp loosened and she turned to jelly in his clutches. The room began to spin. An enormous blast echoed in the concrete space as she fell to the floor. Her ears rang, and a warm, oozing liquid pulsed from her shoulder.

The next thing Katie knew, sirens whined and she blinked against the flashing lights all around her. Bobby appeared at her side, a horribly worried expression on his face.

She struggled to regain her bearings. "Where are we? What are we doing?"

"You're going to be fine," Bobby said. "You've been shot. But it's a clean shot, right through."

"Shot?" Katie's shoulder seared with pain. EMT's bustled around her. She caught flashes of tubes, needles, and portable machines at their side. Slowly, she squeezed her eyes shut. No, she realized, it's not a dream.

"She's in shock. Her pulse is thready. Let's get her to the hospital."

As they loaded her into the ambulance, she cried in fear, "Mark. Where's Mark?"

"You don't need to worry about him."

"Did he get away?"

"No," Bobby said. "You're safe now."

Chapter 36

SAFE AT LAST

June 1970

Katie's mom pleaded with her. "Come to the cottage with us. You've been through too much...we've all been through too much."

From her hospital bed, Katie spoke in a whisper. "Please, I need to be with my friends. My shoulder will heal. I need to follow up with the doctors, appointments and all. I should stay here."

"Who will care for you?"

"Mom, I have Janie and Bobby. They can drive me to the doctor."

"Dad wants you at the cottage with the family. It's where you belong."

Katie's head fell back on her pillow. Her hospital gown itched, and a simple glance at her IV site made her squeamish. Being in the hospital, Mark dead—all much more than a horrible nightmare.

"I don't have the energy to fight, Mom. Please, talk it over with Dad."

Katie's mom gazed at her, the worry lines in her forehead forming deep grooves. She stroked Katie's arm and her touch felt warm and welcome. "Everyone is frantic with worry. Are you sure that's what you want?"

"I'm sure. I need normal. I'm being discharged tomorrow. And plus, the police will need to speak with me."

"Haven't they gotten enough information from you already? What more could they possibly need?"

"I don't know. But it makes sense for me to stay here. It's what *I* need." Katie inhaled a deep breath. Goosebumps rose on her skin.

"You look so tired, honey," Katie's mom said. She pushed Katie's hair back off her forehead and stroked her temple. "Why don't you try to rest?"

Katie closed her eyes and shivered.

Her mom kissed her cheek, firmly tucked her blankets around her, and gathered her purse. "Sleep for a bit. I'll be back after I call your father and plead your case." She walked to the window, pulled the shade and left, closing the door behind her. Sleep came to Katie in a welcome veil.

The next thing she knew, the food cart clanked in the hallway and a hair-netted employee eased open the room door with one of her ample hips, delivering Katie's lunch tray.

She set the food on Katie's tray table and scooted it in front of her. "Here you go, honey. Chicken soup, mashed potatoes, and pudding."

"Thanks," Katie muttered, rubbing the sleep from her eyes.

Katie pushed the button on her bed to raise her head, situated herself, lifted the cover from her soup, and took a sip. Lukewarm and salty, it still tasted like heaven on a spoon. Her eyes lit up at the sight of noodles floating in the broth. She slurped one between her lips and smiled. No more clear liquids. She'd graduated to a soft diet. After she savored the first bites, Katie scarfed the stiff mashed potatoes and runny pudding.

She wiped her mouth and chin, pushed the tray table to the side, and grabbed *The Clue of the Broken Locket*, her favorite Nancy Drew mystery. She and Nancy had a lot in common. In this story, Nancy had been kidnapped, her hands tied, her mouth gagged. She, too, had been held captive in a cellar. Too freaky, Katie thought. But as she read the final pages, she marveled. Nancy unraveled her puzzle, and unwittingly, so had she.

She closed the book, glad for the happy endings in both cases, and committed to never solving a puzzle again.

The heavy room door creaked open once again, and Janie, her round face and smiling blue eyes, lit up the doorway. "Hey, stupid! How you doin'?"

"I can't wait to go home and put all this behind me."

Janie picked up Katie's book. "Hey, Nancy Drew!"

Katie giggled. "Yeah, Mom brought it up for me. I guess I she found an extra copy at home."

"Reading her books prepared you for this. You know, 'you, too, will turn out to be a detective someday.'" Janie's laughter echoed in the small room. "You and Nancy are just alike."

"I hope I never have to solve anything again. It's not like I solved it really. The pieces just fell into place."

"You know," Janie said, "I've been thinking." She rubbed the edges of the book binding between her thumb and index finger. "You should be an author."

"How do you figure?" Katie asked.

"Think about it. You have quite a story to tell."

"I wish I didn't."

"You could call it *The Wrong Guy*. You always said the cops might have the wrong guy."

"You're right, I did. But they didn't have the wrong guy. They have enough evidence to put Collins away for a long time. As Bobby said, Mark was just another guy. Another bad guy."

Janie reached out and tapped her best friend's hand with her long slender fingers. "And you have the right guy. All wrapped up in one spectacular hunk of man."

Katie smiled and closed her eyes. "And he's a good dancer."

35706283R00207

Made in the USA
Middletown, DE
12 October 2016